# WINTER OF THE OWL

## SEASONS OF THE LUKOI BOOK ONE

IRIS FOXGLOVE

BELLADONNA PRESS

# ACKNOWLEDGMENTS

We'd like to thank our editor, Alicia Z. Ramos, for all her hard work editing this book. Thank you also to our Patrons for their continued support, and to our family and friends for being so encouraging! Special thanks to Zach for the hunting advice, and for not laughing too hard at Iris' (incorrect) thoughts of how you quartered a bear. Finally, thanks to Marmolita and Freo for the inspiration and world-building in regards to the natural power exchange aspect of our stories.

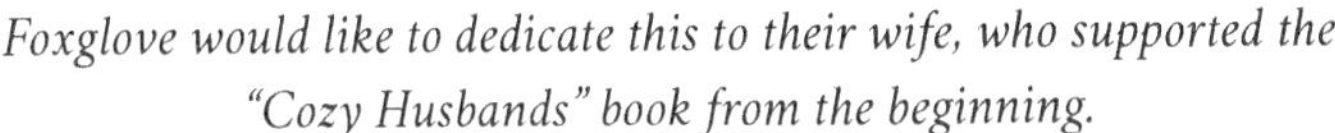

*Foxglove would like to dedicate this to their wife, who supported the "Cozy Husbands" book from the beginning.*

*Iris would like to dedicate this to her mom, for her steadfast support and encouragement. This doesn't mean she needs to read it, though ;)*

*And to the real Speedy cat, inspiration and muse.*

My wings are dusted
    With frost and cold
    For a little thing like you
    I'm too heavy a load
    You'll struggle and falter
    Amble around
    Just follow some other storm
    'Cause I'll only weigh you down
    You carry me home
    My love

— GOOD MORNING, MAGPIE (MURDER BY DEATH)

# AUTHOR'S NOTE

**Author's Note**

Please be advised that the natural power exchange/biological imperative kink element to this story is intended as fantasy, **and should not be considered a factual representation of BDSM as practiced between consenting adults in real life**. The dynamics portrayed in this and other Iris Foxglove titles are entirely fictional, and should not be considered a guideline for the safe practice of any activity described herein.

CW for some non-graphic discussion of suicide and a slight cultural misunderstanding of mental illness. If you would like more information on these CWs, please feel free to contact the authors.

Thank you for reading!

# CHAPTER 1

When Victor had first come to the Two Sisters University in the heart of Gerakia, he hadn't thought that he would spend the last day of his academic career shoved in the back of a cart. He should have been a graduate by now, a proper one, in black robes with the silver laurel of a scholar pinned in his hair. His friends back home were expecting it. They'd had a celebration planned for years, ever since he got his scholarship letter in the mail and old Aunt Grace had burst into tears in the foyer. He was supposed to walk back into town and be hailed as the returning hero, the one kid who made it out.

Outside the cart, the evergreen trees that lined the university rustled in a high wind, bells rang to signal the start of a new class, and students pushed narrow boats into the river. Inside, Victor huddled up against a stack of books and polished his glasses with his shirt.

"It won't be long." David Vitale, adjunct professor of philosophy and the love of Victor's life, leaned over the back of the cart to take Victor's face in his hands. He was hard to see up close, just a blur of pale skin and dark hair, and he laughed softly as Victor fumbled to put his glasses back on. With classes starting, there was no one else on the service road, and for the first time in ages, it felt like they were alone.

"It's all my fault, anyway," Victor said. "I shouldn't have been there."

David kissed his cheek, bumping his nose into Victor's glasses, and tapped the frames. Victor grimaced—his spectacles were enormous, with thick glass spelled not to break, and David always preferred that Victor keep them off. Victor kept forgetting all the same. David removed them again himself, and then all Victor could see were the trees behind him and the statues of the two sisters standing tall on either side of the river, lanterns raised.

"Let me get a better look at that face before you go," David said. "And it wasn't your fault. It's the school's fault for not allowing us to be together. But I suppose we were bound to be discovered eventually. You're not the best at subtlety, Victor. How can you be, the way you are?"

Victor sighed. He knew he didn't fit in. David liked him for his mind, he said, not for his gangly limbs or narrow face, or his feet that were a little too big and his slender hands. David liked to joke that Victor was a fey creature from Kallistos, a changeling someone had dropped off in Gerakia by mistake, but he thought Victor was brilliant and would keep him up all night speaking of old languages and philosophers.

Which was the problem, really, because Victor had just been winding down from one of those late-night talks—with his head between David's thighs while David dug his fingers into Victor's tight curls—when the door opened and Aurelia, another professor, came home early from sabbatical in Thalassa.

That turned into a whole shouting mess, with Victor awkwardly picking up his clothes while Aurelia—who claimed to be David's fiancée—ripped into David for "seducing students" and "ruining her life." Which turned into David being brought up before the board of directors, who decided, thanks to some letters Victor would have sworn David had burned, that Victor had an "unhealthy obsession" with David and would have to transfer out. That, or take classes on how to "master his submissive urges," as though being a submissive was something that possessed him, like a ghost.

But David, of course, had the perfect way out.

"You have all your notebooks?" he asked, as the horses at the front of the cart kicked up dust and snorted at each other. "Your coat? It gets cold out there in Lukos, I hear."

Victor smiled in the general direction of David's face. "I heard something like that, yes. I'll be fine. The expedition you hired, it's only supposed to be there a week, right?"

"That's right."

It was simple. Victor's field of study was the evolution of languages from ancient times to the present, and the Lukoi—a people now known only by their connection to the island of Lukos, who had originally come from a land that now barely had ruins to remember it by—were the perfect subjects for study, one that no one had attempted before. All Victor had to do was walk among them for a week, ask some questions, and come back with the first real primer on their dialect and culture since they were exiled. The Two Sisters wouldn't have a choice but to grant him his degree, and then he and David could be together.

There was still the problem of Aurelia, but David had a plan for that, too. Victor had seen her hanging around the dorm when he was moving out, eyeing him, but he hadn't approached her, not given the look on her face when she'd seen him with David. David said they'd broken their engagement before she left for sabbatical, and she was just raising a fuss because she was unable to let go. He swore that it would all be sorted out when Victor came back, and he hadn't broken a promise yet.

"Just remember to ask for the captain of the *Seahorse*," David said, handing Victor his glasses back. He spoke with a touch of his natural dominance, just as he would when he was wrangling an unruly classroom. "He's an old friend of mine. He'll know what to do."

"Thank you." Victor grabbed David's hand. "I don't know what I'd do without you."

"Be an artist, probably." David laughed. "Good thing you have me to keep you on the right path, eh?"

Victor's smile wavered. He hadn't told David that half the notebooks he'd packed were blank, heavy sketchbooks his roommate, Miles, had shipped in from Kallistos. But David was right. He needed to focus on his degree. "Right. Good thing."

"I'll see you when you've unlocked the secrets of the Lukoi, then," David said, and, after checking behind him to make sure the road was still empty, caught Victor up in a crushing, possessive kiss.

"I love you," Victor whispered.

David laughed and patted Victor's cheek, and Victor put on his glasses as the cart jostled to life, books crashing around his shoulders as it rocked over the dusty road. David stood there for a moment, watching him go, and raised a hand in farewell. Victor waved back, blinked the mist from his eyes, and stared up at the twin statues of the Two Sisters. They stood taller than the college, giants of stone with flowing gowns and slight smiles, like they already knew everything there was to know and were just waiting for the rest of the world to catch up. He'd stared at them for hours when he was younger, sitting on the roof of the dorm with Miles as the sun went down. Leaving them behind hurt almost as much as leaving Miles or David, and Victor shifted to get comfortable in his seat full of books, opened a sketchbook from his bag, and hurriedly started to draw before they disappeared.

VICTOR HAD FILLED two sketchbooks before he realized something was wrong.

It was the captain who made him wonder. Captain Harolt wasn't much older than David and had welcomed Victor aboard his ship quickly enough, but when Victor started asking around for the other members of the expedition, Harolt only laughed and told Victor not to "worry your little head about it."

No one on the crew of the *Seahorse* seemed interested in Lukos, either. Oh, they were interested in passing it, since they had business hunting the seals that frequented the waters beyond Lukos, but no one seemed to care about the island itself.

"But it's where we're headed," Victor said to a sailor taking dinner on the deck. "Surely it holds some appeal."

"Where you're headed, maybe," the sailor said. "Me, I'm going home after this. My tour on this fucking trash heap is almost done."

"Oh." The sailor had rolled his eyes as Victor backed away.

No one else was particularly forthcoming, either. So Victor practiced speaking in the dialect the Lukoi used, the one found in old ruins and on tablets scattered on beaches throughout Staria and Arktos. It was the only remnant left of the nation the Lukoi came from, and only a handful of scholars knew enough to speak it. Victor was one of them because he was a sponge when it came to languages—he always had been. Growing up in a Gerakian orphanage, where kids came from everywhere and spoke every tongue known to man, Victor had become a linguist out of necessity.

With the crew of the *Seahorse* keeping to themselves, Victor found himself almost wishing that he'd accepted the board's decision and left college for good rather than mooning about on a ship that clearly didn't want him there. Still, the plan was already in motion. He just had to see it through for a week, and then it'd be over. He'd be a proper scholar, and David wouldn't have to sneak him through the back door or smile blankly at him when they met in public.

Lukos appeared on the horizon the next day, and Victor could barely catch his breath. It was beautiful, with high hills that crested into small mountains hugging the island like a crescent moon. There was already snow on the distant peaks, and the beaches were pebbled and gray, the hills a mix of green and brown and gold. Victor sat out of the way and took up three pages sketching out the shape of it, and his hands shook as he bound the book in its waterproof casing and stuffed it back in his bag.

"I can't believe we're here," he said as he followed one of Harolt's men into the lifeboat hanging on the side of the ship.

The sailor turned to squint at the beach. "Yeah, it's a miserable fucking place." Victor stared at him, then back at Lukos. Clearly, they weren't looking at the same country. "I hear the people there, they live like wolves. Run around naked in winter, howl at the moon."

"I'm pretty sure no one can run around naked in a Lukos winter," Victor said carefully. This sailor clearly wasn't part of the expedition. "Are the others … are they coming, or …"

"Just you," the sailor said as the boat lurched downward.

Victor's smile was a tight grimace. "Just me … in that I'll be the first one to contact the Lukoi?"

"Just you," the sailor repeated.

Victor looked up at the ship as the lifeboat crashed into the freezing water. "Surely there must be a mistake."

"Look. I'm being paid to row, okay?" The sailor sighed, and Victor sank into the bench, clutching the straps of his bag.

This couldn't be right. David had said that the *Seahorse* was the ship he needed, so why was he the only one on the expedition? Had David arranged the whole thing just for Victor? David never spent money on Victor. He had a rule about it. He said it went against his moral philosophy. Something about buying love.

It had all made sense when David explained it, but with the icy spray flying in Victor's face and the bitter cold digging through his winter coat, Victor couldn't quite remember how.

There were almost no waves on the rocky beach when the lifeboat ground to shore, and Victor stepped out warily, holding his bag to his chest. "Where did the captain say the Lukoi were?" he asked, peering into the beautiful, lonely landscape.

The sailor shrugged, both hands on the prow of the boat. "Fuck if I know. Start walking, I guess."

"But—wait." Victor turned. The sailor was pushing the boat back into the water, cursing softly. "Wait: a week, right? You'll be coming back?"

The sailor said nothing. He just shoved the boat into the gray waters of the Cheimon Sea, and Victor stared in growing horror as the man took out the oars to row away. Victor raced after him, but the moment he reached the water, he cried out as his cheap boots filled with what felt like ice. He staggered back out and kicked the boots off, shaking with a sudden chill.

The boat kept moving, heading slowly back to the hulking shadow that was the *Seahorse*, and it was then that Victor finally understood. David must have been lied to. There was no expedition. Victor was alone on the shore of Lukos, shivering in his best winter coat, and he would never see Gerakia again.

He picked up a stone from the beach and threw it as hard as he could at the retreating lifeboat. It missed the boat entirely, but he threw another, and another, until his arm was sore and his glasses were fogged with steam.

He turned back to the island, wondering whether the ones they called the Exiled had felt like this when they arrived, cold and far from home. He wondered if they, too, had found it beautiful, or if they'd cursed the ones who left them behind. It was hard to say. Some accounts called them survivors of a collapsing empire, others criminals, but regardless of why they went to Lukos, the fact remained that they were trapped there.

Just like Victor.

"I suppose I can ask them which account is true," he said, and laughed. He was bordering on hysterical, he knew, but at least no one was around to watch as he sat down and replaced his sodden, freezing socks. His boots were soaked, and his feet were actually warmer without them, but he thought it best not to discard them. He tied the laces together and swung them from his fingers like he would have when he was a boy walking along the lakeside by the orphanage.

Gerakia was too close to the southern shore to have a proper winter, and the only time the lake by the orphanage had frozen, so many children ran out to throw rocks at it that the shards of ice melted by the next morning. In Lukos, the air felt like it was laced with frost, and Victor stopped by a small pool on the beach to find it iced over. He kicked the ice to see what would happen, instantly regretted it, and had to stop to change his socks again.

"I'm probably going to die out here," he told his socks as he dumped them into his wet boots. "Wouldn't that be an inglorious ending."

He sat there on the pebbled beach and watched the distant rowboat bob toward the ship, a scrap of white on the darkening sea.

David couldn't have known. The captain must have taken his money and lied through his teeth. The only mercy, Victor supposed, was that he hadn't just pushed Victor into the ocean as soon as they left port.

"Some mercy." He sighed. He'd have to start moving soon. The days were short this far north, and the wind was already biting through his thin coat.

Victor was just getting to his feet, which ached with the cold despite his best attempts to chafe them warm, when he heard it.

A voice. A voice, calling out in the language of the Lukoi.

"Fuck," Victor said. This was it. He reached for his bag, where his notes on the language were, then changed his mind and shouted the first phrase he could remember. "I am very sorry!" He winced. "I mean, I need assistance!"

There was a long, pregnant pause. Then, "Why are you sorry?" the voice shouted back.

Victor beamed. "I was right," he said to himself. "They don't have gendered formal pronouns. Fuck you, Professor Gregoris." He cleared his throat. "Where are you?"

"I'm right here, child!"

Victor whirled around. A woman was standing just beyond the scrubby grass at the edge of the beach, her long, dark hair blowing in the breeze. She started forward, and Victor raised his hand in a half-hearted wave, lurching toward her. As she came closer, he realized that she wasn't really as wide as she seemed—she was just dressed sensibly, wrapped in a fur coat and leather gloves, a knitted scarf wound around her neck. She was paler than Victor, whose skin was the red-brown you saw everywhere in rural Gerakia, but she wasn't as ghost-pale as David. She looked like she could be Arkoudai, even, if they ever came that far north.

"What are you doing so close to the sea?" the woman said. She grabbed Victor by the arms, dragging him a few steps as though to keep him from turning back. "Don't you know how dangerous that is? Whose son are you?"

"I don't … know?"

The woman's eyes narrowed. "How do you not know? Do not turn to look at the sea," she snapped, when Victor tried to twist around. Her tone held none of the weight of a dominant, but Victor found himself unable to look away, startled by the panic in her voice.

"I won't. I'm not from here. The ship, behind me? They left me here."

Or that's what he hoped he said. He had the right words, but the order seemed to be all wrong.

The woman kept her firm grip on his arms, glancing over his

shoulder as though she were afraid of the ship. "You don't talk like you're from Lukos."

"I know. Sorry."

She frowned at him and released him to strip off her outer coat. Before Victor could react, she slung it around his shoulders. "You're too small to be out here half-dressed. Come with me. I'll find you new boots and bring you to the kuvar."

"The … the kuvar?" Victor struggled to translate, but he hadn't learned that word in his studies of the language. "Like a leader?"

The woman didn't smile, but her gaze softened a little. "Yes. And my name is Zora. My mate and I, we live nearby. I saw the sails and came to see what would bring a ship so close."

"Me, I guess," Victor said. "I'm Victor. I'm from Gerakia—do you know where that is?"

"I've never heard of it," Zora said, eyeing him as he trembled in her coat. "But it must be a warm place. What did you do, that you would be sent here?"

"Loved the wrong person, I think." Victor tried for a self-deprecating smile, but it probably failed miserably, because Zora slowed her pace, brows furrowed. Up close, she seemed older than before, at least twice Victor's age, and the lines in her forehead deepened as she looked at him.

"Well. You are here now, so I can at least give you warm boots. But you must promise not to try to go back. They are too far, and if you try to swim to them, you will die."

"I wouldn't," Victor said. "I promise."

Zora sighed. "Good."

She stayed close to him regardless, as though Victor were likely to take off and fling himself into the sea at any moment, and only visibly relaxed when they crossed into the grassland beyond the beach, where a small plume of smoke rose over a tiny cabin overlooking the sea.

"What you said before," she said, as Victor shivered and slipped on the damp grass. "You don't know whose son you are?"

"Oh. I don't have parents," Victor explained. "I've never met them. Do you group people by who their parents are, here?"

Zora gave him a bewildered look. "No. I wanted to know who you belonged to."

Victor smiled wryly. "No one."

Zora fell silent for a moment, staring out past the little house. "We have enough food for a meal, before I take you to the kuvar."

"Thank you." Victor tugged the coat tighter around his frame. He hadn't expected the Lukoi to be so welcoming—or so frightened of the sea, but that was a question for another time. For now, he followed Zora toward the cabin and struggled with the warring emotions rushing through him. He was finally in Lukos, speaking to one of the Exiled, being delivered to their leader … but he was also exiled himself, dropped onto their shore like flotsam from a shipwreck.

Which he was. It had all been a wreck from the start, from the moment his scholarship was revoked and he had to turn in his student's robes. He just hadn't realized it until he was caught in the debris.

He jumped as Zora called out to him, already approaching the door to her cabin.

"Come," she said, the wind teasing her hair. "We will have to hurry if the kuvar is to see you before the sun sets."

# CHAPTER 2

The man called Sava Snow-Walker stood in the home he'd built with his bare hands, wishing with all his heart he would not have to spend the winter alone in it.

He'd designed the cabin from the first moment he realized he was a dominant, and he'd lived in it on his own for two winters to prove his worth as a provider and a mate. But the house was meant to be shared.

Most homes were built simply at first—one room, or two at the most, with a pit cellar for food and sometimes a tanning hut a ways from the main structure. Over time, other rooms would be added. The kuvar, the traditional name for the ruler of Lukos, had even built a sunken bath in his home, supposedly for his daughter, who was still wintering with him. She'd heard of the sunken baths in Staria and wanted something similar.

Sava did not have a sunken bath, but he had a bathing room with its own chimney and hearth, to heat the water more easily. He'd lovingly made the bedroom with the suspended bed, smiling as he thought about the cold nights he'd spend beneath the furs with his mate. He'd killed enough bears to make the bed comfortable and warm, placing hooks for the animal skins around the walls to help insulate during the coldest part of winter.

And there was even a hearth-room, separate from the kitchen, with more furs for the best part of all: a pit filled with a wooden frame and insulated with wild grasses. He'd designed it in his head all through his second winter, how he would stretch the animal hides over the frame and the grasses, put stones around the sides and cover them with more skins, then put more furs on top of that. It was something of a sunken bed, warm and cozy, before the fire. He could easily imagine himself and his mate tangled up there, talking or laughing or doing other things.

No other Lukoi had one, and they'd laughed—nicely—when he'd talked about it last spring. But when he'd finished it, plenty of people had traipsed through his house to see "Sava's fur pit" and lie on it themselves. Dragan, the kuvar, said it was likely to catch on in a few winters, when submissives decided their dominants should build such luxuries for them, too. Sava had traded two of his jars of honey for the downy undercoat of goats to fill pillows and the mattress of the bed. Lukos was a harsh land, but there were ways to make the winters more comfortable for yourself and your mate.

His larders were full, both the cellar you accessed down the trap in the floor near the kitchen, and the others in the tanning house. He had enough wood for two winters, by this point, and he'd even built a porch with a roof at the front of the house and had—right when the thaw began—finished a second chair on curved wooden blades, the gift he'd made for his mate so they could sit outside together when the weather permitted it. Those precious few months when Lukos was sunny, everything blooming, and they could spend a few days idle before the preparations for winter inevitably began anew.

"Sava Snow-Walker has the nicest house in Lukos," people said. "His mate will be lucky, next winter."

And then, just as the first of the flowers began to push

through the sodden, fertile ground … Milan, the man Sava had always intended to take as his mate, had walked into the cold sea and drowned.

Winter madness, people said, even if the winter was past. Dragan had placed a warm hand on Sava's shoulder and said that sometimes it took root like a deadly flower, blooming long past when it should have withered and died. Ivan Spring-Singer, the healer, had wept, wishing Milan would have come to him for the tinctures that might have helped heal his mind. What no one said out loud—to Sava, at any rate—was that it was for the best, really, because a man who would follow the fox-maiden to the sea, which was deadly cold even in Lukos's brief summer, was no fit mate for a man of Sava's cleverness and strong, capable hands.

Sava had grieved quietly and thought of all the nights he'd spent making the chairs for the porch, how he'd almost carved Milan's name on the second but had decided to wait. It had seemed presumptuous, even though everyone knew Milan was all but promised to Sava. If Sava had acted sooner, brought Milan to the fields and taken him in the wild grasses before the chill was entirely gone, making the mate bond then … maybe it would have helped. Or earlier still: before the winter, he could have brought Milan to the heated spring and fucked him in the warm water near the cave where their people first came together and shed who they used to be, taking up the mantle of *people of the wolves, the exiles, those who survive.*

But Sava had wanted to wait, so he could finish the fur pit, the chairs. He'd wanted to have the best to offer, and now he had more than he needed and a chair no one would use, and in a few weeks the snows would come once more and he would stay another winter in his house alone.

He carefully cleaned his boots—not thinking about how that would have been Milan's job, were Milan here and not burned on the pyre—and sighed as he went to put a parcel of goat cheese in the cold cellar. He'd been trying to give his extra supplies to others over the last few weeks and had just delivered a hock of smoked deer meat to Ozren and Marta, who were expecting their first child to be born shortly. But of course they would not take something for nothing, and Marta had insisted on sending him home with the cheese, swearing she was "swimming" in goat's milk.

Sava wouldn't kick up a fuss about it; all Lukoi knew better than to argue with a woman in the last few months of pregnancy. It would be a treat, he supposed, to enjoy with the the remainder of the flatbread he'd made a few days ago.

Sava went about stripping his outerwear and starting a nice, warm fire, and he'd just put some stew in the pot to heat when there was a knock on his door. It was accompanied by the rumble of thunder, and that meant the snowstorms would soon come. Winter always started that way, with the mixture of rain and sleet and snow falling from a churning sky. If he wanted, he could go to the stone circle near the kuvar's house tonight, celebrate by the fire with the others, shake fists and hurl laughing insults up at the sky. But he was not in much of a mood to celebrate anything, and he would likely spend the night quietly in his house, alone.

Sava shook off the uncharacteristic gloom of his thoughts and headed for the door. He'd grieved Milan in the spring, and likely would again, when the snows came in truth. But for now, there was no point in it. What happened could not be changed. Milan had opened his heart to the treacherous song of the fox-maiden, and her voice had been louder than Sava's. There was nothing to be done about it now.

"Ah, Snow-Walker. You're home. Good." Dragan Wolf-Breaker, kuvar of the Lukoi, stood on Sava's porch. He was a man of indiscriminate age, with thick, dark hair worn pulled back and braided out of his face and the pale, ice-blue eyes possessed by all those of his line. Wolf eyes, they were called, and according to some they was a sign he was meant to rule the Lukoi. He was clean-shaven, as most of them were before the snows, and dressed in simple leathers and fur, with high, sturdy boots topped with fur, a knife sheathed at his side.

Also at his side was a slight man Sava had never seen before. He had lovely reddish-brown skin, curly dark hair that was blowing about in the wind, and huge brown eyes flecked with gold and green—they reminded Sava of the hills right before winter took them, the faded grasses that looked so lovely in the light of the setting sun—over which he wore two pieces of round glass connected by a wire. He was shivering, dressed poorly in what appeared to be threadbare fabrics and a pair of boots that were too big for him. Sava thought he'd seen Elena—the kuvar's daughter—wear those boots a time or two.

"Zora found a man," Dragan said. "Let us come in before he freezes on your porch, Snow-Walker."

Sava nodded and stepped back, and the pair entered the house. The shivering man with the messy hair looked longingly at the fire but seemed to shy away from going closer.

"Go and get warm." Dragan pointed toward the fire, sounding perhaps a bit exasperated. His dominance was heavy enough that even Sava could feel it, and it made the young man sway a bit before he moved.

"Zora found him?" Sava asked, curious, as the man walked over and knelt before the fire, muttering in a language Sava didn't know. "Where?"

"On the beach." Dragan shrugged. "He was left by a boat. He's a book-writer."

"No, that word is wrong that I am," the man said, glancing up, like he couldn't help himself. He winced the second Sava and Dragan looked at him and immediately lowered his gaze, muttering something to the floor.

"Why would a boat leave a book-writer?" Sava asked. "It is soon to be winter. Snow says nothing; it is silent."

The man's head snapped up again, and he said something in a

language Sava didn't understand. At their blank looks, he added, "Those words pretty are."

Sava glanced at Dragan, who shook his head. "He is from a place, Zora said, where they sit around in rooms and talk about other people."

"Why?"

"I don't know," Dragan said. "But he said he would be here unless another boat comes for him."

"No boat will come here anytime soon," Sava said, as the sky rumbled above them. "Only snow."

"Yes. I think he was a problem. So, you know the laws, Sava."

Sava did know the laws. There weren't many, but one that all Lukoi adhered to was the one that kept their civilization in existence long after the country that exiled their ancestors to this snow-covered island had fallen into ruin: *those exiled to die, survive.* If someone had sent this man here to die, he was now one of them. Lukoi.

"Excuse me," the pretty man said. "Would you kindly, the laws, to tell me."

"He speaks our language well enough," Dragan said. "Even though he has never been here."

"Huh." Sava considered that. "He must be clever," he added, because he'd never heard of anyone from Lukos leaving the island. How would anyone know the language if they had not heard it spoken?

"I can, the reading of it, yes," the man said. "The law you speak of, may I know of it?"

"He uses many words to say a few," Sava said, and the man laughed a bit wildly, raking both hands through his hair. It tousled it fetchingly, and Sava thought again that he was pretty, this wide-eyed stranger.

"You are not the first to be dropped here," Dragan said bluntly. "My mother, her people came from Mislia, they say. They shunned demons and were exiled, so they came to Lukos. Aleks, who lives nearby. In his line, far back, was the unwanted son of an Arkoudai soldier and his Katoikos lover."

"Unwanted," the man whispered, and seemed to wilt.

"That is what exiles are," Dragan said. "Sava, this man's name is Victor. He was not wearing shoes when Zora found him, and he was throwing rocks into the sea, and his socks were ice—"

"I was angry. The boat had with the leaving already made," the man, Victor, said. He winced and muttered something else to himself in his own language.

"Does throwing rocks into the sea summon boats, for book-writers?" Sava asked.

Victor sighed. "No."

"It was pique, I think," Dragan said. "Like Elena, when she would get cross while she was learning to hunt and would throw an arrow at a hare that escaped her."

"But she was six," Sava said. "This man is older than that."

Victor laughed again, louder this time, then put his head in his hands. His shoulders shook.

Alarmed, Sava looked at Dragan.

"This is the thing. He is an exile. So he is Lukoi, now. A submissive with no family, no dominant. The snows are coming." A pause, and then Dragan sighed and clapped him on the shoulder. "I will speak clearly, Snow-Walker. The winter comes, and this man has a very bad coat and wet boots that would be useless even if they were dry. There is no time to find him another place; the preparations have long since been finished. And I know that you have been … trying to share what you prepared, when you thought you would have a mate. I am not asking you to mate him, but … look at him, Sava. Even if you have given away most of the supplies you had gathered, he would only need a third of it not to starve."

Looking pained, Victor spoke in his own language again. He didn't seem to be addressing them, though.

"And there is a little time for you to gather more," Dragan

said. "The snows will come, but you are called *Snow-Walker,* so it should not be a problem. Keep this man alive in your home, which is the nicest of all of ours and big enough that you should not have a problem keeping him out from underfoot, since he is small and slight—"

More incomprehensible words from Victor.

"Maybe you can learn what it is he is saying," Dragan said. "Well, Sava? I would take him, but Elena is in my house for another winter yet, much to poor Aleks's despair. Marta and Ozren will soon have the child, and slight though this one is, I think he will eat more than a baby."

"It is all right," Sava said, because the poor man was shaking again, but maybe not from cold this time. "I will keep him alive until the thaws, Kuvar. But what will become of him then?"

"Well, then we will know if he is meant to be one of us or not. But he is pretty, Sava. Look at him. Maybe Ozren and Marta will want him. They will have a child to look after. If he can hold that sack, there, that he came with, maybe he can hold a baby."

Sava saw something on Victor's face, then. It wasn't anything he needed to translate. He looked as Sava felt when Milan went into the sea. As he felt when people looked at him, when they saw his house, built for two. The empty second chair on the porch.

He would not have a mate this winter, but perhaps he need not be alone.

"All right," Sava said. "Yes, Kuvar. I can keep this man alive."

Dragan nodded. "I know." He turned to Victor, voice booming. "Well, there you go, book-writer. A good outcome, see? And this house, it is the nicest one in Lukos. Probably like your scholar-houses, yes? Bring him later to the fires, Snow-Walker. Maybe get him some warmer clothes first."

With that problem solved, Dragan—practical, as all Lukoi were—turned to go. "He can keep the boots," Dragan called as he let himself out the door. "Elena says she outgrew them two, three winters ago."

And with that, he was gone, leaving Sava and Victor alone, while water dripped from Victor's face that Sava did not think was rain or snow. He politely didn't mention it. It would dry soon enough.

VICTOR COULDN'T BRING himself to look Sava in the eyes. *Dear David,* he thought, *please round up the captain of the* Seahorse *and have him brought up on charges. Do it in my memory, since I will die of embarrassment here on Lukos.*

He knew what this was. He'd experienced something like it before, when his friends at the Golden Street Orphanage waved goodbye from the road with their bags packed and their new parents beaming. When old Aunt Grace pulled him aside after a visit by a potential adoptive family and said, "But you're such a clever boy, Victor—you need someone *brilliant*. Someone special," while the visitors grimaced awkwardly and minced their way out of the sunny hall. When he was assigned to help the younger kids get ready for breakfast and help them learn their letters in the afternoon, like the older staff who began calling him "Vic" and "Teach." When he and the handful of other older kids would ride bicycles through the narrow, winding streets past the lake and would hear grandmothers strumming guitars from the little courtyards between houses, houses where entire branching trees of families lived together.

When he was eight and snuck into the traveling gallery in the square to wander alone through the paneled maze of paintings brought in by Kallistoi artists. He'd stopped in front of one almost the size of Aunt Grace, which featured a boy with black eyes sitting on a wall with a lyre in his lap. He was looking out at a gathering storm on the horizon, and Victor had felt such a pull of *yearning* that he sat down and stared at it until the sun went down and the artists started folding the panels up for the night.

Aunt Grace found him there, and Victor saw a hint of recognition in her eyes when she looked at the painting, hands on her bony hips.

"Well," she'd said. "He looks a lot like you, doesn't he, Victor?"

The boy in the painting didn't resemble him, not at all, but when Victor was older and would find himself sketching the boy's face on the margins of his notes in class, he thought he understood what she'd meant.

Now, he stared at the fire and tried to ignore the sounds of Sava moving around behind him.

"I'm sorry," he said at last. He knew he wasn't speaking as clearly as he wished, and he was probably still fucking up his verb placement—why was Professor Gregoris such *shit* with sentence construction? The man wouldn't know where to put a verb if it showed up with a map—but hopefully the meaning was still there. "I know I'm ..." He sighed and dug through his bag, pulling out his notes on the language. There was only one published work on the subject, so the few scholars who spoke it tended to use their own translations, cobbling the words together out of guesswork.

"An imposition," he said, finally. Sava frowned and moved closer, but he stopped when Victor shifted to make room.

"You don't have to make yourself small for me," Sava said in his low, soothing voice. He didn't bother to modulate the dominance there, but it was a comfort, like a weighted blankct on a cold evening or the currents of the rivers in Gerakia, which would gently push a boat for miles through the countryside. Victor couldn't help but relax a little, some of the tension draining from his shoulders.

"I'm in the way," Victor said with a shrug. "This is your house."

"That's not what the word you said means," Sava said. "It means powerful. Strong. Unable to be moved. And you are not in the way."

Victor squinted down at his notes and quietly cursed

Professor Gregoris to an eternity of teaching introductory classes to bored freshmen.

"Can you sew?" Sava asked, leaving Victor to the fire while he made his way to an adjoining room. "What I have may not fit you."

"I can … change them." Victor glanced up, now that Sava's back was turned. Sava was a powerful figure, with a sturdy frame and dark hair braided out of his face, and Victor had to force himself to think of David—poor David, who would probably get word that Victor had been lost at sea.

"I used to mend clothes when I was younger," Victor said, trying to banish the thought of David mourning him. "In the … house where children lived."

"You have houses just for children?" Sava asked. He came back with a bundle of clothes in his arms, and Victor gingerly took them.

He'd expected Sava to hand him fur-and-leather garments like those Dragan and the others had been wearing, but the first thing Victor saw was a knitted sweater. The soft wool was dyed a dark green, and Victor ran a hand over it, wondering if Sava had made it himself.

"I don't know if you have a word for it," Victor said, tugging on the sweater. "It's a house where children go when they have no parents."

Sava's gaze went dark, troubled. "You lost them? Your parents."

Victor tried on a laughably large coat. "No. I think my mother is alive. She just left me there."

"*Left* you? Did she not come back for you, later?"

Victor laughed. "No. I wasn't one of those kids." Sava was frowning slightly, and Victor gestured, trying to piece together the right words. "The kids who say, 'I don't need new parents. My mom's a queen, and she'll come back for me one day.' If she didn't want children, I'm sure she had a reason. You don't have that, here? People who give their children to someone else?"

Sava was silent for a moment, as though he were trying to translate. Given how badly Victor probably mangled that explanation, he likely was.

"Children are valued here," Sava said.

"I wasn't—" Victor groaned, searching for the words. "I wasn't not valued. There was a woman who was in charge of the house. She valued the hell out of me. She's why I went to … the place where you learn things."

Some of Sava's dark mood seemed to lift. "Ah. So she became your mother?"

"What? No. I don't have one. She was in charge of the house."

Aunt Grace liked Victor. He knew that. But she liked him in the way she liked all the children she took care of, with the knowledge that one day, they would find someone else to love them properly. So she always kept herself a little apart, which made sense to Victor. She was kind, and he loved her in his way, but she wasn't his *mother*.

But there was no way he could explain that to Sava, who was staring at him like Victor had just said, *My mother is a demon and my father is a summoning circle.*

"The point is, I know how to fix clothes," Victor said. "Because I was responsible for the younger kids. And I can clean, and cook a little. I have … books, I guess."

From his bag, he took out some of the journals he'd filled with translations of the Lukoi language and passed them to Sava. After a moment Sava turned his gaze from Victor to the books and opened one.

"This is empty," he said, and Victor's chest tightened in horror as he realized he'd just handed Sava a sketchbook. Sava turned the first page, and Victor grabbed the book back before Sava could see his weak rendition of the Two Sisters.

"Wrong book," he said. "The other one. That's it."

Sava gave Victor another curious look and skimmed through the book. "Your writing is very neat, but some of the words, they're in the wrong places."

"Blame fucking Gregoris for that one," Victor muttered in Iperian. "Yes," he said, in the language of the Lukoi. "I'm going to fix that."

"This is what you do?" Sava asked, turning the pages. "In the place where you lived?"

"Yes. I know words," Victor said. "Other languages. I know four, but yours is the one I study the most."

"Why? Do they know of us, where you were?"

"Not well," Victor said, thinking of the sailor with his tales of naked wolf men. "I wanted to figure it out. Your country is beautiful, and you're the only ones left of the place that exiled you."

Sava smiled, faintly, for the first time since Victor had been dropped on his doorstep. "Yes. We are."

"That's it," Victor said, a little too loudly, and drew back as he realized he was pointing at Sava. "That's why. Your country was massive. Powerful. They ruled from Staria to Arktos, and they exiled you, and you made yourself a new country and you *survived*. Who wouldn't want to know how? Why is no one here, talking to you? Writing it down?"

"Our winters are long, and the waters have sunk more than one ship," Sava said. "When the first Lukoi came, two of our ships sank on the ice. The water, it is death."

There was something odd about the way Sava said that last part, something that made Victor pause. "There's nothing left of the people who exiled you but stones."

Sava sighed and closed the book. "You'll learn to fix the words, I think, after your first winter here."

*Your first winter.* He spoke like Victor would have a second, as well. Victor wasn't sure what was worse: dying of hypothermia two days in, or living while David wept for him in Gerakia.

He didn't realize he'd fallen silent until Sava gently put his book back in his bag and stood to go to a trapdoor in the floor. He came up with some flatbread and strips of meat, which he set in a pan over the fire while Victor tried to wrestle into the rest of his borrowed garments. He was swimming in them, and when Sava made a startled noise, looking at Victor standing there like a child in an adult's clothes, Victor shocked himself with a laugh.

"Yes, I know," he said. "I'm too beautiful to look at."

Sava quickly glanced away, but Victor thought he saw a hint of that elusive smile again.

Sava didn't eat, which made Victor uneasy on a biological level. He was a submissive, and he liked to please people, which was wrenching when he was dating a philosopher who couldn't decide what counted as *good behavior* and he came from a string of rejected adoption visits and distant friends.

He would have been something, probably, if he'd come home with a degree. But that dream was dying by the minute, and Victor doubted the scholar's laurel meant anything to the Lukoi.

"You should eat something," he finally said to Sava, "or I can … do something. Wash the dishes. Do you have things that need to be done?"

"More than you know," Sava said. "Always. Winter will come soon, and there is always something to be done."

"Oh. We don't really have winter in Gerakia. It's too warm. Just summer and spring, a little fall."

"You don't have snow there?"

"Once, when I was a boy. I slept through it, and it melted. But the lake was covered in ice." Victor smiled. "I was so mad, my roommate made snow out of soap to make me feel better."

"Your what?" Sava's brows lowered. "You had a mate, as a …"

"A roommate," Victor said. "That's what it … it means you live with someone in the same room?"

"Mate means something different here," Sava said, and Victor blushed as he realized what he was implying.

"Oh. No. Not that. This was in the house with children. There were a lot of us, so we had to live together."

"Are there … many houses like this, in Gerakia?" Sava's voice was careful, precise.

Victor shrugged as he finished his flatbread. "I think? But it's not what you're thinking. People would come there and pick a child they liked, and bring them home." Victor winced. He was probably painting Gerakia like a nightmare, instead of a place where the most danger he ever encountered involved falling off his bike on the way to the bookstore.

"Every child, they had this experience, then."

"No." Victor smiled to himself. "Not all of us. But it's all right. It means I'm used to it, being dropped off in strangers' houses, eating their food. But it won't be for long. Someone's going to come find me soon."

*My mom's a queen, and she'll come get me and you'll all be sorry.*

Well, wonderful. Now Sava knew what Victor was, and he hadn't been there for more than an hour. Victor pushed the nagging voice to the back of his mind and stood, holding his dish in both hands, and went off in search of a sink before he could dig himself deeper still.

# CHAPTER 3

What a strange man Victor was.

The word he taught Sava was *scholar,* a strange word to use, here. Every Lukoi knew the history of their people. If they forgot, they would go to the caves and see it written there on the walls, etched in stone. But they wouldn't forget. It's why they were still there, still thriving in the place they were long ago sent to die.

He did not entirely understand why Victor was here. He'd said it was to study the Lukoi, to make a primer of their language, but that it was only to be a week's visit before he would return to Gerakia. Someone who claimed to know their people and who *did* know their language—at least well enough to communicate— thought a ship would clear the ice of the bay this close to the first snowfall? That seemed not likely, but what did Sava know of scholars or book-writing or places where people made snow out of soap?

He was not sure he'd heard that right. Perhaps it was a phrase that did not translate. He was certain they would have many of those, over the winter. And he could not stop thinking of the houses full of children, so many they would simply … give them away. He could not imagine that. In Lukos, the birth of a child was celebrated as one more victory against the long-ago king who sent them forth to die.

When dinner was over, Sava said, "I should show you about the food. It is important that you keep this trapdoor, here, closed. If animals get the food, we will not survive the winter."

Victor's eyes went wide. "I won't. I, ah. I mean, yes, of course."

"Do not worry," Sava assured him, when he saw how alarmed Victor looked. "There is a lot of food. More in the tanning house. But we cannot be too careful. Life is harsh here, but it is my fourth winter on my own, and I know how to survive it."

Victor smiled at him. "I don't doubt it. You built this house yourself, is that right?"

"Yes, that's right," Sava said, leaning against the wall. "Do not tell me they make the children build them, where you are from?"

"What? No," Victor said, looking askance at him. "That's—the building was already there."

Sava smiled. "Yes. I was joking."

Victor blushed, which was fetching on him, Sava decided. "Oh, right. Sorry, it's … been a long day."

That made Sava feel bad about teasing him. "Yes. I would think it was. Why would they send you here in the winter? Even if they do not know that much about us, they must know how harsh it is here when it snows. Is it because you do not have snow in your country that you do not know when it comes?"

"I think my … I think someone lied," Victor said, but he glanced away, going tense, and it was clear he didn't want to speak of it. "To the person who arranged my trip here. We don't know a lot about the specifics, no. Maybe I'll keep a record." Victor lifted one of his books. "I can write it down during the winter."

"You will have the time, yes," Sava said. "But we should make sure you have the, ah … what do you use, for the writing?"

"A quill? I have one."

"Yes? Good. And the, ah, what you write with, you have plenty of that, yes?"

Victor blinked his huge eyes at Sava again. Sava wondered if he wore the glass circles because his eyes were so pretty he wanted to show them off. That would make sense. "Ink, you mean?"

"Ah, yes. Ink. Do you have that?"

"I have … some, yes, enough for the week I was supposed to be here." Victor looked concerned. "Now I'm thinking I don't have enough for the winter, so … do you?"

"Me? No." Sava smiled. "Our healer, Ivan, he has flowers that can be ground to make pigments. Marta, she knows how to do it, and sometimes she makes … stretched canvas, to use them on. Do you know this?"

"It's … painting?" Victor smiled. "Yes, I know painting. I … wouldn't mind extra canvas to paint on, if she has it."

Sava smiled back. "That is good. She is big with child now and I think will not come to the fire at the kuvar's tonight, but Ivan will be there. I will bring you to him, tell him about needing the flowers. Tomorrow we will trade with him for them, and with Marta for some of the canvas."

"That … would be very nice, thank you." Victor beamed, and it was so lovely that Sava found his own smile widening in response. They stood there, smiling at each other, and then Sava felt his own cheeks heat and clapped his hands once.

"Good. Now, take off those boots. They are still too big. Your people are very small. I have fur. I will line them for you. New socks. You will not walk in streams in socks; that is not a good idea."

Victor made a choked noise. "I did learn that, thank you. What, ah. What are you called, here?"

"Sava," he said, slowly. If Victor was so clever, surely his name wasn't too hard to say? "Or Snow-Walker, but that—" He almost said, *that isn't what a mate would call me,* before he remembered

Victor was not a mate. "That is not what someone who shares my home would call me."

"I meant, for dominants, do you like to be called … hmm. *Master? Sir? My lord?*"

Sava didn't know what any of those words meant, but he knew they weren't his name. "Just Sava is fine. Those words you said, what do they mean?"

"Oh, they're just …" Victor waved a hand. He gave that same laugh again, the one that sounded more like he wanted to yell instead. "Words dominants like, back home. That show you're important, that we submissives respect you."

"Does a name not mean that, where you are from?" Sava tilted his head and regarded him solemnly as something else occurred to him. "Is there a word I should use to show *you* that you are important, that dominants respect you?"

"How are you … how are you even *real?*" Victor asked, and Sava had no notion how to answer such a thing.

"I am not a book-writer," he said. "Or a mystic, to see stories in smoke and dreams."

"You have those?"

Sava nodded. "Yes. We have a hot spring, and sometimes if you smoke the right sort of herbs, you see things in the mists there. But sometimes it just makes you dizzy and want to lie down."

Victor's laugh was more genuine this time. "Just Victor is fine, Sava. Thank you for … all of this, really. I know you probably didn't want a roommate for the winter, so …"

He'd wanted a mate, but now he knew that word meant something else to Victor, so he simply shrugged. "Let me have your boots, and I will fix them so they are warm."

Sava watched as Victor sat and pulled off the boots. He was shivering again. Sava clucked. "You will, I think, need more fat on you. They do not make you big enough in your warm city, do they?"

Victor laughed, and Sava smiled even though he'd been serious. He found some charcoal he kept to make notes about hunts and supplies, and handed it to Victor to supplement his supply of pens and ink while he went to do something about the boots.

In the tanning shed, Sava found some leftover fur scraps and went about attaching them to the boots. He made short work of it—he'd been doing this since he was practically a child—and then went ahead and quickly fashioned some other remnants into a rudimentary pair of gloves and a hat.

When he went back inside, the thunder had picked up, and there were flakes of snow mixed in with the sleet. It made a gentle sound as it fell, coating the ground in a slick surface that glittered in the muted afternoon light. It was rapidly getting colder as the sun went behind the mountains, which it did earlier and earlier as the season hurtled inexorably toward winter.

Sava knocked his boots on the coarse rug—he'd made it from the quills of a porcupine, and he made a note to warn Victor not to walk on it without shoes—and headed in with his offerings. He stopped as he saw Victor sitting in the furs, head bent, writing with the charcoal in one of his books.

Only he wasn't writing—he was drawing. Sava crept closer and heard Victor mutter as he raised his arm and rubbed at the charcoal with his sleeve. When he noticed Sava standing there—which took him quite a long time, to be honest—he startled, and Sava saw he had smears of charcoal on his nose. "Oh! You … walk so softly, I didn't hear. You must have taken your boots … oh." He flushed, seeing Sava was still in his boots, and muttered something in his own tongue.

Sava was too taken by the image sketched on the page of the book in Victor's hand to worry about the words he didn't understand. He realized with some surprise that he knew what it depicted. "Those are the hills, from the shore."

"Yes." Victor beamed at him. "I thought they were beautiful. If I had colors, I would draw them … Did you just *make* those?"

It took Sava a moment to realize Victor meant the furs he was holding, fashioned into a few things that would hopefully keep him warmer. "Yes. That is very good, your drawing. Is this how you write books, in Gerakia? You will like the caves, I think, that tell the story of the Lukoi. It is in pictures, but not like that."

"Sure. The images in the caves are probably better."

"No," Sava interrupted, frowning. "You are doing that thing again. Making yourself small. This, it is much better than the caves. I will take you to them, before we are snowed in. Maybe you could draw the story better."

"Better than the Lukoi?"

Sava shrugged. "Spite made us survive. It did not make us artists."

Victor smiled at him. "Can you teach me to walk that quietly?"

"Hmm. Maybe if I carry you." He smiled to show he was kidding—or, no, he wasn't, but he didn't mean it unkindly.

"Is that a … family name, then?" Victor asked, setting the book aside to inspect the new fur-lined boots. He slipped them on, and the grin on his face told Sava they fit well and were warm. Good.

"Snow-Walker? No. It is a sobriquet. Do you have them?"

Victor stood up, got tangled in the furs he'd rolled in, and blushed as he wriggled out of them … only to forget the area was slightly sunken and bang his ankle on the side. He grumbled a few things that Sava would guess were curses, then climbed out of the fur pit and shot it a victorious glare, like he'd felled a bear.

Sava hid a smile and waited for him to answer.

"I … no. I don't know. The word, I mean. Sobr— What was it?"

"Sobriquet," Sava said again, slowly, then spelled it out. Victor repeated it twice, the second time flawlessly—he was clever, even if a bit clumsy. "It is a name you earn, not one you are given at birth. The man who brought you here, he is Dragan Wolf-Breaker."

"I … yeah, he would be," Victor said, slipping the hat on his head. It was a bit too big for him, but he shook his head when Sava offered to tighten it. "Did he really … break one?"

"Well. No. We revere wolves. But he came upon one while he was hunting, and it howled to summon the pack, maybe to bring him down as prey. Dragan howled back, fierce enough that the wolf stopped, showed its belly, and followed him home. Now he has wolves of her line as pets. His daughter, whose boots you have now. She has two, pups both, that follow her everywhere."

"Sure," Victor said weakly and then added something in his own language.

Sava had learned the little asides were not meant for him, so he let it go. "I am called Snow-Walker because once, when I was wintering with my mother, a wolverine—do you know these creatures? They are small, wily, have fangs that tear things, and are very tenacious?"

"I do … not," Victor said, eyes wide. "In Gerakia, we have house cats. Tame dogs."

"Ah. Well. One caught the scent of food up in a tree, where I was storing the fat from fish I had caught, and it climbed the tree and ate the fat. My mother was not well at the time. It was shortly before she went back to the sea—that is what we call it when we die. She was weak and needed fat. You will need fat, too." Sava wondered why Victor winced at that. "So I hunted a bear, which is not easy to do. I had to walk quietly, both to find it and to bring it home safely when I had killed it. The wolverine, eh? It would have liked that meal. Lots of fat on a bear, early in the winter."

"I might, hmm." Victor put a hand on his forehead as if he was going to crumple.

"Do you not feel well?" Sava asked, concerned. "Maybe it is too warm in here."

"No." Victor gave another slightly wild laugh. "No. So, the bear?"

"I brought it back, and then I had to wait outside in the snow for the wolverine. I did not want it to eat the bear fat. And I was, ah." Sava cleared his throat. "Perhaps it will not make you think well of me, but I was angry at it."

"Why would … Go on, please."

"Try on the gloves," Sava urged, and watched him slip them on. "Too big. I will make you better ones out of deer hide, I think. Maybe lined with fur. But they will work for now. So I waited for the wolverine, and when it came, I took it with an arrow. That winter we had bear meat thick with fat, and I made that blanket, there, you were huddled in. And the wolverine, its meat does not taste good, but I used the fur to line my favorite boots. So that is why I am called Snow-Walker, as I hunted in the snow."

"And it's easier to say than—what was the animal called, again?"

"Wolverine. Not a wolf. Different animal. Smaller. Meaner, I think."

Victor smiled at him, laughed, and shook his head. "I've seen one bear in my life, and it was not alive. It was, how do I say it … propped up, in a place that shows things. A *museum*, we call it. We put art there, and, ah. *Artifacts.*"

Sava was not as quick with the new words as Victor, but he tried to say them. They felt clumsy, like the too-big hat on Victor's head, or the gloves. But Victor didn't seem to mind, and Sava soon forgot about it. He did remember to warn Victor about the rug, then spent a few minutes describing a porcupine, which Victor finally understood when he realized it was covered in quills.

"I will find you tools to write with, so you can draw more mountains," Sava said gallantly. He headed to the door and opened it for Victor.

"Thank you." Victor beamed, then promptly slipped on the sleet-slicked wood of the porch and landed, with a squeak, on his ass. "This isn't going to make me *Victor Slippery-Feet*, is it?"

"Not if we do not tell anyone." Sava helped him stand and

patted him awkwardly on the arm, all too aware of the heat of Victor's body next to his. Sava had not touched anyone since a hunting trip weeks ago, when he and Vasily took a moment to find pleasure under a tree.

It thundered again as they walked, slow and steady, toward the kuvar's fire.

WIND HOWLED over the valleys as Victor followed Sava in the direction of the kuvar's house. There weren't really any roads, just a few hunting paths, and everyone lived far enough away from each other that they could go ages without seeing a single lonely house in the distance. It was as though Lukos wanted to remind Victor that he really was rather small in the grand scheme of things, just one more creature struggling to survive in a land that would long outlast him. It was the kind of philosophy David hated the most—he preferred the ones about the strength of a man's mind, the immortality of thought. He would have called Victor's theory too depressing to consider, but Victor thought, secretly, that there was some good in it. The land survived, just like the Lukoi had survived. Empires rose and fell, but winter still came to Lukos, with snow clouds that thundered like a summer storm, and wasn't that important, too? Wasn't it beautiful that he could be around to see something immortal, even if he wasn't?

*Leave philosophy to the masters,* David would have said, laughing softly, and for some reason, that didn't make Victor smile with the same kind of fondness as it would have, back at the Two Sisters.

But Victor's mind had been acting strangely when it came to David. It was like there was a vast, yawning pit around David's name, one that Victor kept skirting because if he thought too much about it, he would have to stare into it. So he didn't. He tried to push David out of his thoughts … but when he did, there was Sava, competent and thoughtful and strong enough to kill a bear with his own two hands.

Sava was the nicest dominant Victor had ever met. They'd met less than six hours ago, but Victor *knew*. Some people were inherently good. The universe deposited them on Earth sometimes, maybe as a way to compensate for all the petty squabbling the rest of the world got up to. Or maybe it was a curse. Maybe Victor was doomed to find competence hot in other people, only to be tossed into a small cabin with *Sava*, who built a house on his own and took in strangers who fell out of the ocean, *and* had the kind of natural dominance that would put any submissive under at a touch. If Victor weren't mostly sure that someone would come for him eventually, he might even …

No. No, that was terrible. He tried to force himself to think of David, but there was that pit again, threatening to swallow him whole.

"We're almost there," Sava said, clearly not aware of Victor's skittering thoughts as they trudged through the dying grass. "Maybe you'll see the wolf pups tonight, eh? You said there are dogs where you come from?"

"Sure, everywhere." Victor smiled to himself. "There's at least one street dog in every town. Everyone takes care of them, but no one owns them. There's an old story about that, how every street dog is actually the same one, a dog who waited for his boy to come back from war. He's still waiting, so that's why he never settles down with anyone. His heart belongs somewhere else."

"We have stories like that, too," Sava said, in a soft tone. "But the spirits in them, they're not always so kind."

"I used to believe it, when I was a boy." Victor struggled to keep up in his enormous boots, and Sava had to grab his arm to keep him from falling. "Thank you. I used to go up to the dog in the town where I lived—where the orphanage, that's what they called the house for the children, was—and I would get down close and say, 'It's me! I'm home!' I thought maybe the dog would feel better if he thought I was his lost boy."

"That was kind of you," Sava said, looking down at Victor with a curious expression.

"Foolish, maybe. Is that the fire?" Victor gestured to a spot of light over a slight rise in the ground and grinned when he saw figures there, sitting around the flames. One of them stood and waved, and Sava nodded back, glancing at Victor.

"That's Ivan Spring-Singer," he said as the figure started marching toward them. "Named for his gift with plants. He is … enthusiastic. You'll see."

"Sava!" A warm voice called out over the whistling breeze, and Victor caught a glimpse of brown hair in a narrow face, wrapped in a red cap that covered his ears. "I hear you have a new exile! A book-writer, is he? Hello, book-writer!"

Victor raised a hand, and Ivan flashed a grin. He had the kind of face Victor had seen at the university too many times to count. This was the Lukoi version of the unexpectedly perfect senior classman, the one who threw the best parties, blacked out in the fountain at least once, and then turned around to write a dissertation that had half the faculty singing his praises. He beamed at Victor and walked over to clasp Sava by the arm.

"Where did you find him again? The sea? He looks like one of the bird people in my mother's old stories, only human for a day."

"The feathers are hidden," Victor said, and Ivan's grin came back, broader than ever.

"Oh, good. I was worried I'd have to dislike you." He glanced at Sava. "But if you're a bird person in disguise, that's all right. Sit with me. I brought my best cider, grew the spices myself."

Oh, yes. Victor had definitely met people like Ivan before.

There were a handful of others at the fire, which looked like the kind of bonfire Victor used to run around on lakeside beaches as a boy, drawing pictures in the sand with sticks while teenagers tried to secretly get drunk and other kids dared each other to jump in the water. A young man Ivan called Aleks was there, seated on a stone next to a girl who looked like a mirror image of the kuvar, only a little more inclined to smile. Or maybe it was just that Aleks was staring at her fervently while two people who had to be his parents laughed quietly to each other and shot him sympathetic looks.

Zora was sitting by the kuvar, but she didn't rise when she saw Victor and Sava approach. She smiled tightly at Victor, but her gaze went hard when it slid past him, and Victor found himself struggling just to say hello.

Ivan dragged Victor away from Sava, who stepped forward as though to stop him, then hesitated just a moment too long.

"Everyone," Ivan said, an arm slung around Victor's shoulders, "this is Victor, who survived a terrible shipwreck when his captain was eaten by sea ghosts. He's haunted by them still."

"Shut up, Spring-Singer, you didn't even find him," Aleks said. "And his ship *left*, it didn't *sink*."

Ivan rolled his eyes. "Sinking is better." He took a seat on the other side of the fire, pulling Victor with him, and Sava sat next to Victor. For a man who very obviously didn't have a dominant bone in his body, Ivan was determined. "If your ship sank, it means they didn't leave you."

"Oh." Aleks's cheeks colored. "Victor, I'm sorry."

Victor was glad, at least, that he didn't show a blush as easily as Aleks. "It's fine."

Ivan introduced the rest of the circle. Elena was the kuvar's daughter, and she did have wolf pups, which were asleep under a discarded coat at her feet. There was Ozren, who had a mate at home who wanted the house to themself for a time, a dominant named Vasily who passed Sava a drink and tried to get Aleks caught up in a game of dice, and the kuvar.

"And you two have met," Ivan said, gesturing to Zora. "The one who rescued you from the sea!"

Zora shifted uncomfortably in her chair, and a silence descended over the gathering.

Victor could feel the weight in the air, charged as if with an oncoming storm, but it was like he was reading only half of the script of a play he didn't know. He bowed to Zora and held out his hand, and she startled, just a little, like she'd forgotten he was there.

"I didn't thank you properly before," he said. She took his hand in both of hers, and he smiled when she squeezed his fingers.

"That's all right," she said. "We protect exiles, here."

She glanced behind Victor, to where Sava was sitting, and Sava looked into the growing dark. Victor glanced between them, and Ivan pulled Victor aside, lowering his voice.

"I'll tell you later."

"Right," Victor whispered back.

As the biggest news on the island, Victor spent most of the evening trying not to stumble over his words while more people started to ask him questions and Ivan plied him with cider. Aleks wanted to know about the university. Ivan wanted to know what the ship was like. Elena wanted to know *everything*.

"Is it true it's always summer in the desert?" she asked. Victor tried not to shrink in on himself, clutching the bottle Ivan had given him.

"In Arktos, maybe," he said. "But I hear at night, it gets so cold that it's like winter, and you can see every star in the sky."

Elena went quiet, and Aleks darted in with, "So what did you do there, in the south? You wrote books?"

"No, I … learned things. Some people, that's their job." Victor scratched the back of his neck. "I wasn't very good at it. No, I was, but I messed it up, at the end, and that's why I'm here."

"Maybe that's enough questions," Sava said, in a low rumble.

"One more," Ivan said. "How'd you mess up? Were you exiled, then?"

"No, my … my dominant. I have a dominant, at home." Sava went very still next to him. "But people didn't want us to be together, so I had to come here so I could …" He tried to remember David's plan. "Become important, like him. Except they left me, and now he probably thinks I'm dead."

There was a stark silence in the circle, and Ivan carefully took the bottle back from Victor, patting his hand. "You have a mate," he said. "And people separated you?"

Victor shrugged. "It was his idea for them to bring me here. Not … not to *leave* me."

"Maybe your mate wasn't very smart," Ivan said, not unkindly, "sending you here so soon before winter."

"Oh, no, he's very smart. Smarter than me." Victor smiled wryly. "But maybe he'll come for me."

"Yeah," Ivan said, patting Victor again. "What's his name?"

"David." Victor stood up, wobbling a little. "Sorry, I need some air. Lots of it, here."

As he staggered a few paces away from the fire, he heard Elena hiss, "Good job, Spring-Singer."

"I didn't know!"

Footsteps crunched on the grass behind him, and Victor crossed his arms tight over his chest as Sava walked up next to him, a bulky shadow against the fire.

"I didn't know you were mated."

"I'm not really," Victor said. Mated felt permanent, weighted, the way Sava said it. "Not for real, yet. We were supposed to be together after I came back. Really together."

"But you love him?"

Victor lifted his glasses to rub at his eyes. "Fuck."

Sava reached out slowly, and when Victor didn't pull away, he laid a hand on his shoulder. "I'm sorry. Do you want to go back?"

"I want to go home," Victor said miserably. "I want him to hold me. I want him to say he didn't know they would leave me here."

There was a short silence, and Sava's fingers curled slightly. "You don't mean—"

Victor's mind frantically skidded around the edges of the pit. "No. No, I don't mean that. Of course I don't. He wouldn't know. I'm sorry—you're taking me in, and I'm crying over a man who will forget me if he's smart."

"He could still come for you."

"I know you're just being kind." Victor put his glasses back on, but they were completely fogged. "I'm not going to see him again, am I?"

"I don't know," Sava said. "But we'll be here, and so will you. You'll endure."

"The way you say it, I almost believe it." Victor turned away and let Sava's hand fall from him, the warmth of the fire bleeding away into the bitter cold. "I wish I could."

# CHAPTER 4

Of course Victor had a mate. He was clever and could draw mountains with charcoal, remember new words, and speak many languages. That was not the sort of man who would remain alone for long.

The rest of their time at the fire was pleasant enough, but Sava was aware of Victor's valiant attempts to hide his shivers as the night wore on. Ozren promised to ask Marta about the canvases, and Ivan instructed them to come by the next day for some pigments and a few other things he swore would make the winter pass easier for Victor.

"He said he lived alone," Victor said, when his shivers had grown more blatant and Sava decided it best to return home. "Ivan. But he's a submissive—or did I get that wrong?"

"He is, yes. He lived with his mother, but she grew weak and did not survive the last winter." Sava remembered standing with Milan by the fire after the thaws as Ivan crested the hill alone. It was always a joyful event, greeting the others around the kuvar's fire to celebrate their endurance, another winter in the past. But the moment he'd approached them, Ivan's smile had faded and the light in his eyes had dimmed. The Lukoi had been sympathetic, but Ivan had grown angry at his murmured condolences and stormed off—one of the few times Sava had seen Ivan anything less than cheerful.

"So he'll be … alone?"

"It is uncommon, but it happens. Submissives do not often build their homes—that is a dominant's responsibility—but if they inherit one, as Ivan did from his mother, and they are not mated, it isn't unheard of. You'll see, tomorrow. He has gardens, all sorts of … tinctures, potions? Do you know those words?"

"Medicines, yes?" Victor nodded and deftly maneuvered around a tree stump that had almost sent him sprawling on the way there. He made a triumphant noise, but a moment later Sava had to keep him from tripping on an exposed root, and it gave way to a sigh.

"Yes. He also makes cider, as you know, and it is very good. Mostly, we put fruit to ferment at the end of summer, and by the time we are miserable in our homes and waiting for the thaws, it is potent enough that we can forget the darkness and the boredom and the sound of the ice against the roof."

"The … ice," Victor said, repeating the word slowly. "Is that— You don't mean—"

"Yes," Sava said, amused at the look on his face. "It begins with the thundersnow: that's what you heard today. Then we have sleet, freezing rain, mixed with the snow. When the snow comes to us in truth, we go inside, and that is where we stay. Eventually it goes away as it comes, with the snow turning to rain, the little pellets like we have now. But before it is over, the ice comes. We call it *false rain*, because by then you can see the ground and it looks only wet, not frozen."

"Wonderful," Victor said dryly, but there was a glimmer of interest in his eyes, curiosity that apprehension couldn't bank. "And that's when you drink?"

"Yes. The urge to go outside then, it is very strong. That's when you hear—" Sava stopped. He did not want to tell Victor about the fox-demon spirit. If he did not know of it, maybe he would not hear it. "You start to again hear the sea, and the sound of tree limbs as they crack and break. The world looks safe, but it is not. One last test for us, we call it. Where the kuvar's house is, that is where it is the worst. The urge to go outside is strong, but it is so cold, so still, that a breath in feels like needles in your lungs. False spring, false thaw … it is when you must be careful not to catch the winter madness. You've survived indoors so long that you think you cannot possibly bear it any longer, not when the sun shines as it does in the ice. So we draw animal skins over the windows, keep the fire burning, and drink so we can't go forth from our homes. When the real thaws come, you know by the sound of the *drip, drip* as the ice melts."

Victor smiled a bit. "The way you say it, it's almost romantic."

Sava laughed shortly. "No, no. Well. Maybe the first time. My first winter, I was … hmm. Enthralled by the quiet. It is why dominants have to face a winter alone, at least one, before taking a mate. To prove they can survive, that they will not give in to the temptation of a false spring and leave before it is time. It is why most do two winters, and … I did three." Much to Milan's mother's disapproval. Zora made no secret of her belief that if only Sava had mated Milan sooner, Milan would not have fallen prey to the fox-maiden's song.

"And you were going to have a mate, but he … went outside too soon?" Victor placed a hand on his arm. "You don't have to talk about it, if it's painful."

Of course it was painful, but Sava shrugged. "Soon we will live many months in a cabin together, Victor. There is very little that will be kept from each other. Milan did not succumb to the false spring, no. It was after that when he went into the sea."

"You don't mean—" Victor swallowed. "You don't mean he … literally went into the sea, right? It's just a saying?"

"No, he did. The waters after the snows are beautiful, clear and blue. We say, when we die, that we let the sea take us. That is true. But Milan … one morning, his mother woke up and he was not there. She thought perhaps he was with me. It was after a fire like the one we were at, at the kuvar's. After the thaws, we come together and feast, share what we have left, drink together. But Milan did not leave with me that night. In the morning, he woke early and went into the water. He drowned."

"Oh, I'm … so sorry," Victor said softly, his eyes very wide behind his strange mask of glass and wire.

"What is this for," Sava asked, touching it lightly. Not to change the subject, or not only that. He genuinely wanted to know. "To make your pretty eyes look bigger?"

Victor gave a sharp inhale. "You think—ah. No, it's so I can see. There's, oh boy. Um. How do I … There's something about the glass, the way it is bent, that makes me see better with my glasses than I can without them."

"Oh. Is that how you can see the mountains so clearly, to draw them?"

"I … no, not really. My problem is things that are too close, not far away. And then, of course, there are forests that I cannot see because I am looking at the trees."

"What?" Sava blinked and looked around. "The forest is made of trees, Victor. Is it different, in your land of soap snow and scholars?"

The smile Victor gave him made something tighten in Sava's chest. "No. It's an expression. It means … that sometimes you get so caught up in the small details, you miss the bigger picture."

Sava pondered that, but he was more interested in the way Victor's soft smile faded and his eyes went sad and bright behind his glasses. His melancholy, almost pained, expression made Sava's protective instincts kick up. "What? Did something hurt you? Did your ankle twist, one of those times you nearly tripped?"

Victor shook his head. "No." His voice sounded strange, a mix of tears and anger. "I think I finally saw the forest, that's all." At

Sava's expression, he shrugged and wrapped his arms around himself. "And I'd rather keep looking at the trees."

Sava almost asked him to explain, but if Sava wanted to keep his guilt for not mating Milan fast enough to prevent his death close for now, Victor could do the same with his … trees.

"Let me tell you how to find the way back," he said, pointing to the stars. "In case you're ever out alone. If you can see the sky, there is a formation the stars make, see? It looks like a knife, so we call it the Dagger's Blade. The tip of it: follow that, and it will lead you to my home."

"Thank you." Victor blinked up at Sava, and Sava fought some restless urge in himself, smothering it like the embers of a fire. Victor had a mate. Sava would have him only for the winter, and then he would leave when the thaws came. Milan was not to be his mate, and neither was this strange, pretty, clever scholar from beyond the shores.

"But I don't think I should be out here without you," Victor said, then proved why two seconds later, when he tripped again. The disturbance sent something furry and fast skittering out of the underbrush, and Sava laughed as Victor gave a startled yelp and moved almost as quickly in the other direction.

"That was just a snow hare," Sava said, grinning. "He saw your big eyes, perhaps, and thought you were an owl." That was a good comparison. Owls were wide-eyed and clever, like Victor. "Maybe, if you see one in the daytime, you could draw it, like you draw the mountains."

"Sure," Victor said weakly, adjusting his glasses. He shivered again. "Unless I freeze before we get home."

"You won't freeze, little owl, because I will carry you." Sava laughed again, the sound echoing loud in the chilly night, as he grabbed Victor and tossed him onto his back like a deer. "And this way, we will get home before spring."

❄

VICTOR HAD THOUGHT, when Sava slung him over his shoulder, that he would spend the rest of the walk in private mortification. Instead, he was laughing himself hoarse as he was carried into Sava's lovely house. He hadn't laughed so hard since he and Miles had taken a one-man canoe together across the lake, wobbling and shrieking as disgruntled professors watched them from the shore. He was crying with it, pushing up his glasses to wipe his eyes as Sava gently set him on the floor. Even Sava was smiling, his beautiful, quiet smile that lit up his whole face, and Victor was still grinning as he leaned over to help Sava out of his boots.

It was instinctive—a habit built from years of helping younger kids in and out of their shoes, snickering on the floor as he helped Miles out of some strappy leather sandals, removing David's boots for him after a clandestine night out. His hands seemed to move on their own, and he already had Sava's laces undone before he realized.

"Oh," he said. "Sorry. Is this too forward?"

"The word you just used means to fall from a height," Sava said, but his smile faltered. "But you can, if you would like to. Is it something submissives do, where you are?"

"Mostly submissives named Victor." Victor wriggled the boots off and squinted at the dirt still clinging to the soles. He went to knock them on the door frame like he did with his own at home, most evenings, and Sava gently stopped him, handing him a pick. "Oh. You care about your shoes, here."

"You don't, in your warm country?"

"I was always barefoot." Victor started clumsily cleaning the boots, sure he was doing it wrong but too embarrassed to ask. He knew he was trying to run from the truth he'd seen on the way there, the pit in his mind, but he forced his voice to be light, amiable. "Imagine it, Sava. Summers that last four months. The streets are clean, and there are carts everywhere, selling food and ice flavored like fruit, dough fried in hot oil and dipped in …

something wonderful, and you're ten and there's no one to tell you to put your shoes back on. That was Gerakia."

"It sounds like you love it," Sava said.

"Of course. It would be awful not to love where you are. Aunt Grace, the woman who ran the orphanage, she said you could drop me in the desert and I'd find something to like about it. I used to pick out houses I wanted to live in. That one! No, that one! I couldn't decide."

"There are that many, where you come from?"

"More than you can count." Victor set Sava's boots on the floor next to the door and gently kicked off his own. They were muddy, but it was fine. He was still too buzzed to care. "All pushed up next to each other. Big families all living together. Everyone knows each other's business. Don't lock your door, because what are you hiding?"

He chuckled as he stumbled into the pit before the fire. "But everyone knows each other here, too. And your hills! Your houses! We could fill libraries with books about you. I hope that isn't rude. I don't think you're, oh, what, a shark in a fishbowl."

"You said that last part in your own language," Sava said, and Victor groaned. "Come, you should bathe before you sleep."

"Just roll me into the fire." Sava startled, staring at him in alarm. "I didn't mean that."

"Good. You should still come here. I will show you how to heat the water."

Sava's dominance was strong enough to tug at Victor's incessant need to please, so Victor clambered out of the fur pit and followed him into a room with yet another fireplace. Sava showed him a clever trick he used to heat the water over the fire so that it rolled down a small trough into the tub, and the room was soon warm and so full of steam that Victor took off his glasses and fumbled for the bath.

"Not in your clothes," the blob that was Sava said in a bemused voice. "You'll need help, I think."

"I haven't needed help to take a bath since I was seven," Victor said, but went quiet when Sava eased him out of his coat. It wasn't the playful sort of undressing, the kind he and David used to do, with David leaning back while Victor unbuttoned David's trousers with his teeth and trailed his fingers up his chest. It was polite, no-nonsense, and it made Victor slip right back into the dark pit he'd been desperately trying to avoid.

David.

David had known. David had known all along that there was no expedition, and he'd sent Victor to Lukos anyway. He probably didn't think there was anything wrong with it, either.

*Individual ambition is the only thing that will serve the common good, Victor.* He'd said it so many times Victor could quote it in his sleep. He always trotted out that phrase when Victor would ask why he didn't make a case for him to the board or do something as simple as hold his hand in the street. He couldn't do those things, David insisted, because he was *serving society* by earning tenure, and pushing Victor to the side was something he did for the greater good, not out of malice.

Strangely, though, any time *Victor* talked about *his* ambitions, David was quick to shut him down.

It made sense that David would quietly do away with a student who put his tenure at risk. He would expect Victor to understand, to *sympathize*, because David was always bigger than he was.

"Steady," Sava said, and Victor came back to the world with Sava's calloused hands on his arms, easing him down to sit on the edge of the tub. Sava was tall enough that he had to bend a little to meet Victor's gaze, and Victor found it hard to catch his breath.

"Do you need help with the rest?" Sava asked. "You drank Ivan's cider. It is always very strong."

"I'm fine," Victor lied. *My boyfriend sent me to die so he could be a philosophy professor.* He couldn't say it. What kind of fool let that happen to them? What kind of man fell in love with someone who would cast him off?

"I'm a fraud," he said, in his own tongue. "I was supposed to be the smartest kid in town, the *scholar,* and I let David lead me around on a leash for years."

"Your face, at least." Victor closed his eyes as Sava brought a warm, damp cloth to his cheek. Sava gently touched the back of Victor's head to hold him there, and Victor leaned into it.

"I'm sorry," Victor whispered. There Sava was, mourning his lost love, and Victor was mooning over *David.*

"It takes people like this," Sava said, his voice soothing as he cleaned Victor's face and neck with the cloth like the mother Victor never had. "Do not drink so much, next time."

Victor barely remembered Sava laying out sleeping clothes for him, leaving Victor to scrub the rest of himself down in the bath while he thought of David back at the Two Sisters, finding some other young student to fuck in secret. Once Victor was dry and dressed, Sava showed him how to lower the suspended bed full of furs, and Victor realized, belatedly, that there was no other bed in the cabin.

"I can take the pit in front of the fire," he said, carefully. "I don't want to take your bed."

"You are new to Lukos." Victor's breath hitched as Sava lifted him onto the furs. "You should be comfortable."

"I should be dead," Victor muttered.

"What was that? Those words, what did they mean?" Sava climbed in the other side, and Victor burrowed under the fur blankets.

"They mean I'm not as clever as you think I am," Victor said, turning away.

Sava was quiet for a moment, and the bed shifted slightly, creaking on its tethers. "You speak four languages and you can draw mountains," he said. "Whoever told you that you are not clever, they are wrong."

Thunder rolled overhead, and Victor hunched under the blankets, closing his eyes tight, until sleep finally took him.

The truth was still there in the morning. Victor stared into it when Sava showed him the medicinal sticks they used to clean their teeth, when Victor tried to fix breakfast and had to sigh as Sava gently showed him the proper way, when he looked into his bag and saw his sketchbooks thrown to the side as though he were ashamed of them.

Which he had been. David had always been disdainful of artists, so Victor had held his tongue and kept his sketches and watercolors to himself. He'd made himself small, as Sava had said, to leave room for David.

"We should go to the cave today," Sava said, as Victor struggled into his boots. "Before the snows come. You can see our history, copy it in your book."

"I can?" Victor rose out of his glum mood for a moment. "I'm allowed?"

"Why wouldn't you be? But we should go to the hot spring first, and then to Ivan, for the inks. There will be time for work today, but you should see the spring before the winter snows make travel difficult."

Then Sava opened the door to the most magnificent landscape Victor had seen in his life.

It was snowing. Real, thick flakes of snow, the kind Victor read about in children's books, drifted in a slow-falling curtain over Lukos. Victor stumbled forward, all thoughts of David gone, and tugged off a glove to catch some in his hand. It melted, but he grinned up at Sava anyway, unable to contain his delight.

"You're right," Sava said, and Victor blinked as Sava gave him one of his quiet smiles. "You are a man who loves everything."

"You say that like it's a good thing," Victor said, but the low mood couldn't settle over him entirely when the world had transformed into one of the entrancing balls they sold at glassblowers' shops, the ones with little pieces of silken snow that swirled around miniature houses.

"Why would it not be good?"

"Maybe I love too easily," Victor said. "We're walking in that?"

"Yes, it's not bad."

"Not bad, he says." Victor stepped out into the snow and tipped his face up to it, shaking flakes of it out of his hair.

Sava smiled and strode over to fit a hat on his head, and Victor thought of what it must have been like for him to live alone for so long. Back in Gerakia, he would have had a veritable following of suitors, submissive *and* dominant.

Then Sava, eyes bright with good-natured wickedness, leaned down to haul Victor over his shoulder again, and Victor made a squawking sound like a kicked duck in his attempt to retain some dignity. Which didn't work, because he twisted too far out of Sava's grip and fell on the ground, where he lay and watched the snow spiral from the clouds.

"Victor," Sava said, concern threading his voice. "Are you injured?"

"No, this was planned," Victor said. "Lie down with me, Sava. It's comfortable. Did you know the snow moves in a pattern when it comes down?"

Sava blinked at him, and Victor patted the ground like it was a warm coverlet. Then, to his surprise, Sava stretched out next to him, radiating warmth at his side. Snow fell on his face and in his hair, and he squinted up at it thoughtfully. "Yes," he said at last. "It does."

"Right?"

They lay there for a moment, quiet, and Victor found he could almost forget that he'd fallen for a philosopher who'd shipped him off to Lukos the moment Victor threatened his career. He was just Victor, transported somehow to this strange island where winter meant death and ice and false spring, staring up at the falling snow with a man big enough to pick him up without breaking a sweat.

"I want to be your friend," he said in his own language, and Sava turned to look at him, snow glittering on his eyelashes.

"That was different."

"Different how?"

"When you speak like that, you usually sound … like you're unhappy with something. Yourself, maybe. But that was different."

"Maybe I'm turning a corner," Victor said. Sava narrowed his eyes. "It's a phrase we have. It means making a change. Figuring it out. Doing something new."

"You'll be doing many new things today," Sava said. Victor groaned as Sava stood up. "But you should do it standing."

"Or on your shoulders."

Sava leaned down to hold out a hand. "Or that."

Victor risked one more glance at the snow, then up at Sava, standing there with a gloved hand extended. "Lead the way," Victor said, and took Sava's hand in his.

# CHAPTER 5

Sava had never in his life seen someone so enamored of a little snow.

This was hardly a dusting, by Lukoi standards, yet Victor was as astonished as if the snows had arrived in truth. It was clear to Sava that Victor had no inkling of what winter here would be like, how this light dusting would become something brutal, a living, snarling, howling creature of cold and thick-packed wetness.

Victor, with his infectious laughter and keen eyes, would probably find that beautiful, too. It was, in its own way. Every Lukoi knew to fear and respect the weather in equal measure. Winters were endured and summers were celebrated, but they were equally striking in their own ways. It was good, Sava thought, to remember that.

The spring wasn't far, but the walk took twice as long as usual because of Victor. Not because he couldn't keep up, but because he stopped, often, exclaiming over this or that, asking questions, trying to learn words he didn't know. His grasp of the language was already improving. He really was very clever. Sava still wanted to know what Victor had said when they lay in the snow together. But the foreign words all sounded the same to him. It was only the way Victor's face looked when he said them that was different.

"So, tell me again how you— What's that over there?"

Sava smiled as Victor dashed off again, scrambling to pull out his book and sketch something with the rapidly dwindling piece of charcoal. Luckily, Sava had brought another, thinking it might be this way with someone who was so quick-minded. Victor was sketching a group of trees, their branches curled around each other like they were embracing.

"Do they have a name?" Victor asked, voice hushed.

"Yes," Sava said, straight-faced. "*Trees.*"

Victor's face went pink, and he smiled. "They looked … significant, maybe."

"They burned, I think, two summers ago. Lightning from a storm."

"Everything really wants to kill you, here." Victor's smile faltered, the light in his warm brown eyes dimming. Whatever had taken hold of him thanks to Ivan's potent drink, it hadn't yet let go.

"Come," Sava said. "You will like the spring." Victor, on the rare occasions he sat still, was shivering, even though it was a relatively mild day. He would need to eat more. Maybe while Victor visited Ivan, Sava would find another porcupine or try his luck fishing. Find something with more fat on it.

"Does it have a name?"

He asked that a lot. They must name a lot of things, where he was from. Sava shook his head. "Just the spring. There is no need for a special name, I think, because it is the only one here. Maybe there are others, beyond the mountains, but we do not go there."

"Why?"

Sava blinked at him. He pointed to the snowy, jagged mountains rising in the distance. "They are mountains. Rocky, ice-covered, dangerous. Why would we cross them?"

"To see what's on the other side, maybe?"

"The sea *is* on the other side." Sava smiled, pleased with his little pun. "If you want to climb the mountains, you will need better shoes."

"No, thanks. I trust you. So it's the hot spring because there's only one, got it." He dashed off something in his notebook, and they went on their way.

The air was chilly enough that it was obvious when they reached the spring, the heated steam visible in air that smelled of sulfur. Victor's expression was so eager that Sava tried for a moment to see this familiar place as he did, as if for the first time.

The spring itself was ringed with rocks and nestled among a copse of thick-trunked trees that arched over it, forming a protective canopy. The embankment was slippery, but the water bubbling up from beneath the ground had carved natural benches into the rocks. The water was a clear blue, almost turquoise, and the steam was warm and inviting.

"This is beautiful," Victor breathed, and immediately sat down to sketch it.

"We can swim in it, if you like," Sava offered. "The day is warm enough."

"Maybe for you," Victor said. "I like the idea of it, until I think about getting out again. I'm surprised there aren't more people here."

"It is too close to winter, and most do not live as close as I do." A pang hit him as he remembered why he'd chosen to build his house where he had. "I … Milan loved to swim here. I'd thought —" He stopped, shaking his head. Milan was gone, and it would not do to get lost in what could not be.

"I'm sorry." Victor glanced away and drew in a breath. "If you want to leave, it's all right."

"No." Sava thought for a moment before he continued. "It helps, to see how much you like this place."

"Oh." Victor smiled. "Good. I do. It's beautiful."

They didn't swim, but Victor did take his boots off and wade into the water, which he said was almost *too* hot. The weather took a turn, dark clouds rolling in and the imminent thundersnow an ominous rumble in the distance.

"It can be nice, when it snows, to sit in the waters," Sava said, waggling his eyebrows.

"I'll take your word on that." Victor wrinkled his nose and then cleaned off his glasses, which fogged easily. "Maybe after I've gotten used to the cold. What's the story about this place, this spring? Surely there has to be one."

Sava drew himself up, unsure whether he were the best person to tell *any* of their stories. The kuvar was good at it, and some others. Sava was a quiet man by nature; he'd spoken more to Victor in the last few hours than he'd spoken to anyone in months. "When the Exiled came here, they came from the beach —just as you did—and moved inland toward the forest, seeking shelter from the weather. When they found the spring, it warmed them enough to continue, to find the caves beyond. That is where we sheltered that first winter, while we became one people and drew up our laws."

"Were you not all from the same place, then?" Victor sounded eager, and Sava realized he'd never thought much about what others knew of Lukos.

"Yes and no. Come, we can go there now if you like. It might be best to do that first, given the weather, and then we will warm up at Ivan's." Sava narrowed his eyes playfully. "Where you will not drink as much cider."

"But if I do, maybe you'll carry me back home." Victor batted his eyelashes.

"Is there something wrong with your eyes? The steam, maybe?"

Victor snorted, said something in his language, and shook his head. "I'd like to see the caves first, yes, please."

The caves were a bit of a walk from the spring, but it went by pleasantly enough. As they neared the entrance, the air shifted and the light spilled strangely through the grove. Victor went silent, standing in the middle of a gentle flurry of snow and murmured, "It feels … sacred, here."

Sava nodded. "Many feel that way when they come here. We are brought when we are small, to make offerings of honey or flowers. To see the story of our people, where we came from." Sava had never felt much when he visited, but he would not consider himself a mystical man in any sense of the word. "Maybe because it is the first time you are here."

"Maybe, yes." Victor's voice was hushed. "You're all a mystery, really. And I feel like I'm about to solve it. It's … amazing." He laughed, still quiet. "I don't feel worthy of seeing what you're going to show me."

Sava put a hand on his shoulder. "I do not understand much of what you said about the reason you are here. Why your mate— or the man who would have been your mate—sent you to us. But I believe you should know that the kuvar thought it was … to die. I do not mean to speak ill of your people, or your man, but to send someone here in the winter is a death sentence."

From the small, tight smile on Victor's face, it seemed as if he knew it, too.

"If you do not know about our weather and think this is some great amount of snow, or very cold, you will be surprised at what's to come. The king who sent us here long ago did not know, either. Our most sacred law is that exiles are welcome among us. You might not have thought that was what you were, when you stepped from the boat, but what you were before … well, you will see, when we go inside. You can leave it behind. Come from the cave—like a rebirth, you know this word? It is what we call it when we leave our homes when the true spring comes. We were all as you are now, once. Uncertain, afraid. The winter unknown. You loved the place you walked barefoot, the houses full of people. Maybe the exiles loved their kingdom, too.

But you loved the snow, saw the patterns in it, and think this place is sacred. You can be one of us. Enter the cave as an exile, emerge as Lukoi."

It was a long speech, for Sava. Inelegant and clumsy, probably. But Victor was staring at him, wide eyes shining, and he looked … as if he wanted nothing more in the world than for that to be true.

"Your people are survivors," Victor said, after a moment. "I'm just someone no one wanted."

The ache in his voice echoed in Sava's chest. He shook his head. "You are here, alive. You are a survivor, too. And Lukos, it … well. It is not the most welcoming of places. But that does not mean you are not wanted." Feeling oddly as if this moment were somehow profound, like a mating ceremony, Sava held out a hand. "Come see our story. I think you will understand more, when you do."

Victor seemed momentarily incapable of words, but he took Sava's hand and let Sava draw him into the cave.

Sava lit a torch that was kept at the side of the entrance and beckoned Victor toward the back, where the carvings were. "Here," he said, waving a hand. "Our story."

"Oh," Victor breathed, and said something quickly in his own language as he looked at the wall. "These must be very ancient."

"Yes. We do not know how long ago we came here, and others who have come from various places in the world say they do not know, any longer, the name of the king who exiled us. But here you can see the story. I will tell it to you as it was told to me, if you like."

"Please," Victor said, eager as always, pulling out his charcoal and a sketchbook full of all sorts of new drawings. "And you said it's really all right if I write it down?"

"Yes, of course. History is meant to be known, isn't it?" Sava started at the first of the images, which showed a crude figure of a man seated on a throne, a five-pointed crown atop his head. On the ground before him lay a figure with what appeared to be a knife protruding from his chest.

"This, here. This is the king, and that, there, is his son. He was found murdered, and—there, see, the king was despondent and wept."

The next carving showed exactly that, the king with hands over his face, drops like tears falling on the body. Sava pointed to the next carving, which was the king standing before his throne, arm extended, pointing at a group of men with swords. "He summoned his royal guard and demanded to know who'd done this, but there was no answer. So he sent the guard forth to question the prisoners in the jail—there, see?"

The carving depicted simplistic square buildings with bars on the windows and, outside, something that looked like a stake with flames and a hangman's noose on a gallows. "The prisoners, the guards of the jail, and the torturers likewise knew nothing about who had taken the life of the king's son. So the king turned next to the witches, the scryers, those who knew magic."

He indicated the images of figures with longer hair seated around fires, staring into what might have been mirrors or pools of water. Some held bottles with skulls on them, as if to signify poison.

"But the scryers knew nothing, or if they did know, they would not speak of it. The king, enraged, said that if no one would answer for this crime, he would simply banish all those who were capable of committing it … or who failed to stop it."

The next image showed a ship and a line of people waiting to board it: the guards with their swords, the prisoners in chains, the torturers, the witches with heavy collars of metal around their necks, and the people with their jars of poison. "He thought if he exiled any who could do violence, whether in his name or against him, those banished would have to include the one who had killed his son. So all of them were sent away on a ship, never to return."

"No one *knows* this." Victor's voice was still soft, but it was trembling with reverence and excitement. "No one—they don't have any idea, Sava. They only know you were exiled, but not why, or from where. For all we knew, you ended up here by accident."

"Well, it was sort of an accident," Sava conceded. "See this, here? The waves took the ship, and it came upon Lukos, and whoever was sailing it forced those aboard to disembark and then sailed away." This was shown with a group of people huddled on a beach, with sails in the distance and snowflakes falling from simplistic clouds depicted above the huddled figures.

"That looks familiar," Victor said.

Sava nodded. "That is what I was trying to say, before. Now, see, here is the spring that the exiles found. Do you recognize it?"

"They're putting their feet in it, just like I did," Victor said, not quite touching the figures on the cave wall.

"Yes. They, too, had poorly made boots. Look, here is the cave, and this is where they gathered that first winter."

The rest of the story played out on the rocks: how they fought among themselves, each trying to rule, the prisoners and guards and all the others separating into factions and arguing, the disagreements sometimes turning violent. One figure followed a crudely drawn wolf from the cave while the groups clashed, and Sava pointed to him. "It is said one of the men left the camp and told them all that he would come back with a plan, bidding them to promise not to kill each other while he was gone. And here he is coming back, with the skin of a wolf over his shoulder, see?"

Victor nodded, drawing frantically.

"That was the first kuvar of the Lukoi. The word means *wolf-leader,* and it is said that he spent twelve nights and thirteen days with the wolves, who taught him the ways of survival. We must make dens, he said, and find a mate we can shelter with that we will not kill out of boredom or anger." Sava grinned. "Not very romantic, eh?"

"Maybe not, but it's fascinating, and he was probably right." Victor grinned back. "That's it, that's your secret to who you take as a mate?"

"Well, it is a bit more than that, now. But, see, here—the kuvar, he split them into dominants and submissives, then told them that if we would survive what had been done to us, we must be one people, and it must not matter who wore a witch's collar, or who wore shackles, or who held the keys to both. So that, there, is the pile where those who followed the kuvar's advice discarded their old trappings and joined together as one."

"Who are these people?" Victor asked, pointing to a small group over to the side.

"The ones who did not listen," Sava said. "When the kuvar brought his people out, they would not follow. Instead, they went to the mountains. We call them *those who left.*"

"Did they come back? Ever?"

"No. It is thought they died in the winter, for they did not know about the false spring or the ice or any of it." Sava pointed. "Here, you see pairs, yes? Dominants building a home, submissives going with them. Sometimes two dominants, sometimes two submissives, sometimes three or more. But wolves mate for life, and pack is the most important thing to them: it is how they hunt, how they help each other, how they live. So we did that, too. Our law was simple. It did not matter if you once pressed a hot iron to the flesh of a man in your pack or would have hanged a woman who was a witch or a poisoner. You left it behind, or you would not survive. And we wanted to survive. See, here?"

The next wall showed nothing but tick marks. "This, it is said, is the mark made by each exile who chose to follow the kuvar and live the life we still do, today. Life would be sacred, mate bonds would be sacred, the strong would protect, the submissives would serve, the dominants would lead. Each mark shows a person who cast aside their old life and became new." Sava indicated the following cave walls, which were full of more tick marks, uneven and jumbled but clear against the gray stone. "Every Lukoi, when they are of age, makes a mark here. To show we will live by the laws." He picked up a sharp bit of stone and handed it to Victor. "Soon you will live as we once did. An exile who has never known winter or the long, cold dark that it brings. But if your mark is here … you will think of it, when it seems as if the snow might drive you mad. You will remember choosing to be one of us, and it will give you strength."

That's how it was supposed to work, anyway. Sava knew that some of the marks on the wall belonged to people for whom it hadn't been enough. Milan had made the mark. And it had not helped, in the end.

But Victor was staring at the rock in his hand. "I'm not strong, like these people were. Like you are."

"You are strong in different ways, I think. Look. You are the first to ever draw this, to put it on paper. You came here from a faraway place, and you did that. Do not diminish your own cleverness, little owl, or you will fade away like those who left. You will find all the strength inside you, this winter. That is how it works. And you will have me there, a dominant, to help you."

Victor wiped at his eyes, trembling. "I can't believe you're just letting me do this. Add my mark. As if I deserve it."

Sava frowned, trying to understand. "You deserve to survive, like we all do. It is not a promise that you will, only that you will try. Will you try, Victor of Gerakia?"

Victor drew himself up, chin lifting, and his trembling eased. There were still tears on his cheeks, but he nodded. "I will try, Sava Snow-Walker." With that, he turned and pressed the rock to the cave wall and, as Sava watched, added his mark there. The newest, but one among thousands. When he stepped back, he stared for a long time at the wall, then traced his mark with his fingers.

Sava had done the same when he made his own. He smiled. "Now you are Lukoi. No longer an exile. And I can feel from the wind that the snow will come soon, so we should go. But we can come back in the spring. Leave honey, flowers, to show that you kept your promise to live through the worst of what the island brings. We all do this the first year after we come of age. When it seems too much to bear, think of the others who survived, and you will, too."

So simple, and not always true, but hopefully it would be enough.

WHEN VICTOR STEPPED out of the cave where the first of the exiles once lived, its shadow slipped past him like a living creature, releasing him into the light snow of Lukos. He was almost afraid to turn around, as though the cave would disappear if he looked back, gone like a ripple of air in the height of summer. But it was still there, dark and oddly welcoming, when he turned to check.

Perhaps he should have thought it over more. Others would have. People didn't just decide to join an ancient society of exiles because their boyfriend left them on an island and they heard a pretty story. But Victor knew he was still the boy who had seventeen favorite houses while everyone else had one, who fell in love too easily and too entirely, and he couldn't deny that something in what Sava had said, there in the dark, rang true.

"You know, you're not the first person to call me an owl," Victor said, as he carefully followed Sava down the slope. "Not because of the glasses. There was a story about an owl Aunt Grace used to tell me, when I kept sleeping on the roof or making tents by the lake. It's an old Gerakian ... tall tale? Not tall as in high, but ... it could be true if it weren't impossible?"

"I don't know if we have those stories," Sava said. He was probably being diplomatic. He grabbed Victor before he could jam his boot into a rock and end his brief tenure as a Lukoi, and Victor grinned up at him.

"Gerakia has hundreds. This one, it was about a girl whose brothers were turned into birds and eaten." Sava made a face, and Victor shrugged. "She has to be tragic. It's required. She'd been promised—in marriage—to the giant who ate her brothers, but when she found out what he'd done, she poisoned him and wove a coat of feathers that turned her into an owl."

Sava made a soft, concerned sound. "Where did she find the feathers?"

"Don't ask." Victor gave up trying to be self-sufficient and steadied himself on Sava's arm as they navigated the rocky ground before a thicket of trees. "She flew to the next village, looking for a home. She found someone who took her in as a pet, but she knew that wouldn't work. So she squeezed through the cage to escape, losing some of her feathers in the process. Then she went to the next place, where a falconer thought to use her to kill smaller birds, but she didn't like that, either. It reminded her of her brothers, and the falconer still didn't see her as a person, so she left, and more of her feathers broke off when she tore off the hood he used to train her to fly. She went to half a dozen places like this, to people who wanted her as a pretty pet or a piece of decoration or a tool, but never as a girl."

He ducked under a low branch as they crossed the line of trees. "Finally she found a witch and her boy. By this time, almost all her feathers were gone, and she could barely fly. But the boy saw her resting by the well, and he had enough magic to know who she really was, so he ran and found his mother. And they took off her coat of feathers and gave her something to eat, and in the morning she was the witch's daughter."

"And this owl, they said she was like you?" Sava asked.

"Yes. I hated it as a kid, but I suppose … The point is that sometimes you have to make a long journey to understand who you are or to find out where you belong. So I was Aunt Grace's owl, because I left town to find myself, and I didn't belong to anyone yet."

Sava nodded slowly. "I think I see it. But do you still hate the name? I can stop saying it, if it hurts you to think of it."

"No. I think it's nice. But I don't know. Maybe I can take my own feather coat off one day." He looked around, trying to imagine settling into a new skin, a new place, no longer in between.

"So long as you don't take off the one I gave you," Sava said sternly, eyeing Victor with suspicion.

"I'd never. It's too cold out here."

"I have a feeling you'll try it, before the first snows come. Just to see what it feels like."

Victor squinted at him dramatically. "You shouldn't know me so well this soon."

Sava chuckled, and Victor looked away, his cheeks warm against the chill breeze.

It wasn't a long walk to Ivan's house from the cave. He lived near the woods, surrounded by a clearing peppered with stumps and lines of twine framing a dead garden.

"You'd think he'd want the cover," Victor said as Sava led him past where the trees ended and into the open.

"These trees are full of sap," Sava said, gesturing to a wooden tap someone had placed in one of the trunks behind them. "In winter, they can freeze and burst, and then, maybe, the tree comes down on the house. Ivan's mother was wise to make this clearing. Ah, he's home. See the smoke?"

There was indeed a plume rising from the chimney. Ivan's house was considerably smaller than Sava's and painted in shades of dark gray and black. Victor assumed that was meant to absorb the heat, but it made for an odd look when there were also rows and rows of dried flowers hanging from the roof in garlands.

Before they reached the door, Ivan opened it, dressed all in knitted wool with a coat patched with moons. His dark hair was braided back like Sava's, and he smiled warmly at both of them.

"You came at a good time, Snow-Walker," he said. "I have your paints ready. And the inks, but those will freeze, while all you have to do with the paints is grind them down and add oil." He was already back inside the house, rummaging around, and Sava gave the long-suffering sigh of someone who was used to it and gestured for Victor to go in.

Ivan's house was much lighter on the inside, and it was fragrant with dried herbs and flowers, which hung from the ceiling in little bundles. The walls, like Sava's, were lined with furs, but the house felt more like an apothecary than a place where someone actually lived. Victor kept to the side, close to the fire, as Ivan ran around gathering jars marked with dabs of paint.

In Gerakia, most of Victor's paints had been watercolors, but when Ivan handed him a jar for inspection, what he saw inside looked like the expensive oil paints Kallistoi artists used. Victor held his breath, examining the perfect indigo shade of the paint Ivan had given him.

Ivan flicked his nose to get his attention. "You look like you're in love," he said. "I'm going to be your favorite person if you want more of this. We can get more in the spring, maybe. Together."

"Oh. That'd be nice."

Ivan jerked his head toward a side room and glanced slyly at Sava. "Submissives only, Sava. Pick a bottle you want. I have mead for you."

Sava smiled, but he didn't answer. He just started packing up Victor's paints and let Ivan drag Victor off.

"He's so quiet around people," Victor murmured, as Ivan pulled him into what had to be a storeroom. It was full of bottles and herbs, but Ivan didn't reach for any. He sat on a crate instead, looking at Victor.

"He'll talk to you eventually," Ivan said. "He's always quiet, our

Sava. He only talks a lot around me or Milan—" He pulled a face. "Talked. Sorry. Sometimes I forget he's gone."

Victor glanced at the door to the storeroom. "He really loved him."

"I think so. Milan was special." Ivan sighed. "But he followed the fox-maiden. It was hard, seeing him in the water. Even his hair was frozen."

"I'm sorry. But … you said he followed someone? Was he killed? I thought he—"

"No." Ivan was pale as he fiddled with a sachet of flowers, and Victor wished he knew him well enough to comfort him, somehow, without it being awkward. "The fox-maiden is a spirit, they say, who leads people into the false spring and sends them into the sea. But she isn't real. She's just a story we tell to make death seem less … meaningless. Sudden."

"I think I understand," Victor said. "We don't have to talk about it, if it's too much."

Ivan shook out his hair and laughed hollowly. "Sorry. I came here to make plans. Real ones, for spring." He gave Victor a searching look. "Like the two of us. We can help each other find dominants, maybe. I'll show you how to make paints, and you give me pretty foreign words to charm a dominant into building me a house. Or you can put in a word for me with Sava—have you seen his bed?" He raised his eyebrows and laughed at Victor's expression. "You have!"

Victor covered his face with both hands, and Ivan laughed again.

"No, no, it's good! It's fine! You aren't mates, and Sava is too good a man to take advantage. Enjoy the bed, and tell me if I should find my way into it when the ice thaws, eh? It's Sava or the kuvar, Victor. I'm a man with high ambitions."

Victor sighed. Ivan would have fit in *perfectly* with his friend group at university. They were always eyeing attractive dominants like they were cakes in a pastry store window. "Fine."

"Yes! I knew you were a good man, Victor." Ivan slapped him on the shoulder and towed him out the storage room door, saying loudly, "And remember you need air when you paint, so the fumes don't make you dizzy and sick."

Victor nodded, and Ivan deposited him at Sava's feet.

"Collect your guest," Ivan said. "No need to give me anything; Victor and I struck a deal." He grinned when Sava gave him a curious look. "Nothing he can't afford!"

"I will at least repay you for the drink," Sava said, and Ivan gave Victor a weary sigh as he accepted a length of tanned hide.

"Now I'll need to get you something else." Ivan dropped the hide next to the fireplace. "Go. I know how you are before the snow falls. Prepare your house, Sava."

Sava smiled pleasantly enough at Ivan as they were ushered out, but he only waited a few moments before he leaned down and whispered to Victor. "So. Did he ask for help courting the kuvar?"

Victor snorted, and Sava shook his head sadly. "Is this common?"

"He's predictable, that's all. Milan said he was always asking questions. Well, it's lonely in that house."

Victor thought of Sava's house, built so lovingly, and Sava sitting there alone as the snow rose around the windows. "Maybe he'll find someone."

"Not the kuvar. Dragan has enough to handle with Elena. She is like a storm, herself."

The clouds rumbled with thunder as though they agreed, and Victor and Sava glanced at each other, then away.

David would have hated Sava. Partly for the simple fact that Victor found him attractive—David was always quick to glare when Victor mentioned maybe finding someone else until things died down—but also because Sava was intrinsically tied to the other Lukoi. David believed that a person had to be an island, dependent on no one, but everything on Lukos was connected.

When they got back to the house, Sava pulled out wool that had been traded from a neighbor, needles made by his mother, a knife forged by the kuvar. His house had probably been built using plans engineered by Lukoi generations before him. For all that the Lukoi lived in their small houses isolated by the storms of winter, there were signs of each other everywhere.

And now Victor was one of them. Or he could be, if he survived the winter.

Sava gave Victor clothes to mend while he went about the house, checking for weaknesses Victor couldn't see. Victor curled up in the pit before the fire. It had been years since he'd tailored anything to fit, but he was pretty sure he'd remember how if he got started, so he set to ripping seams and hemming sleeves, glasses slowly falling off his nose as he worked.

"This might be wrong," he said, holding up a wool shirt with a weave so fine it was soft to the touch. "Do you think this is wrong? It's wrong. I'm trying it on."

"What?" Sava came up from what Victor thought of as the cellar just as Victor started stripping off his own shirt. He stared at Victor, brows raised, and Victor quickly threw on the mended shirt. The seam ripped along the side, and Victor slumped.

"Perfect," he said. "Now I can be shirtless whenever I want." He flipped his shirt open by the ripped seam, posed, and winced. Sava probably didn't want to see more of him than he had to.

Except Sava hadn't looked away, and Victor found himself unable to break his gaze.

"I'll show you how to fix it," Sava said, and Victor went still as Sava climbed into the pit. There was enough room for both of them, but Victor was suddenly very aware of how much space Sava occupied. He really was built like … well, a house, and when Sava gestured for Victor to hand him the shirt, Victor didn't even think before he shrugged it off.

"Here," Sava ordered. "Come close so you can see."

"Of course you know how to sew, too." Victor moved just a

fraction. Sava looked at him, and Victor pressed up against his side, remembering too late that he hadn't, in fact, put his other shirt back on.

He sat there, frozen in helpless panic, as Sava leaned over him and carefully threaded a needle.

"There's an easier way," Sava explained, and Victor tried valiantly to listen as Sava showed him how to stitch the seam back together. He stopped halfway, and when Victor blinked at him like the owl he apparently was, Sava took Victor's hands in his and guided him through the motions. It wasn't condescending, it was careful, and Victor looked up and found Sava was so close that he could count his dark lashes as he looked down at Victor's hands.

Sava met Victor's gaze, and Victor turned toward him, lips parting slightly—and jabbed him with the needle. "Oh, damn and blast," he hissed as Sava flinched back, not in pain, but with the mild embarrassment of someone jolted out of a daze. "I'm sorry."

"You're all right," Sava said, but he didn't seem to know where to put his eyes, and Victor only barely resisted the urge to shove his face in a pillow and scream as Sava got out of the pit. "I'll make you something to eat."

"Yeah," Victor said weakly, holding the shirt to his chest. "And I'll just…"

Burrow into the earth, maybe, and live there like a confused rabbit until Sava forgot all about the scrawny, gangly would-be scholar who poked him with needles. But Sava was already turning away to go back into the stores, so Victor just sat there, needle in hand, while the fire crackled and laughed in the hearth.

# CHAPTER 6

Winter never came with a bang in Lukos. It crept silently like a fox toward a henhouse, and you often didn't notice it was there until suddenly the snow was thick enough to block the door, ice forming patterns on the window that didn't melt by afternoon. Not that there was much afternoon; the mountains trapped the sun at half past three, making the days short and the nights long even before winter properly arrived.

Victor was, of course, enamored of each new turn the weather took, often sitting on the chair on Sava's porch—bundled up in furs—and drawing. He tried to help Sava with the preparations, but it quickly became apparent that he needed careful guidance to do chores that came easily to Sava. Sava didn't mind explaining, and Victor's smile when he mastered some new skill was almost as bright as the sun that was shining less and less often. But Sava would never understand how a person could grow to adulthood without knowing how to start a fire.

That was one task he insisted Victor practice from the outset, over and over, because if something happened to him during the winter, Victor would not survive without it. Their first lesson ended with Victor lying facedown on the floor, bemoaning his lack of talent with firecraft, while Sava laughed and asked whether all scholars were so dramatic.

Which didn't help Victor learn how to light a fire, but that night he did entertain Sava by telling him about theatrics from the school where he was a student. Sava wasn't sure he believed there was an entire discipline focused on pretending to be someone else, loudly, in front of an audience. He thought perhaps it was one of those tall tales of Victor's, like the woman in the owl feathers. But if anyone could be a scholar of such a thing, Victor could. He was better at it than at lighting fires, but Sava thought it unkind to say so. Maybe after Victor figured out the fire starting, it would not seem as if he were making fun.

Sava could not pretend to be anyone else, so he did not want to demean the idea of it being useful. Maybe it was, in a land where you could dash about with no shoes most of the year. He wondered if Victor would miss the warm sunny homeland he'd been made to leave, in the dark months to come.

Victor did not speak of whatever truth he'd found in the cave. It was all right. Sava knew the time would come when they would sit before the fire and the wind would howl, and they would tell each other secrets because there would be little else to do. Victor seemed happy enough to put whatever it was behind him, to have made his mark on the cave wall and spend the nights in the pit of furs, wrapped up in blankets, sketching. He always seemed surprised when Sava wanted to see the drawings, and he blushed when Sava praised his skill. Which was very silly. Victor praised Sava's skills often enough.

In addition to helping Victor learn to start a fire, Sava gave him an overview of the house and everything that made it not only a home but a way to survive the winter. He showed Victor the food storage in the cool place beneath the kitchen, the firewood kept safe and dry, the tanning shed, and the processing shed beyond that—far enough off to keep predators from the house—which he didn't often use in the winter. He showed Victor how to salt meat and explained how to use the hooks in the ceilings for the skins that would help insulate the house when the coldest temperatures came.

They had some time to walk to the spring and, on what might have been the last nice day of the year, took the waters there with the rest of the Lukoi. Victor was warmly welcomed in that everyone assumed he would be staying—why put yourself through a brutal Lukoi winter and then leave?—and Ivan was there, smiling his bright smile and splashing about in the water with him.

Zora was at the spring, too, watching Ivan and Victor with an odd look on her face. She was distant to Sava, but Ivan made much of her and seemed to be introducing her to Victor properly. All she said to Sava, though, was, "He needs a warmer coat."

She wasn't wrong.

Sava wanted it to be a gift, then remembered that Victor was not his mate and it would be better if he learned how to do some of this himself. Even if he found a dominant mate to take care of him, he should know how to do some cooking. Many submissives did much more—like Ivan with his flowers, herbs, and ciders, or Ozren and his many uses for goat's milk—and Victor, of course, had his sketches and his quick, clever mind. But he should know the basics, and it would be unfair of Sava not to teach him what he could. So he pushed aside the pang of wishing he had a proper mate to give gifts to and showed Victor how to make a coat lined in fur, and boots that fit him better, gloves, and a hat that didn't fall over his glasses so much. Even if Sava thought he looked fetching in the other one.

Victor took some time with most tasks, his hands not accustomed to the work, but he was deft with the needle and did understand the patterns, which Sava had difficulty explaining. Victor nodded along when Sava showed him how to lay out the hides and cut them with his bone knife, the sharp one that made clean, neat edges and would save time in the sewing.

It went well enough, though a few times Victor sewed the hides too thick or not securely enough, as the thread used—made from animal guts, mostly—tripped him up a bit. Three times he cut himself and sheepishly showed Sava the strips of cloth he'd used to stop the bleeding.

Attaching the fur was harder and frustrated Victor at times. But he kept up with it, sitting before the fire as the thundersnow gave way to sleet and freezing rain, wielding the needle and cursing softly in his native tongue *and* the new one, occasionally flinging his arms up in victory when he finished a section. He would bite his lip when he sewed, and Sava could only watch him for so long before he was distracted by those nimble fingers and thoughts of how Victor's lip would taste if *he* did the biting instead.

It was even worse when he saw Victor painting, humming to himself, making Lukos come alive on canvas with the paints Ivan had given him. Victor would make a good mate for a dominant, and Sava briefly entertained the thought that it could be him … until he remembered Milan's still, cold body, Zora's face when she accused Sava of waiting too long to take Milan as his mate, the guilt he'd felt as he'd stood by the pyre.

He would not make a mistake with this clever young scholar, who deserved to be cherished by a man who was good enough, *strong* enough, to keep him safe.

"So," Victor asked, one night, working on his gloves. "When you want to be mates with someone, what exactly do you do?"

Sava, who had been thinking of just that as he sewed a thicker set of hides for the wall, had to chastise himself before he answered. "You take them, and if they like it, you are mates. You cut your hands for the kuvar, to show your blood is as one, and then they live with you."

"You just fuck someone? That's it?"

Sava laughed despite the rush of heat that went through him at hearing Victor speak of it. "Well, yes and no. The word you used—it is that, yes, but … with your mate, you do things you do not do with others. Kiss them." He cleared his throat, feeling his face heat. "Other, ah. Things that are pleasurable."

Victor glanced at him and grinned, firelight glimmering on his glasses. "Like … make a flute of their organ?"

*"What?"* Sava laughed so loud it echoed off the glass of the window where he was hanging the newly shaped hides. "We do not make instruments of our cocks, Victor."

"That definitely didn't translate," Victor said, then made a crude gesture that *did*, and Sava nodded, grinning despite himself.

He ran a hand over the slight growth of a beard on his face and said, "Yes, that. Those things, they are for your mate. Dominants and submissives, they can find pleasure with each other. But other things of, ah, a flute-playing nature …"

Victor said, his eyes very wide, "So you've never kissed anyone?"

"No, I am unmated," Sava said. Of their own accord, his eyes went to Victor's mouth. The air in the small room turned heated, charged. It happened more and more, as of late.

"So you just … take someone? What if there are submissives no one wants?"

Sava blinked. "Submissives can live on their own, as you have seen, and so can dominants. It is rare, but it can happen. There is a man, a dominant, who lives alone far out of town, but it is his choice to do so. "

"What if some dominant tries to fuck you and you don't want them?"

Shame burned through Sava, and he told himself firmly to keep his attraction to Victor in check through the winter—surely he would not ask this, if he was not trying to make sure that Sava did not try to mate him? "You tell them *no*," Sava said. "Is that not what you do, in Gerakia?" He still tripped up a bit at the name.

"No, you do," Victor assured him. He said, wincing a bit, "I guess I assumed that … it's probably wrong, and also not very nice."

"That the dominant could take them anyway?" Sava shrugged. "I think, back when we first came here, that happened out of necessity. Because the way it's always worked is that you pin the submissive, bite the back of his neck, and when you fuck him, if he moans for you … Or she, or they," Sava added. "Whoever they are, they must want you for it to work."

"So back when the first exiles came here, some dominant former prisoner found some pretty former guard …"

Sava grinned again. The way Victor said it, it sounded like one of the theater tales he would perform after their chores were done for the day. "Yes, but they both had to want it for it to happen, or else it would be force—and that is not allowed. If they agreed to the laws, they could not kill each other *or* take someone who did not want to be taken."

"How romantic." Victor's smile faded, but he asked, hesitantly, "So it's always up to the dominant?"

"Oh, no," Sava chuckled. "My father was a submissive, and he courted my mother for months. Brought her food to show how he could cook, tanned hides he'd sewn, all that sort of thing. But she said what made her push him to his back in the green grass was when he had too much cider at the kuvar's fire and recited very bad poetry about her eyes."

"Fan of bad verse, was she?" Victor asked, smiling again.

"No," Sava said, shaking his head. "But it made her laugh. She said that would get them through many more winters than his bread, as good as it was."

"That's …Why is every story here so great?" Victor shook his head. "I can't bake bread, and I think my poetry is too earnest to be properly bad, but you laughed when I tried to sing the coals back to life the other day, so, hey, maybe I'm funny."

*You are clever and quick-handed, and you can paint our hills, and our stories delight you.* "Well," Sava said, pointing at the glove Victor was sewing, "unless you used my bone saw again and had an accident you did not tell me about, you are making that for fewer fingers than you have."

Victor glanced down, saw he'd sewn the third and fourth finger of his new gloves together, and swore—he'd tried to teach Sava the words in his language to no avail—and Sava laughed as Victor reached for his ever-present seam ripper, a tool Sava had to make for him after he saw him worrying at the glove like a dog.

"As I said, at least I can make you laugh," Victor said, and Sava thought about what it might be like to tumble him back on the furs … but also that his mother had been right, maybe, and laughter was more important than he realized.

But Victor was not for him, and it was best he got that through his head before he did something foolish. Victor might think Sava was owed something, for sheltering him through his first winter. And he was a good actor. Sava did not want them both miserable due to gratitude and a misplaced desire to say *thank you.*

But the wind howled outside, and Sava could feel the snow in his bones, sweeping down from the mountains and the cold northern sea. It would be a long winter, and he would have to stay in control to keep from taking Victor. Like every winter before, his hand and his imagination would have to do. And he would have Victor's company, which was more than he thought he'd have.

It would have to be enough.

THERE WAS no light in the morning.

A storm swallowed it, brought by a wind that sounded like a pack of wolves, and Victor woke with a start as the ropes suspending the bed trembled. It was like the ghost stories they used to tell at the orphanage, the ones that would send kids clambering under their beds or running for the rooms where the older kids were, sobbing about ghosts at the windows. Victor stared at the door for a while, half expecting Gerakia's famous childhood specter, Wide-Mouthed Abbie, to come sliding through, and he jumped as the house groaned, shivering in the storm.

He slipped out of bed and over to the fire, where he spent a good minute with the flint before he sparked the coals to life. It was the quickest he'd ever started the fire, and Sava was asleep for it.

"Well, *I* know it's a victory," he said, and stood to climb back into bed. The wind howled again, and something in the walls rattled, just enough like the bones of a long-dead specter that Victor sat back down with a wince.

A shadow shifted on the bed, and Victor startled before he realized it was Sava, blinking in the firelight.

"You did well with the fire," Sava said, voice low. "But you should sleep. It will be dark today. It storms like this before true winter starts."

"I can sleep here," Victor said, a little too lightly. "There's plenty of furs."

"I am warmer than the furs, yes?" There was a smile in Sava's voice, warm as the blankets, the furs, the fire—warmer than all of it.

Victor let out a slow breath. "You could come here," he said, finally, and Sava swung himself out of bed.

He brought blankets, and an extra pillow, which he wedged behind Victor's back before draping the furs over him. "The house always makes these sounds, in the storm. It will hold."

"I'm not doubting that. I'm being silly, I suppose. Doesn't your mind ever play tricks on you? Make you see things in the shadows that aren't there?"

Sava's breath went harsh, and his gaze looked distant for a second. "No. Don't follow those things, if you see them. Stay by the fire."

"I wasn't saying they're real. They're like … stories. Ghost stories. You don't have those?" Victor had to crane his neck to look up at Sava, who was so much larger than him even when Victor wasn't curled up in a pit by the fire. "Can you come down here? I mean, because you're probably going to get cold, and I'll strain my neck like this."

It was a weak lie, and he knew Sava could tell. Sava climbed into the pit next to him and carefully kept his distance, sitting so that they barely touched.

"We have ghost stories. The kuvar tells them better than I would, but I don't think I should tell them right now."

"Really? Is it because I'm so calm and composed?" Victor gestured to himself and was rewarded with Sava's small smile. Or he thought he was—his glasses were still on the mantel, and it was hard to tell. "I must be the worst submissive in Lukos. Can't cook, can't start a fire, scared of ghosts—" He jumped again as the wind howled outside, and Sava raised a hand as though to steady him before drawing away again.

"I don't know why you say these things about yourself," Sava said. "When you just started a fire, and you've shown yourself to be clever and eager to learn."

"Sorry." Victor wrapped his arms around himself. "Can you believe I used to be *too* confident?"

Sava frowned slightly. "Did something happen to change that?"

"More like someone." Victor sighed. "As long as we're talking about unpleasant things. You know I spoke of a … mate, before. Someone I thought would be one."

"The one who sent you here. You don't have to speak of him."

"I know. But I should." Victor huddled under the blankets. "He was my teacher, I guess. I took a class with him, on … we call it philosophy. It's where a lot of people argue about how to think."

Sava narrowed his eyes. "Don't they already know how?"

"Yeah, you'd think so. But David taught it, and he always left these really critical notes on my papers. Usually—in my other classes—I got top marks, so I was mad about it. If I failed, I'd have to go home, so I went to his office. Where we could talk alone. And he offered to give me lessons, and I … oh. Oh, no."

Sava sat up as Victor covered his face with his hands. "What? Did he force you?"

"No. It's that I'm embarrassed at the thought I'll now be a cautionary tale to other students, about the dangers of seducing your professors." Victor groaned into his hands. "But I thought I loved him, and then when I became too much trouble for him, he got rid of me. He said there was a trip planned to visit Lukos, and he'd arranged for me to join the group. So. Well. Fuck."

"He thought you were *trouble*?" Sava's voice was colder than Victor had ever heard it. "So he sent you here to die? You?"

"You say that like it's surprising."

"Is he the one who did this?" Sava leaned closer, and Victor fell back, catching his breath as Sava lifted his chin with one hand. "Made you feel small?"

"I don't know. Maybe. Yes. I think so." Victor was finding it rather hard to think with Sava radiating warmth over him, holding him still. "I didn't think about it at the time, but he was always saying how, you know, ugly I was, and—"

Sava made a sound so close to a growl that Victor shivered. "I do not know this man, but I know you enough, Victor, to know he is a liar. If he were in Lukos, he would be punished for breaking our laws and casting aside a man like you. I would cast him out myself if I could."

Victor couldn't speak, and Sava looked him in the eye, his

calloused fingers firm but so gentle on Victor's chin. "You forgot how valuable you are, little owl, but you can learn again."

"Fuck," Victor whispered.

"You are clever and beautiful, and a worthy submissive. This man, he did not deserve you." Victor tried to shy away, and Sava turned his cheek again. "Do you know me to be a liar?"

"No."

"Then know I am telling the truth," Sava said. "And I will tell you again, if you need it."

Victor raised a hand to touch Sava's arm. He slid his fingers to Sava's shoulder, closing the space between them, and Sava cradled his cheek as Victor kissed him.

There was a moment of quiet, as though even the howling winds had stopped to consider what Victor had done, before Victor drew back. "Sorry," he said. This wasn't Gerakia. Only mates were supposed to kiss, and Sava didn't want to be his mate. He would have said something by now if he did, even if he had just called Victor *beautiful*.

"I don't think you understand," Sava said, and Victor wished he could crawl into the earth and *die*. "This David does not deserve you, but neither do I."

Victor peered at him. "It's Milan, isn't it?" Sava looked away, and Victor lowered his voice. "Sometimes people leave us even when we do all the right things."

Sava's eyes were bright, but he gently ran a thumb over Victor's cheek. "You deserve to be loved properly, by someone who doesn't have this weight on their back."

"Well, maybe you deserve someone who can lift it," Victor said. "You never thought of that?"

Victor fell back as Sava leaned down to kiss him, still holding his cheek. The pillows lining the pit before the fire were soft, and Victor sank into them as Sava deepened the kiss, hungry and desperate in a way Victor had never seen before.

"I wish I could deserve you," Victor said, when they came up for air. Sava was hard to see up close, but his brows seemed to furrow.

"You do," he said. The dominance in his voice was heavy, and Victor felt his pulse race as Sava stroked his hair. "Tell me why."

"What?" Victor gasped as Sava bit him high on the neck, still holding his face in one hand. He rucked up Victor's shirt, and Victor grabbed at his broad shoulders.

"Tell me why you deserve it," Sava ordered, and Victor made a sound against his mouth.

"I don't know, I—" Victor groaned as Sava pressed up against him, over him. "You're so … I'm good at languages, I guess."

"Yes, good." Sava couldn't have missed the shiver that ran through Victor at that. "You like it, the praise? Or being good, being taken care of, cherished as you should be?"

"All of that," Victor said, breathless, and he could feel Sava's smile as Victor kissed him again.

"Then tell me why I would call you beautiful." Victor hissed out a sharp breath as Sava turned him around in his arms, leaning Victor over a pillow. Sava helped him out of his shirt, trailing kisses up his back.

"I don't know. I really don't. My … my eyes. You said I had pretty eyes."

"Because they are," Sava said behind him, and Victor turned to look at him and was rewarded with another kiss. "You deserve this and more, Victor. Little owl. You don't need to hide how lovely you are beneath a coat of feathers. Anyone should see it."

Victor groaned as Sava tugged at his pants, both of them equally desperate, Victor's fingers curling into the fabric of the pillow. Sava held his fingers to Victor's mouth, and Victor sucked on them, wetting them with his tongue.

"You call yourself too thin, but look at how well you fit beneath me," Sava said, watching Victor carefully. Victor could feel Sava's cock nudging against him, and he rocked back into it, eyes half-lidded.

"You always … talk about feeding me, though," he said, when Sava removed his fingers.

"Because I want to. Let me take care of you." Victor let out a sound that could have been a sob, biting his own wrist. He didn't know why the thought of Sava taking care of him was so perfect, rolling through him like fire while the storm raged outside.

He writhed beneath Sava, gasping and pressing his face into the pillows, and when Sava kissed the back of his neck tenderly, reverently, Victor shuddered.

"You want this?" Sava whispered, and Victor groaned into the pillows.

"Yes, please, fuck."

Sava kissed him behind the ear, and then he was leaning over him, pressing into him, filling Victor as he panted against the pillows. Sava was breathless, too, and he paused when Victor had taken all of him.

"Please," Victor said again, and he cried out as Sava started to move, pleasure spiking through him. He pushed back against Sava, but Sava soon overtook him, fucking into him so hard and deep that all Victor could do was hang on.

When Sava reached forward to wrap his hand around Victor's cock, Victor howled as he came, and Sava leaned in to bite the back of his neck, hard, as he followed Victor into release. He held him there a moment longer, a comforting weight, before he drew away and rolled Victor onto his back.

"Shit," Victor whispered, his voice muffled as Sava kissed him. "That was … Did we …" He ran a hand over the mark on the back of his neck, meeting Sava's gaze.

"Oh," he said, and even though he still didn't quite believe all the kind things Sava had said, he couldn't hold back the smile breaking over his face. "I guess we did."

# CHAPTER 7

*W*ell. So much for self-control.

Part of Sava wanted to ignore this. Tell Victor it was fine, they were just pleasuring each other, it was the same sort of thing that Sava got up to with other dominants on a hunt.

But he knew that wasn't true. He'd heard Victor say those things, and he hadn't been able to stop himself from embracing him, kissing him, *taking* him. And Victor … the way he'd looked at Sava, the way he *always* looked at Sava, as if he could do nothing wrong. Despite all Sava's earlier protestations about how Victor deserved someone better, he'd been caught up in the moment and had taken him even though he didn't think he was worthy of such a clever, brave mate.

But Victor didn't think much of himself, and that must mean he didn't think he deserved a better mate. Sava was suddenly beset by doubts, because Victor had only just become a Lukoi. What if he'd made a mistake, moaning so prettily for Sava? What if Sava was supposed to control himself, let Victor be? What if he'd ruined Victor's life?

"Did you say we have to, ah, go see the kuvar?"

Sava glanced at him and forgot what he'd been thinking.

Victor had Sava's teeth marks on the back of his neck, and he was still a bit sweaty, and he *smelled* like Sava. That made Sava almost unbearably hot, and he pressed his face against Victor's neck and inhaled, then bit him again for good measure.

Victor wriggled underneath him, and that was the end of any theoretical conversation. Sava wanted so many things—and he could have them, now that he had a mate. He kissed down Victor's chest, biting his lovely skin and thinking he really *did* need to eat more.

"What are you ... Wait," Victor moaned, fingers lighting like hummingbirds on Sava's shoulders as he pressed hot, open-mouthed kisses on Victor's stomach and then lower, his intentions clear. "Sava, shouldn't I do this for you?"

"Greedy thing," Sava murmured, nipping at Victor's hip bone, which was far too prominent. "You will wait your turn."

"But I'm—ohh," Victor moaned, as Sava took his cock in his mouth. He thrilled at the weight of it, the salty taste, the way it grew hard as he sucked and swirled his tongue. Sava was new to this, and he choked when he went too far, but Victor was thrusting up, and his hands on Sava's shoulders were no longer light but tense and desperate. It was a newfound pleasure to tease him, to hold his hips steady and drive him wild until Victor sobbed and begged Sava to let him come.

Later, once the edge had worn off their sudden passion, Sava heated a bath and laughed outright when Victor simply climbed in and settled atop him, falling asleep while Sava gave in to the urge to draw his fingers through Victor's dark curls.

"I will be a good mate," Sava told him as he slept. "You deserve that, clever owl." He was stunned at his sudden good fortune, but he couldn't shake the eerie sense of impending disaster that seemed to howl along with the wind. "I will prove myself worthy of you."

Suddenly, Sava wanted to get up, get dressed, and find a sleeping bear to get his mate the warmest fur in all of Lukos. If he could do that, make a comfortable home here, maybe Victor would not regret having moaned for Sava. He might never love Sava like he'd loved his David, but perhaps Sava could make this enough that Victor would not leave and go into the sea, chasing a life that was no longer his.

"Mmm. This bath is the best," Victor said, blinking up at him. His glasses were on the table, and his eyes looked soft and fuzzy. He smiled, the steam from the bath making his hair curl even more. "It's so *warm*."

Ah, but he was lovely. Sava tipped his face up and kissed him. "That is, I think, me, not the bath. Come, you should dress and eat—do not make that face at me. You will put on weight this winter, as a good Lukoi should."

Victor's smile went wicked, and he wriggled on top of Sava, reaching down to grab at the soft part of Sava's stomach. "It won't look good on me, like it does on you."

"How can you know this, until you try?"

"David thought putting on weight made you slovenly," Victor said.

Sava narrowed his eyes. "Like a bear sleeping in the cave for the winter? That is not being lazy, that is how they survive."

"I ... can't tell if you're joking." Victor kissed him. "I can do this now, right?"

"Of course. We are mates. You can do whatever you like to me."

"What if I did ... this?" Victor shoved his hands under Sava's arms, which did not make much sense. Perhaps this was some strange Gerakian gesture of affection, and Sava should reciprocate?

But when he did, Victor shrieked and kicked and sent water flying, then gave Sava's shoulder a wet *smack*. "You're supposed to be—what's the word? When you touch something, and it, ah. Makes you shiver?"

"We went over this," Sava said, and made the same gesture Victor had, earlier, mimicking sucking cock.

Victor laughed. "No, no." He wiggled his fingers. "When you do this, and … here." He dropped his hand to the skin behind Sava's knee. This time, it made *Sava* kick, and then he knew the word Victor wanted.

"Ticklish." He smiled wickedly. "And you may do it, but I think I will get revenge, and you might not like that."

Victor laughed. "There will be no water left in the tub, and something tells me it's the submissive's job to clean it up."

By the time they had finished bathing, cleaning up the water, and dressing warmly, it was nearly time to eat. Sava went to prepare dinner, since they'd spent half the day wrapped up in each other—and that was, so he'd heard, how it was supposed to be when you found a mate.

Victor's mood seemed to dim as he watched. "Shouldn't I do that?"

Sava frowned. "You seem to think there is a list of things you must do for your mate. It is not that way. We do what we are good at, each of us."

"So I'll make a mess and talk too much, and you'll do every-thing else?"

Sava heard a somber note beneath Victor's attempt at light-hearted teasing and shook his head. "You will have time to learn these things, yes? Trust me, little owl, there will be very few things to do when the snows come in truth."

"Oh, speaking of, I kept meaning to go check and see why it's been so dark outside," Victor said, standing up.

Sava thought he was just going to look out the window, but instead, Victor opened the door. It happened too fast to tell him not to, and then he heard Victor's shout of dismay as the door flew open and the wind pushed in a drift of snow, sending the cold, slushy mess all over the floor.

It took all of Sava's considerable strength to get the door shut again, pushing against the wind as he was, and by the time it was closed and latched the fire had gone out, he and Victor were both soaked and shivering, and the floor was a mess of mud and melting snow.

"Like I said," Victor wheezed in the ensuing silence. He would not look at Sava. "I'll make a mess."

Sava just sighed and went to get a bristle broom. "I should have warned you. Not very much snow has fallen, but the wind makes piles of it. This passes before the first real storm—"

"There's a mountain in our living room," Victor interrupted, hands on his hips, water dripping down his nose. His glasses were spotted, and his teeth were chattering as he spoke.

Sava smiled despite the unexpected chores that had blown in. "No, no. Just a hill. But it is my fault. I should have told you."

"Maybe I should be smart enough not to open the door in a Lukoi winter," Victor said, raking a hand through his curls. "Not everything is your fault, Sava. Especially foolish things I do because I'm not thinking."

"You are curious. And this is not yet winter, little owl. Not even close." Sava thought about it for a moment. "In true winter, you will not be able to open the door."

"Because the wind will be too strong for my lackluster muscles?"

"Well." Sava cleared his throat. "Mostly because the snow covers the door to the roof and will fall on you. Go and get warm. It will do you no good to shiver there like you are made of ice, not feathers." He thought of Milan, of his earlier dread, and ignored the ominous sound of the wind outside. "Tomorrow it should be clear. We will go and make the mark for the kuvar if we can."

"What if we can't?" Victor asked.

"Then we will show him the scars in the spring," Sava said, as the wind rattled the eaves and rushed down the chimney, trying to smother the fire he'd only just restarted. "You will eat twice as much at dinner as you usually do, mate. To give you padding for warmth. Do not argue with me."

"Yes, yes," Victor groused, and moved off to the bedroom.

Dinner was late that night, since Sava insisted on cleaning all the debris and water from the floorboards first. He explained why to Victor, that everything needed to stay dry and not spoil the food in the cellar below, then had to pin him against the wall and kiss him when he tried to apologize—again—for opening the door.

"I will be exasperated if you do it again, now that you know," Sava said. "But you did not know, so how could I be angry? Is this not how scholars learn, in your place full of knowledge?"

"We memorize things out of books, mostly." Victor was bundled up in furs and eating a second portion of stew under Sava's watchful eye. "Did you make this bowl *and* this spoon? Of course you did."

Sava was not sure whether he was supposed to answer, but he nodded. "I carved the spoons from the antlers of a stag. It is smoother to eat stew with, I think, than rougher wood that is sometimes used for utensils. And the bowls, these are clay that Marta made. She is, like you, good at art. I made some from the skull of a bear—"

"Why is that hot," Victor muttered, shaking his head.

"And wood, too. I will show you how, if you like."

Victor's smile was shadowed, and he looked away from Sava's gaze, down at his bowl. "He really did mean for me to die."

Sava frowned. He did not want to speak badly of a man Victor had feelings for, but in Lukos, the punishment for what David had done would be exile—a death sentence, for it meant no resources, no one to trade with, and the land was too unforgiving to survive that way. "Like you with the snow, perhaps he didn't understand how harsh it was here."

"Oh, I'm sure he didn't." Victor's voice was bitter. "But I'm sure he didn't care, either." Victor took his bowl, and Sava's, and spent some time cleaning them with the hot water from the kettle hanging over the fire. Sava showed him how to store the rest of the soup, and it was late by the time they finished getting everything tidy for the next day.

When they got into bed, Sava expected Victor to sleep; his mood was pensive, and it had been a fairly momentous day, all around. But Victor climbed on him immediately, kissing him with a heated purposefulness that made Sava's cock grow hard in seconds.

"I'm an awful cook, I can't start a fire, and I—literally— opened the door and welcomed in winter," Victor said, pushing Sava to his back and settling between his thighs. "But there's something I *can* do, and I'm almost sad no one's ever done it to you before, just so you could recognize how truly gifted at it I am."

"What are you—" His words fell away as Victor took his cock in his mouth, the pleasure hitting him like the snow had earlier, sudden and overwhelming. But it was warm, not cold, and Sava's calves tensed, toes pointing as he felt, for the first time, the incredible pleasure of being taken into someone's mouth. And unlike Sava's earlier efforts, Victor took *all* of him and didn't choke.

It felt so good that Sava didn't get to enjoy it for long; the wonderful sensation had him gripping Victor's curls and coming down his throat in an embarrassingly short time, gasping for breath as Victor sat back on his heels and grinned in triumph.

"I'm good for something, see?"

Sava wheezed and managed a nod before he grabbed Victor and drew him close. There was something there, beneath the pleasure and Victor's admitted skill, that they would need to address. But as the wind howled and ice pellets fell in sheets over the snow of Lukos, Sava and Victor were lost in each other, and Sava had forgotten it by morning.

❄

THE WORLD WAS quiet when Victor woke. He stirred slowly, loath to leave the warmth of the bed and the comfort of Sava's arm over his middle, and stared at the strong lines of Sava's face. He raised a hand to stroke Sava's long, dark hair and let his fingers linger at his temple, momentarily thrown by the way his brown skin compared to Sava's, which had an undertone of gold in the light.

As a child, Victor had been taught to be proud of the way he looked. He came from the people who'd always lived in rural Gerakia, the first scholars and philosophers who wove crowns out of grape leaves and started the public schools that dotted the countryside like trees. Of course there were other kinds of people from the region now, but back when Gerakia was more isolated, all the great scholars looked like Victor. There were statues of them by the schools, sometimes, and while Victor never thought much about it, Aunt Grace had reminded him when he went off to college that he was part of a legacy.

"Maybe you'll revive it," she'd said as Victor unwrapped his bespelled glasses, a costly gift from a woman whose house ran on donations. "There was a time this village was full of scholars."

But Victor hadn't returned to the village, and somewhere along the way, he'd been trained to think of the parts of himself that were previously beautiful and valued as useless. How could one person's influence break all that down so thoroughly?

Sava opened his eyes and smiled at Victor so warmly that Victor rolled to press his face to Sava's shoulder. Sava's chuckle felt like the rumbling purr of a giant cat, and he kissed Victor's curls.

"You've experienced your first storm," Sava said. "While the sky is quiet, we should go and see the kuvar."

Right. They had to finalize it, whatever it was they'd become. Victor looked at his palm, unmarked and uncalloused, and wondered if he was cursed to fall hard and fast for the first person to show him kindness—and whether Sava would regret it, mating a man who couldn't survive a Lukos winter on his own.

"Maybe we can stay in until spring," Victor said.

"There will be plenty of time for that later, my owl. We'll eat, now, and I'll show you how to walk in the snow."

Victor groaned as Sava climbed out of bed, but he followed, padding into the bathing room. He dipped into a precious bottle of hair oil he'd brought with him from Gerakia, then twisted his curls into tight braids that would probably freeze over the moment he stepped outside. Sava watched him from the fire, clearly trying not to look like he was spying, and Victor flashed him a nervous grin. David had always accused Victor of being vain when he did this.

Breakfast was decadent, the last of Sava's store of eggs and thick bread with strips of venison, and when Victor gave Sava a baleful look at the amount on his plate, Sava just shrugged.

"If you want me to finish this, you'll have to start feeding me by hand," Victor said, half to himself, and stopped as Sava's gaze went distant. "Oh."

It was like when he was a freshman and he'd first met Miles, his best friend at the Two Sisters. Miles was a bit wild, the son of a Kallistoi muse. He knew how attractive he was and didn't mind throwing himself into the arms of anyone who would have him, and Victor had suggested that Miles tie himself to one of the statues for a day and get his need to be controlled and restrained out of his system. Miles's eyes had glazed over in the same way.

"I mean …" Victor cleared his throat. "If you want to." He didn't know how it would feel—David had certainly never shown any interest in caring for Victor that way—but Victor had always believed he should try something at least once before making up his mind about it.

Taking bread from Sava's fingers was awkward at first—Sava was so careful, so watchful, that Victor felt heat burn his cheeks and he looked away—but when he licked Sava's fingers and Sava took him by the back of the head with his free hand, it was so intimate that Victor couldn't help but be drawn to Sava's gaze. It reminded him of that night after the fire circle, when Sava gently cleaned his face and neck while Victor stumbled and fumbled just to undo his bootlaces. This was a different kind of dominance, a different kind of control, and Victor felt the same tug of interest as he had when he saw the marks on the cave wall, curious and soothed all at once.

He and Sava moved to the pit before the fire when they were done eating, and Sava stared down at him for a breath before taking Victor's hand in his. He kissed Victor's knuckles, an oddly genteel gesture, and Victor reached up to touch his dark hair.

"All right," Victor said. "I'll eat more next time, I guess." Sava let out a breathless laugh, and Victor kissed him, warm and content. "You learned something, didn't you?" he asked.

"I think so," Sava said. "It's as though I didn't know the shape of it, before. Does that happen to you, with what you like?"

"I don't know. I'm not sure what I like." Victor reached out to grab his glasses. "That was nice. And I like people who are … good at things. Like you. Someone, uh. They put a thing in my mouth? A …" He gestured.

"A gag?"

"Yes." Victor repeated the word. "I liked the feeling of not being in control. Knowing the person I was with knew what I wanted, when to stop, how to tell when I was into it."

"Of course a man like you would need a mate who is just as perceptive." Sava kissed him softly. "Maybe this winter we will try covering your eyes. Or your ears, or both. If you trust me to."

Victor shivered. "Why wouldn't I?"

Something sad flickered in Sava's eyes at that, but he just kissed Victor again, and they lay together while the sun rose over the snow beyond the windows, filling the room with light.

They didn't lounge for long. Victor was just starting to drift off when Sava shook him gently awake and left their warm nest of furs.

"Nooo," he whispered, as Sava laughed and tossed him his coat. Victor grumbled as he bundled up, and when he reached for his glasses, Sava stopped him.

"The metal," he said. "It will burn your skin in the cold. I can make a cloth to cover the part that touches your face, but for today, these will have to be left behind."

"You'll have to hold my hand, then," Victor said, only half joking, and set them down by the fire.

Sava showed Victor how to open a hatch in the wall next to the door, high enough off the floor that they had to climb up a stepladder to go through. The snow and ice from the night before had drifted halfway up the door, and Victor stared agape at the blanket of white draped over the hills like an unfinished quilt.

"It's beautiful," he said, eyeing the trees with their naked branches twisting to the sky, the clouds still roiling over the mountains.

Sava shrugged. He must have seen this landscape all the time, enough for the glitter of light on the snow to seem ordinary, but Victor couldn't look away. He kept getting distracted as Sava showed him how to put on his snowshoes, which were wickedly difficult for Victor walk in, and probably would have been even without his wandering thoughts.

As they headed up the slope to the kuvar's house, Victor heard a shriek in the distance and nearly fell on his face. He turned, clutching Sava in alarm, but it was just a child clinging to a wooden frame of some kind as they rocketed down the hill. A man stood at the top, bundled in furs and wool, and he raised a hand in greeting as his child went, rolling and giggling, into a snowbank.

"This happens, before the first long snowfall," Sava said as the child started dragging their frame up the hill again. "Children don't have much opportunity for play during the worst of winter."

"What do they do, then?" Victor couldn't imagine it. Even when storms would roll through Gerakia, they were never so dire that Victor couldn't run into the village for sausage rolls at the bakery or catch frogs with the other kids from the orphanage, scrambling barefoot by the lake.

Sava was silent for a minute. "When I was young, I spun wool. Carved figures out of wood—many children carve spoons, forks, simple tools. But you know a child has been bored in the winter if you see carvings on the beams of their houses."

"I wish I could see the things you made." Victor watched the child fling themself down the hill again.

"They weren't very good. But I liked to hunt, and my mother made games for me to keep me occupied. They say it is easier when you have more than one child."

"Sounds lonely," Victor said. "I was always surrounded by kids, growing up. It wasn't the same as having a sibling—the other kids left, when they were taken in by new parents—but there was always something to do."

"You, I think, were not a child who could easily tolerate being bored."

Victor grinned at Sava, even though his face was covered by a scarf. "Boredom was torture."

They passed another family on their way—parents with a teenager, this time, showing a little boy how to hold on to the frame and not cry when he fell. Victor applauded when the kid got up again, and he caught Sava looking at him with open yearning in his eyes.

"Do you want children?" Victor asked before he could stop himself. Sava seemed momentarily thrown, his gaze shifting from the family on the hill to Victor.

"Did you?" There was a note of panic in Sava's voice that made Victor smile. It was easy to forget how young Sava was, but now he truly did sound like a man in his midtwenties. "I do not know whether that is possible. That is, if there were a child without a home, and—"

"Easy," Victor said, reaching out to pat Sava's arm. "It was only a question. I know we can't, between us, but I was an orphan. If a child needed a home, I wouldn't mind. Once I figure out how to walk in these things, of course. So at least two, three years from now."

Sava tugged on the flaps of Victor's hat. "I will keep that in mind. We will see plenty of families when the snow thaws. Children run from house to house in the summer. Everyone is an aunt or an uncle. We will have no choice."

"Uncle Victor." Victor snorted. "I'm not old enough for that."

They left the family laughing and tumbling down the hill and made their careful way to the kuvar's house in the heart of Lukos.

The kuvar's daughter was already out, marching over the cold ground with two wriggling balled-up blankets in her arms. A massive gray wolf walked alongside her, staring at her like she'd hung the stars, and Elena called out to Sava as he and Victor approached.

"Snow-Walker!" she shouted, in a booming voice that echoed over the snow. "I've caught these two vicious wolves. Look at them."

"Oh my gods," Victor breathed, as a small nose poked out from inside one of the blankets.

"You don't have to wrap them up like that," Sava said, and Elena made a face at him, hefting her bundles.

"No, I don't, but this teaches them that I'm the one who will care for them, when it's time to see who will listen to whose commands. I'm stealing them from Father," she added, in response to Victor's frown. "He thinks he'll have three wolves following him around just because he can bark like them? Please."

She maneuvered around to slip a piece of jerky to the adult wolf, who continued to stare at her in adoration.

"Father's inside." She looked from Victor to Sava and smiled. "If you're here to, you know. Announce anything."

Victor watched, mildly bemused, as Sava's cheeks reddened. "Yes. Well. Thank you."

"Yes, that's right," Elena said to the pups, as she and her wolf walked past Victor. "They're nothing more than two big, ridiculous men, aren't they? Aren't they? Oh, yes, they are."

"I think we might be obvious," Victor muttered, as they reached the front door of the kuvar's stone house. Sava knocked, while Victor hung back. Dragan had the kind of dominance that tended to leave Victor feeling tongue-tied and abashed, like he'd been caught filching chalk and was about to be sentenced to writing lines again.

The door swung open, and the kuvar stood there, broad and taller even than Sava, dark hair pulled back from his blue eyes. He stood in silence for a breath, staring at them, and then burst into uproarious laughter.

Sava blushed darker still, and Victor tugged his scarf up to cover more of his face.

"Ah, yes," Dragan said. "You are here to, what, trade hides? Comment on the weather? Some storm, eh? Perfect for taking in a new mate, not that you would have done that. How long did it take you? One day? Two?"

"A few weeks," Victor mumbled, but thankfully, Dragan didn't hear.

"We can come back," Sava said.

"No, come in. Tell me what it is you want of me, Snow-Walker."

Sava drew himself up as they stepped into the kuvar's house, with its stone walls and high ceilings. Victor edged in behind him, marveling at how the heat of the fire reached even the doorway.

"We have come to make the vows, declare ourselves as mates."

Dragan snorted, arms crossed over his chest. "Well. I can't say

I am surprised. When I brought him to you, I thought you would take him. Good, good. He understands what it means to be one of us?"

"I took him to the caves," Sava said, then added, in a tone of pride, "He drew the stories we have there, copied them. He is very clever."

"He came from a place where they are supposed to be clever, yes?" Dragan drew a knife from the wall, one with a bone handle and what looked like a recently whetted blade. "He knows that, as your mate, he is to be yours and only yours, unless you decide between you to have a third? And that for either of you to harm the other is a crime that is not forgiven?"

"He does, yes."

"All right, then, Victor who came from the sea. Take your place beside your mate, and hold your hand out. We stand on little ceremony here."

Sava turned and took Victor's hand, patting it. "We will each cut our hand and grasp each other's, showing that our life depends on each other and the work we do together."

"Oh, I—all right." Victor squeezed his hand. "Are there words?"

"Just say what you want to say," Dragan said. "We are not known much for our pretty words, eh, Sava?"

"Sava says them," Victor murmured.

Dragan laughed, and it sounded a bit like a wolf's bark. "Yes, he would, wouldn't he? Sava, go first, show him how. Sava will cut his dominant hand, and you, Victor, you will cut your nondominant one. Then, when the thaws come, you will return, stand before me again, and give me the name Victor will be known by."

He handed over the knife. Sava took it, nodded at Dragan, and turned to show Victor. "This is the dagger they say the first kuvar used, when he slew the wolf that brought us here."

Victor's eyes went wide.

Sava took the knife, pressed the tip to his hand, and gently cut a line down his right palm. "I will give you shelter in the winter, Victor. See you through to the thaw. Show you the beauty to be found here, the way I did in the caves."

With that, he handed the knife to Victor and waited with his hand bleeding, the sincerity of his words hanging in the space between them.

If Victor were a good man, he would have given the knife back.

If he weren't hopelessly and desperately selfish, he would have told Sava all the things that would tear away at his image of Victor over the winter: his countless weaknesses, ones that others had no problem noticing and picking apart. He would have spared Sava the embarrassment of taking back his vow.

Victor pressed the blade into his left palm. The cut was sharp, almost painless, and only started to twinge when he pulled the knife away and saw the line of blood well up from his skin.

He looked at Sava. His breath left him in one enormous rush, and he held out his hand like an offering, blood in his palm.

"I'll ..." He didn't know what to say. He knew so many languages, but he couldn't piece together anything that could describe how he felt, standing there with Sava looking at him like he was something beautiful, something wanted. "I'll be yours. I'll be worthy of you."

It probably wasn't what a mate was supposed to say, but it was all he had. Sava clasped his hand over Victor's, and Victor tightened his grip like a man drowning.

"So it is done," Dragan said, deftly taking the knife from Victor's free hand. "You didn't have to kneel, but it was pretty enough."

"What?" Victor hadn't realized he'd gone to his knees. "Oh."

Sava looked down at Victor like he was ready to throw him to the floor then and there, Dragan or no, and Victor hastily pulled himself back to his feet. Dragan gave them strips of cloth that smelled vaguely medicinal to wrap around their palms, then waved them off.

"If you're going to make him scream for it, don't do it here," he said. Victor didn't have to point out to Sava that Dragan had clearly prepared the bandages ahead of time, expecting them to come. "I have work to do."

"We should go," Victor whispered, hastily tying off Sava's bandage. "As soon as possible."

Sava smiled and kissed him, swift and hard. "Yes, mate. I like this plan."

"Disgusting," Dragan said cheerfully. "Go on. Get out."

Victor practically fell into his snowshoes at the door, and Sava walked carefully at his side so Victor could grab him by the coat every time he stumbled or swayed.

As they approached the snow-laden field that led to Sava's home, Victor stopped. Sava turned to look at him, and Victor squinted up at the sky, which was thundering again, low and dark.

"You know," Victor said. "If I were at the college right now, I'd probably be in the middle of being lectured for, I don't know, drawing my notes instead of writing them in proper script. I'd be sneaking around behind the school's back with a man who didn't love me. And I could have just ... left him and concentrated on something more fulfilling, that whole time."

"Is this the place to reflect on this?"

Victor smiled. "Maybe not. I didn't realize how stressed I was, before, not knowing where I was going. I thought David was the only thing I knew for sure."

Sava gave him a bemused look. "You're going home. With me. Know *that*, my mate."

"Right." Victor took an unsteady breath. "Can you say that again?"

"You're going home with me," Sava said.

Victor breathed out. "Yeah. Okay. Let's go home."

There were more people out now. Victor considered waving, showing his hand with the bandage peeking out of the glove, but as he and Sava made their slow way through the snow, it was nice to think of it as a secret. One that everyone else seemed to have guessed before they did, sure, but a secret nonetheless. A mark, like the one he'd made on the cave wall, that said he belonged to someone.

They were nearly home when Sava pointed out several people on another frame—a *sled,* he called it—rocketing down the slope. Victor jumped back and fell on his side as the entire group went tumbling past them, children screaming with laughter, the sled tipping over in a snowbank. Sava caught one child before she could land face-first, and her brother fell onto his back. Another figure stood up a few paces away and strode over to hold out a hand to Victor.

"Well, hello there," Ivan said. His eyes twinkled with amusement. "How's your first winter starting, Victor?"

"Wet," Victor said, and Ivan laughed and hauled him up. "Are these … your cousins, or …"

"No, I'm Mitri," the boy said, dusting snow off his back.

"And I'm Anya!" the girl shouted, from Sava's arms. "Put me down, Snow-Walker, I'm grown up now."

"Oh, of course," Sava said, as Ivan winked at Victor.

"I'm taking them out while their parents fix the roof," Ivan said in a low voice. "It started buckling, so Kosta's there now, with that glue he makes. And no, Sava, you don't need to go. There are too many dominants already."

"Ivan's taking us sledding all day," Mitri said. "Over and over and over and over."

"Help," Ivan whispered to Victor, and Victor tugged his scarf up to hide a grin. "How are you two? What brought you all this way? Not a hunt."

"Victor and I just returned from the kuvar's," Sava said, with a note of pride in his voice that made Victor feel so warm that he could have melted half the snow in Lukos. "We swore ourselves to each other as mates not an hour ago."

The children immediately started bellowing questions, Anya grabbing Victor's arm while Mitri bounced on his toes, making Sava blink and struggle to pick a single comment to respond to. Victor laughed, but his voice died as he saw Ivan staring at Sava. For a moment, Ivan was transfixed in shock, and Victor remembered his promise to Ivan with a pang of regret. He knew what it was to be heartbroken, and even without his glasses to help him, the look on Ivan's face was unmistakable.

"Ivan," he said, softly, and reached out. Ivan jerked his hand away and stepped back, his features sharpening with the distance. His forlorn look vanished so quickly that Victor almost wondered if he'd imagined it, and then Ivan smiled just a little too wide.

"Look at you, Victor," he said. "Only a few weeks on Lukos, and you already found a dominant. Well, you're so unique, you know, with your big eyes and those funny languages you speak, it was bound to happen."

*You're not the best at subtlety, Victor,* David had said, what felt like a lifetime ago.

Victor stood very still as Ivan turned his too-bright smile to Sava, and the sounds of voices piping around him seemed to blur. He had been sure, for a minute, that he had lost Ivan's friendship, but now Ivan was grinning and clapping Sava's arm, promising to come by with a mating gift soon.

"For both of you, of course," Ivan said, but when he turned to Victor, his eyes were blank. They showed no sense of betrayal. No anger. Not even sorrow. His smile was warm, but his eyes were like glass, and even as Ivan walked off with the kids in tow, laughing and singing a marching song, Victor couldn't shake the feeling that behind the cheery grin and the kind words, there was nothing. Nothing at all.

# CHAPTER 8

*V*ictor was quiet as they walked back to the house, and Sava told himself it wasn't because he was regretting becoming his mate. It would not do to spend the winter convinced his mate wished to be with someone else.

"Would you like a sled?" Sava asked him, stretching his fingers to feel the sting in his palm where his cut was fresh, new and hot on his skin.

"I would break my neck, probably." But then Victor said, "I might try a smaller hill. Maybe with no kids at the bottom."

Sava turned his face up to the sky. "I will make you one, and we will find the smallest hill. No children. Small bushes only."

"Nope," Victor said cheerfully. "I'll land in those, and you'll have to pick brambles out of my hair."

"Well. That would be all right, but I could keep you from falling into them."

"You say that now." Victor patted him on the arm.

Sava wanted to throw him down and fuck him, there in the snow—which Victor would probably not like, as it was very cold. But he was so charming like this, with snowflakes in his lashes, that it was hard to keep his hands to himself.

"What was that?" Victor tilted his head. "Did you hear that? Was it a bear?"

"A bear." Sava shook his head, amused. "Where? I hear— Oh, you mean that sound, from there? The rustling?"

"Yes, is that … bear rustling?" Victor edged closer to him. "You're carrying me home, if it is."

"I— All right, but no, it is not a bear." He could hear the sound now, like a creature was in distress. "Hmm." Sava moved closer, nodding as he saw the arrangement of brush and sticks in the snow. "Ah. I was afraid of this." He reached down and brushed the debris aside, revealing a hole in the ground from which a very small, angry white snow cat was yowling. Snow cats weren't common—not here, anyway. Mostly they lived near the mountains.

"Oh, *no*," Victor breathed, eyes wide. "Someone put a kitten in a hole?" Before Sava could explain, Victor was reaching out to pick the animal up.

Sava moved to stop him. "No, no. If you do that, its mother will not come back for it. We should cover it and—"

"Just *leave* it?" Victor chewed on his lip. The snow kitten mewled, big-eyed, scruffy and far, far too thin.

"I think, maybe," Sava said, carefully, "its mother has already left it."

"It's so small. If its mother— Does that mean—"

"It would be best," Sava said, as the kitten tried to climb out of the den and failed, "if I … attended to it."

"What does that mean?" Victor picked up the kitten. He winced—it must have bitten his glove—but he stroked it, and the kitten stopped screaming for a moment to peer up at him with big, wide yellow eyes.

"It means it will not survive," Sava said. "The mother, maybe something happened to her, maybe she abandoned this one, but—"

"But, what?" Victor demanded, and he looked *angry*. "So it

should just, what, die?"

"Well," Sava said. "I could make it easier, painless. It will suffer if it is left there."

"Can we, I don't know, find its mother?" Victor continued petting the snow cat, which hissed and yowled at first but eventually calmed as he held it protectively to his chest.

"I do not think so, Victor. It is very kind of you to want to save the kitten, but …" Sava cleared his throat. "The kinder thing would be to put it down, gently." There wasn't even enough fur on the kitten to make a pair of gloves, but Sava did not say that to Victor.

"So because no one wants it, and it's weak, it just … gets its neck broken." Victor's voice was shaking. "That's not—it's not fair."

"Well, no," Sava said. "But it is nature. Things are not always fair here. Once, a few winters ago, my mother and I found a den of—"

"No," Victor interrupted, eyes narrowed, while the kitten tried to scratch his coat. "Whatever sad story you're going to tell me about baby animals that didn't make it, I don't want to hear it, Sava!"

"All right, I will not tell you. But this is not an easy land, Victor. This kitten, it is not meant to survive."

"I don't *care*. The winter is *not getting this kitten*," Victor breathed out, slow and steady. His nose wrinkled. "I'm sorry. I know I'm being dramatic."

Ah. Now Sava understood. Victor thought he, too, was small and helpless. "You are not a snow kitten left in a hole, Victor."

"Oh, but I am, though. Ouch, little cat, that's my finger …" He shifted the kitten, which went from chewing happily on Victor's gloved finger to trying to climb up on his shoulders. "Look. I can't let you kill it. Can we … keep it?"

"Keep it," Sava said, staring. "You want to keep this snow cat? Alive?"

"Yes, *alive.*" Victor winced as the kitten attacked his hair where it stuck out under his hat. "Is that not … Do they get really big, or something?"

They did, in fact. Snow cats weren't as big as wolves, but they were big enough to be formidable. "They can, yes. That one looks to be a runt, which might be why it was left."

"We're keeping it," Victor said, in a firm voice. He had no natural dominance, but it didn't matter—the snow was falling faster, and Victor was cradling the kitten while it tried to gnaw on his ear. "I, ah. I mean. May we keep it?"

"I think I am too afraid of what you will do if I say no." Sava smiled when Victor looked at him askance, trying to remove the kitten from his shoulder … which wasn't easy, considering it had dug its claws into his coat and wasn't letting go. "We can keep the snow cat, mate." Sava reached out and gently removed the cat, turning it around and looking at its rear. "He. It's a he. If you were wondering."

"You know everything." Victor smiled at him. "Thank you … mate."

Sava smiled, pleased. "Let me have your scarf."

Victor gave it to him, and Sava wrapped the little kitten in it and handed it back to Victor. "We will need to feed it. There is milk at home, and maybe we can trade for a goat. Or perhaps we can ask Elena what she uses for her wolf pups."

"You're really going to let me keep him," Victor whispered, eyes big and bright.

Sava nodded. "You asked me. Is that not what you want? Did you think I would say no?"

"I— Yes? I don't know." Victor looked at him, smiling, and his expression was so sweet that Sava felt his whole body flush with heat. "It's so cold out, and he's so small."

"Yes." Sava glanced up at the sky, which was turning darker, the snow falling harder. "Let us take our kitten home, then."

Victor spent the remainder of the walk back to the house

trying to come up with a name for the kitten, who was yowling and trying to chew his way out of the scarf. By the time they reached the house, the snow had turned into sleet and thunder was starting in the distance.

The house was dark and cold when they entered, and Sava lit a fire while Victor unwrapped the kitten and watched with a laugh as he raced around the house, digging his claws into the wood floors. The kitten went screeching into the pit before the fire, where he lay tangled up in the blankets, meowing piteously.

Victor watched him, laughing, looking so happy that Sava's heart felt full. His mate was so clever, so pretty, and so kind he would save a kitten abandoned in the snow by its mother.

"You will do well here," Sava said, unable to put into words the pride he felt toward Victor, even just standing up to him about the kitten. "The kitten will need a name, but first, some food, I think."

The kitten screamed and flung himself about the living area. It took both of them to catch him, and they were both laughing by the time Victor snatched him around the middle. "Gotcha, you speedy thing." He picked the kitten up, stared at him, and smiled. "Speedy. That's a good name, don't you think?"

"I do," Sava said, finding a cheesecloth and the milk. "Come, I will show you how to feed Speedy. Then he will need a box filled with sand, so he does not make a mess on the furs. I will put it in the bathroom. You can show him where it is when it is set up."

"Oh, right, of course. Thank you," Victor said, putting a hand on Sava's arm. "For understanding why I needed to do this."

"Of course. It is good practice, this kitten." Sava tipped his face up, leaned in and kissed him. "For the children we might have in … two, three years, was it?"

Victor stared at him, Speedy meowed piteously for food, and Sava threw his head back and laughed, loud and long.

❄

Victor had never been allowed to keep a pet. There were always kids at the orphanage who tried to bring a puppy or a kitten home, which usually led to tears, and the dorm at university was about as strict. Victor knew it wasn't guaranteed that he could keep an abandoned kitten alive through the winter, but Speedy took to the makeshift bottle easily enough, and Victor let a sliver of hope peek through. Soon, his lap was full of sleepy kitten, tiny claws extended and belly taut as a drum.

Victor almost protested when Sava picked Speedy up off his lap, but the kitten was so out of it that he didn't move when Sava set him on a pillow near the fire, bristly fur finally lying flat.

"He should sleep for a time." The promise in Sava's low voice made Victor shiver deliciously. "Come, mate. You, too, must be made warm."

"I'm not a kitten," Victor said, or would have, if not for the fact that Sava cupped his cheek with one hand and pressed his thumb to Victor's lips. Victor went quiet, and Sava leaned over him to kiss his temple, his cheek, the sensitive spot below his jaw.

"If you are like the owl in your story," Sava said, kissing his wrist, "then I would have you take off your coat, rest your weary wings, and find a home here. I will take care of you, my mate, as you deserve."

Victor cursed under his breath and tipped his head back to look at the ceiling. Sava's earnest gaze was too much, just then.

Good thing that his glasses were too fogged to see anyway. The spell on the lenses was supposed to keep them clear as well as safe—it was a very complex spell—but apparently whoever made it hadn't considered things like *steam.*

When Sava reached for the glasses, though, Victor couldn't help but wince at hands coming toward his face. Sava was quiet and still for a moment, then he touched the edges of the frames.

"I'm going to clean them for you," he said, and his face became more of a blur than ever as he lifted them off.

"You don't have to."

"I said I would take care of you," Sava said. When he put Victor's glasses back on, they were less cloudy.

"I can't help it," Victor said, managing a small smile as Sava adjusted the glasses. "I'm so used to taking care of myself, I feel bad when someone else does—especially if it's something I could do just as easily."

Sava looked at him, then tipped his head up for a kiss. "We could change that," he said. "I can … bind your hands. Cover that pretty mouth of yours for a time. Or your eyes. They're beautiful, but if it helps you …"

"Helps me feel helpless?" Victor asked. Sava seemed to be figuring himself out, testing the waters of his own dominance. "Yes, I can try that. I'll … kick, if I don't like something?"

"Twice," Sava said. "To be safe. Which you will be, with me."

He stripped Victor first, lovingly, taking his time to kiss his exposed skin and comment on how lovely Victor was. Then, when Victor was avoiding his gaze *again* and flushed with the heat of his praise, Sava retrieved a leather strip that he placed between Victor's teeth, and a soft rope for his wrists. With his wrists bound behind his back, Victor felt off balance, and he had to rely on Sava to move him to a more comfortable position against the pillows.

The last thing Sava did was remove Victor's glasses and tie a dark cloth around his eyes. Panic crept in for a moment, bringing an edge to the thrilling helplessness of being gagged and bound, but Victor settled at the touch of Sava's hand on his chest, Sava's warmth as he moved over Victor. Victor felt Sava's fingers more acutely as they slid down his belly toward his cock. He heard the pop of a bottle and felt the slick touch of an oiled hand massaging his skin, parting his thighs.

When Sava started working him open, Victor let out a sound that made him want to roll over and press his face to the pillows. Except he couldn't. He had to lie there with his face burning, making urgent noises against the gag as Sava curled his fingers and found the spot inside that made Victor *ache* for it.

"You're beautiful like this, too," Sava said as Victor shivered under his touch and tried not to beg through the gag. "And still so tight." He teased at Victor's balls, making him writhe and whine, and leaned down to kiss his neck. "Don't worry, little owl. I have you."

And oh, he did. When Sava thrust into Victor at last, Victor felt it in a way that made him see stars and rip the sheets off the mattress. Victor couldn't even control how he moved against Sava—he was practically lying back in his lap, Sava gripping his hips to fuck into him slow and hard.

He felt every thrust, every touch, heard Sava's breath quicken and his own go ragged around the leather. He whined when Sava touched his aching cock, falling apart in seconds under Sava's hand, and when Sava came over him, all Victor could do was lie there and pant.

Sava took Victor's blindfold off first, kissed his cheeks, then reached behind him to take off the gag. "Was it good for you, my mate?" He kissed the side of Victor's mouth.

"Can't do words," Victor said, and Sava laughed. "Yes."

"Good. You did very well. So good for me, always." Sava murmured praise into Victor's neck as he untied Victor's hands, and Victor didn't even protest when Sava picked him up to carry him to the bath.

Clearly, Sava had been planning for this while Victor was feeding Speedy, because the water was steaming when Victor slipped into it. He smiled lazily as Sava rubbed his sore wrists and scrubbed him down, and when Sava asked him how to tend to his hair, Victor showed him how to protect it against going frizzy. They left the bath warm and sated, Victor wrapped up in a blanket and carried to the bed.

Where Speedy was watching them, tail flicking and wide eyes deeply judgmental.

Victor laughed. "We have a critic." He grinned as Speedy scampered over him, attacking his knee only to go rolling off as though he'd lost the fight.

"When he wakes us in the night," Sava said, climbing in next to Victor, "you will have your own judgment to make of loud creatures disturbing your sleep."

Victor sighed as Sava rolled him into his arms. "I've never slept so well before. It has to be you. You have some Lukoi magic in there." He slapped Sava's arm lightly, and Sava grinned and kissed him until Victor was pleasantly tired, drifting off in his hold.

They *did* wake to Speedy yowling plaintively in the night, but Victor prepared the milk and Speedy again drank greedily. They watched him stumble about for a while before he settled down on Victor's shoulder and fell asleep, purring. Victor hadn't realized that large cats could purr, but maybe snow cats were different, a small comfort in a world of snow and ice.

When he went back to sleep, he dreamed of owls. Hundreds, *thousands* of them, filling the sky with white feathers and sharp, curved beaks. There was no reason to it, not even a sense of self —Victor was swallowed by them, drowning in them, lost among them. It was oddly comforting, drifting in the silent, swift-moving blanket of feathers, and Victor woke feeling as though something had shifted inside him in the night.

"It was a snow dream," Sava said, as Victor tried, with some success, to show Speedy where he was and was *not* supposed to leave his *gifts*. "We have them sometimes, when the snow falls. Strange dreams that make no sense, but do. The witches used to interpret them, before their lines waned and their power was lost. Maybe you should paint it, eh?"

Victor looked up at the beam over the fireplace. When Speedy clawed at his arm, he started and frowned down at the cat, who just meowed and went tipping over on his back.

"You were somewhere else, my mate," Sava said. "You were looking at the fire for a while."

"Was I?" Victor reached down to rub Speedy's belly, then drew his hand back, wincing. "Ow, okay, I should have known better than that." He pondered another moment. "I think I want to carve it. A beam, maybe—a plank of wood covered in owls. It sounds silly," he added quickly.

"No. You should try it." Sava took down a small knife. "I can teach you to carve, if you like. Spoons, at first."

Victor smiled. "Then owls."

"Yes. One step at a time."

The carving lesson was painstakingly slow, but even Victor had to admit he wasn't that bad at it. The clumsiness of his feet in the snow of Lukos didn't transfer to his hands as he swept the knife over the wood, and he only cut his finger once, when Sava smiled at him like Victor had just carved a statue out of marble. Sava insisted on bandaging his finger, and then he insisted on feeding Victor lunch, which led to the two of them making an unholy racket in the bed while Speedy glowered at them from his place by the fire.

Victor was just slipping under—brought there by his hands tied to the ropes suspending the bed while Sava fucked him so hard he thought he was going to have to be carried everywhere for a *week*—when a knock at the door made Speedy yowl and Sava force himself to slow, breathing hard over Victor's back.

"No," Victor whispered into the blanket.

"I'll see what they want, or else they may come in anyway to make sure everything is all right," Sava said, drawing back and pulling a fur over Victor's nakedness. "Do you want me to untie you?"

"No." Victor watched Sava as he pulled on trousers and drew a coat over his bare chest. "How did they even get to the door?"

"The snow could have melted. It does, this early in winter." Sava opened the door.

"Oh!" It was Ivan's voice. Victor sighed. "I hope I'm not interrupting."

"No, not … anything that can't be resumed again," Sava said, giving Victor a heated look.

Ivan's cheery face appeared, swathed in hats and scarves. "Hello, Snow-Walker, I've come by just as I said I would. Oh, oh wow, hello, Victor."

"Hey," Victor said, waving his fingers. Ivan waved back. He was far enough away that Victor could see the blank look in his eyes.

"I'll be quick," Ivan said. "Just bringing a gift for your mating day." He pushed a bottle of golden liquid through the doorway, and Sava took it. "Drink it when the false spring comes, and think of me. I'll already have a few bottles in me by then."

"Thank you," Sava said. "That is very kind. I would invite you in, but, ah, now is not … the best time."

"He does look very comfortable there. Don't worry about it." Ivan flashed a bright smile. "I'll come again later, before we all have to stay indoors forever. Have fun, Victor."

Victor grimaced, and perhaps he was too close to under to conceal the reaction, because when Sava was done trying to give Ivan some of his own mead and had shut the door, he turned to look at Victor and frowned. "Is something wrong?" he asked. "Do your hands hurt?"

"No, I'm fine." Victor sighed as Sava started untying his wrists anyway. "I was just thinking, I've probably lost Ivan as a friend. If we *were* friends."

"Of course you are. He follows you like a puppy every time he sees you."

"I don't know." Victor sat up, rubbing his wrists. "It's something about his eyes. When he saw we were mated, it was like everything shut off behind them. His smile stopped before it reached them."

"Ivan is unmated," Sava said, stroking Victor's hair. "Perhaps it reminds him of that, and he had to push the sadness back."

Victor struggled to put into words how it felt, standing there with Ivan smiling so blankly at him. "That's not what I mean. I mean it's like … it's like how when David would say he loved me, the look in his eyes …"

"Not everyone is your David. Maybe that's how it is in Gerakia, where they don't depend on each other to survive."

"That's how it is *everywhere!*" Victor flinched at the sound of his own raised voice, but the frustration was too powerful to ignore. Why couldn't Sava *see* it? "People rely on each other, but they betray, too. They lie and they cheat, and maybe some of them are kind and loving, but you can't assume everyone is good."

"I'm not making that assumption." Sava's brow was furrowed, his mouth pressed in a hard line. "I know that we are not all good. But it sounds as though you think we are all in danger of doing the worst. I understand, when parents abandon their children and men their mates, that it can seem that way."

"I know what good people look like," Victor said. "And maybe David is still … it still hurts, but I'm not seeing him everywhere, I swear." He sighed. It was no use. Maybe he *was* overthinking it. He didn't have proof that Ivan was anything but a lonely man who pushed through it to deliver mating gifts and babysit kids in his spare time.

"You're still a new Lukoi," Sava said. "Live with us for a time, and you'll understand us better."

Victor only just resisted the urge to groan into his hands. Was Sava being too trusting, or had Victor gone too far the other way? He rolled off the bed and grabbed a blanket to wrap around himself. "I'm going to check on Speedy." He went to the fire to curl up while Speedy clambered over him, wide-eyed and so trusting, with his helpless cries and awkward stumbling. Victor held him to his chest, and Speedy purred and rumbled in his ear, kneading his little paws back and forth, steady as a heartbeat.

# CHAPTER 9

"Speedy," Sava said, for the fourth time, "*no.*"

The kitten stared at him after his latest failed escape and cried softly. He blinked big yellow eyes at Sava, who had to smile at how he looked simultaneously adorable and threatening. Speedy, who lived up to his name, wanted nothing more than to run across the floor and fling himself through any and all doors—including the one to the cellar where they kept the food and the front door to the porch.

The kitten had provided a great amount of amusement, which was nice and helped defuse the tension from his … discussion … with Victor about Ivan. What did it mean, that thing he'd said about Ivan's smile not reaching his eyes? Smiles were smiles, weren't they?

Speedy meowed again, then tried to climb up Sava's trouser leg. He laughed despite himself and reached down, detaching the kitten and placing him on the floor. "You cannot hunt with me quite yet, little one."

The kitten screamed at him, but Sava managed to slip out the door without Speedy following. It was early, and Victor was still asleep, but Sava didn't expect to be gone too long. He found some of Victor's writing supplies and carefully noted where he was going in clear, concise words, making sure to take time so his writing was legible. But his mate, he was clever. He would be able to read the note.

It was a chilly morning, his breath a spill in the air as he readied himself for a simple hunt. There was a pleasure in hunting when it was cold. He felt the sting of the winter in the air, the true winter that waited in the low-hanging clouds, a storm gathering, but this was lovely, quiet: the part of winter he liked best. Though perhaps it would be different this winter, with a mate at home waiting to warm him when he returned.

Sava was thinking of Victor, how lovely his skin looked in the light of the fire, when he noticed the trap.

It was haphazardly set in the way children placed them when they were first learning how to trap, but at least it had been hidden well, only the top edge visible, and *that* only because the wind had blown off the snow and leaves. Sava frowned and picked it up—it was far too close to the house to be anything but a danger, which likely meant one of the kids had been practicing and then forgot it was there. He slung it over his shoulder, glancing around, but there was no sound of anyone nearby. He'd have to figure out who it belonged to, have a word with them.

Hunting had always been one of Sava's favourite activities. He liked the quiet of early morning, the routine that was so familiar to him by now he could probably do this half-asleep or under the influence of Ivan's ale. Thinking about the ale, he smiled as he imagined a tipsy Victor in front of the fire. It was quite distracting, being mated. Now he understood why most Lukoi took mates shortly before the winter, as it would be far too difficult to prepare for the winter when all you wanted to do was celebrate and strengthen your mate bond. Sava's mate was so pretty and clever, even if he sometimes behaved oddly and had an active imagination. Maybe that was how it went, with people who were good with books and learning as Victor was.

Sava put Victor's strange words about Ivan out of his mind and concentrated on hunting. Speedy was young enough that milk would be fine for a bit, but they would be confined by the time the kitten became a cat and wanted meat. Better to find something for him now, dry it, and keep it stored, than wake up to find a snow cat eating their reserves.

He settled in his favorite hunting spot, a copse of trees near a hill a little ways up from the hot spring. He saw a few deer but let the does pass by—the meat wasn't worth one less breeding doe in the spring. Sava watched them scamper off, then took down the buck that followed after. He also found a porcupine, which would provide a good amount of fat, and Victor could use the quills for his drawing or writing.

There were precious few other animals about, this close to winter, but Sava headed home with the buck and the porcupine, as well as two snowbirds that would provide the kitten with some sustenance if nothing else. He was halfway back to the house when he saw bear tracks, and he shifted the weight of the buck on his shoulder and wondered whether he should go after it or let it be. Bears who weren't yet hibernating this close to the first major snowfall usually wouldn't make it through the winter, and Sava didn't feel too bad at the thought of taking one for its fur. Victor could use another blanket. And Sava thought his mate would be proud, having a warm bearskin coverlet of his own.

Sava found one of his trapping rigs, a net strung up between two trees to keep other predators from stealing his kills. He put the deer, the porcupine, and the birds up and out of the way, then started to follow the bear tracks. It took a long time, as he had to move quietly and study his surroundings, and he realized he was heading back toward the caves where their history was etched.

"Ah, someone else needs a new blanket," a quiet voice said, startling Sava so badly he nearly dropped his bow. "Not fair, Snow-Walker. Leave the furs for those of us without a pretty man to warm us."

Sava breathed out slow and easy through his nose, his heart racing. Dragan had *snuck up* on him. No one had snuck up on Sava since he was twelve. He couldn't glare at his kuvar … could he?

Dragan laughed. "Boy, they don't call me *Wolf-Breaker* for nothing. I am the kuvar. We are as silent, and as deadly, as the snow."

Sava stared at him. "Did you practice that?"

Dragan grinned. He was a handsome man, with his dark hair braided back and his pale, wolf-blue eyes, and when Sava was younger, he'd had an embarrassing crush on him—but who could blame him? The kuvar was everything a Lukoi dominant should be: competent, strong, a good protector, and a fierce hunter. It didn't matter that he was older, though Sava wasn't sure exactly *how* old he was—it was said that the kuvar would live long enough for a successor to pass the Trials, and whatever his age, Dragan was hale and hearty. He'd been the kuvar since Sava was born, though Sava seemed to recall he'd been new to it when Sava was first allowed to sit with his parents at the fires.

"My mate is not from here. He needs to be warm." Sava nodded at Dragan. "But I will concede the hunt to my kuvar, if you wish."

Dragan snorted and waved a hand in the air. "I am not fit to be kuvar, Snow-Walker, if I need such concessions. No, we will hunt together, and you will keep the gifts this bear will give. We have plenty."

Sava nodded. He didn't ask why Dragan was out hunting if he wasn't planning to kill anything; this close to winter, it was common to see Lukoi enjoying the last few weeks outdoors, even if the weather wasn't quite hospitable.

"Elena is going to be on her own soon," Dragan said as they made their way deeper into the forest. "Maybe not next winter, but the one after, I would guess. She is drawing plans for a house already." His voice was low, so as not to startle the wildlife, but full of fatherly pride. "She might come ask you for some thoughts, eh, since yours is the nicest. The palace of Lukos." He chuckled.

Sava smiled, but not without some tightness. "Maybe she should ask someone else. I think perhaps mine is too much."

Dragan clicked. "Nonsense. Your house is meant for your mate, and your pretty Victor needs comfort as he learns to be Lukoi. You built your house for him."

"I built it for Milan," Sava said quietly. He was tired, he realized, which was strange—he hadn't been hunting that long, and the weather was still holding. "But I waited too long to mate him, so he died."

"Ach, Snow-Walker, that is not the truth." Dragan narrowed his pale eyes at him. "Milan was not meant for you, or he would be yours."

"He was not meant for the fox-maiden, either."

Dragan sighed. "Ours is not an easy life, Sava. I know you grieve Milan. But that he listened to her, followed her … it is not your fault. Your house was built to give safety, and that is all there is to say about it. It was not your doing that Milan listened to the wrong promises in the dark."

Sava smiled grimly. "It was my fault that my voice was not there for him to hear."

Dragan put a hand on his shoulder. "He was a good man. But the way of our people is to look ahead, not behind. You are mated now, with a good man who is much an exile as we all were, once. I would not have *you* listening to her, if she comes calling, do you hear?"

"Yes," Sava said, as Dragan's dominance fell heavy over him like a cloak. "I understand. I know you are right."

"Yes, I am. That is why I am the kuvar. And I would have you and your mate at the fires in the spring, celebrating that once again, we thrive when we were meant to die."

Sava nodded, and that was that. They followed the tracks and droppings to a small cave near the one where the Lukoi drew their story on the stones, but it was empty of anything save some old bones from the bear's last meal. The droppings were fresh enough to suggest it would return, though, so they hunkered down in a tree nearby to wait, bows at the ready.

"Now that your daughter is planning a home of her own, will you take a mate, again?" Sava asked Dragan, giving him a sly smile. "My mate says Ivan would not mind spending the winter on his back for you."

"Ha, he is too young for me. And always trying to get me to drink his potions and tinctures. One, he swore, was like the wildflower liquor from the hot desert where the bear-soldiers live. It tasted like dirt." Dragan paused. "Maybe that is how the wildflower liquor tastes. But it is supposed to get you drunk. Ivan's just gave me a headache. A hangover without the fun part, eh?"

Sava shook his head. "He brought something for us. A mating gift. Victor—" He stopped himself before telling Dragan about Victor's odd reaction to Ivan. Between that and Milan's death, what if Dragan decided Sava was the problem? He had to prove himself a proper Lukoi, a worthy mate for his clever owl. "Victor put it away. I think he worries he will have to cook if I am too drunk to do it."

If Dragan noticed the hesitation, he didn't mention it. "Ah, not a cook, your scholar? Well, he is clever. He can learn."

"Yes," Sava agreed, and now his voice rang with pride. "He is. And I will have time to teach him."

"Yes. Plenty of it, but for now ..." Dragan's voice went quiet, and he nodded, picking up his bow. "The bear is small, but your Victor is not so large that he will need a giant one. If there's another, maybe I will make a bed for Elena's pups."

There were two bears: the first, whose fur was a bit scraggly and who appeared underweight, and a juvenile, born only that spring, stumbling about after it. In a few weeks, all the bears would be tucked away—the first sign to a hunter that real winter had arrived, not just an early snowstorm that mimicked it.

He glanced over, startled to see Dragan was watching *him*, not the bears. In a few moments the animals would move on, and the hunters' chance would be lost. Daylight was short now, and soon it would barely be light enough to hunt at all. Sava remembered Speedy, crying in the snow, and told himself firmly that bears were different. The adult wouldn't last the winter; it wasn't bulky enough, and without reserves the young one would starve. You did not survive in Lukos if you forgot how nature was both nurturer and murderer, her whims capricious and the only law *the strong survive; the weak do not.*

Sava readied his bow, aimed, and took down the larger bear with two quick shots. The smaller one took off running, and Dragan vanished without making a sound. He was serious, perhaps, about making a bed for the wolf pups.

Sava heard something deeper in the woods, like a howl, and thought of the myth that the kuvar was part wolf—but it was likely just his imagination. Sava turned his attention to the bear dead on the snow, thinking how best to get it back to the house for processing before dark. He would have to drag it, then collect his other prey from where he'd left it, and take everything to the shed—

Sava yawned, which was odd, as there was much to be done and he had spent years processing animals from distances that were farther away from home than this. But he was newly mated, and perhaps this was just the way it went. He had a reason to be tired, and perhaps—when Victor saw the results of his successful hunt—he would have more reasons, later. Sava might have lost Milan, but the kuvar was right. Victor was his mate now, and Sava needed to think of the winter that was coming fast, not the spring that was already behind them.

The bear was sickly, though, and it took only a quick glance to see that its meat was spoiled, spotted with a disease that meant it would make any person who ate it sick. The organs, too, were speckled … but that was all right. He would take the skin. That, at least, was usable enough to make a blanket for Victor. He left the meat for whatever scavenger could eat it safely.

Victor was all smiles when Sava returned, finally, tired and aching as he carried the bear skin, along with the buck and the porcupine, to the shed. Victor bundled up in his new boots and warm coat and traipsed into the small building to see—and he only went a little white-faced at the sight of the animals skinned and hanging from the ceiling.

"Did you—is that a *bear* skin?"

"Yes," Sava said, pleased at the awe in Victor's voice. "The meat, though, it was not good. The liver had spots. It means it has some disease. But the skin will dry and make you a nice blanket."

"You killed a *bear* for me," Victor said, sounding dazed. "A huge, scary bear—"

"This one was smaller and diseased," Sava pointed out, then added quickly, "But it is only because it is late in the season. I will kill a bigger, healthier bear for you, mate."

"Wow." Victor laughed wildly. "And David wouldn't even hold my hand in public."

"I would hold your hand, but mine are, ah." Sava held them up. He'd washed them off as best he could in the snow after dressing the other animals, but they needed a proper scrub before he would touch his mate with them.

"Yeah, that's fine, you can hold it later." Victor reached out to touch the fur Sava had stretched on the rack. "Where's the rest of it, if it's … diseased?"

"I put it out beyond the hill, near the caves and the hot spring," Sava said. "Something will eat it. Carrion creatures."

"And they won't get sick?"

"No, not the things that feast on the dead. Disease takes more animals than people do, here."

"I guess jackals and buzzards need to eat, too," Victor

murmured. "Still, I hope the bear didn't have a little family waiting for it. I'd feel guilty. And I'm not sure Speedy would get along with a baby bear. I think he's meant to be an only child."

Sava decided not to tell him about the younger bear, the one Dragan took down. Victor seemed a bit sensitive about animals. He would outgrow it in time, probably. It was hard to think of a baby bear as a pet like Speedy. Perhaps Sava should be grateful it had not been a bear left in a hole, that day.

"When you come in, I'll help you get nice and clean, you big, fierce hunter, you," Victor teased, and Sava smiled at him, glad that Victor's earlier moodiness seemed to be gone. "And maybe you'll forgive Speedy for what he did to your other pair of boots."

"I could still make him into socks." Sava laughed when Victor hissed in faux outrage and punched him on the arm.

"I've seen your feet, and no, you couldn't. Unless they were for me, and I refuse to wear socks made out of my cat." Victor ran his fingers over the bear skin again. "Sometimes I can't believe that you just … make all of this. Survive here. Off nothing but what you can take from the land. Maybe I shouldn't have insisted about Speedy. I'm sorry that I got attached. Is that going to be a problem?"

"Wait until he chews up *your* boots. Then you will know," Sava teased, gently.

"Oh, he didn't chew them, he— Anyway," Victor said brightly, "I'm teasing. I love him. Thank you for not making him into socks."

"The winter is not over yet, mate." Sava laughed. In truth, it hadn't even started yet. "I will finish up here, and if you want your big, fierce hunter to ravish you, heat the water for his bath so he can do it with hands that are not stained and slick with blood."

Victor blinked, then shook his head and said something in his language. His expression made Sava think it was a compliment.

Sava just stood there, and Victor smiled again and rubbed his face on Sava's shoulder. "Water, bath, ravishing, got it."

Except there wasn't any ravishing that night. After he was finished bathing, they ate before the fire and watched Speedy dart around the house, meowing at them and pouncing on pillows and Sava's socked feet, each of which was twice his size. Sava fell asleep with Speedy curled on his chest, paws twitching as he dreamed of mice or birds or whatever things snow cats dreamed about when they were warm and safe and full of goat's milk fed to them by a sweetly concerned Gerakian.

Sava only meant to nap, but though he was vaguely aware of Victor's attempts to rouse him, he did not wake until morning … when the fire had dwindled and the house was cold and dark, the wind mournful through the flue. Both Victor and Speedy were on top of him, wrapped in furs to stay warm. Sava heard what was likely sleet on the windows and the roof, and he yawned, wondering what had woken him and whether he should disentangle himself and stoke the fire or maybe close his eyes and go back to sleep—

Someone banged on the door, and he heard Zora Star-Finder, Milan's mother, shouting, "Snow-Walker, open that door so my man can speak to you!"

VICTOR WAS NOT PREPARED for guests. Neither, it seemed, was Sava, who stared, dazed and quiet, at a bear of a man looming in the doorway. The man was both stout and broad, with a round face and scars running up his hands and arms that were exposed by his rolled-up sleeves. He seemed impervious to the cold, and when he slapped Sava on the shoulder, Sava actually wobbled.

"I'm Pavel Storm-Chaser," the man said to Victor, in a voice that sounded like rocks grinding together. Speedy immediately went racing to hide under the furs in the bed. "I was this close to being this one's hearth-father. So I thought, here now, little Snow-Walker has a mate and I've not seen him once."

*Little Snow-Walker?* Victor glanced at Sava, then at Pavel. Sava could be little only in a world of giants. Zora, meanwhile, looked uneasy, her arms locked together. Neither she nor Sava would look at each other.

"I'm Victor," Victor said, holding out a hand. Pavel stared at it, then took it, squeezing his fingers. Victor tried not to wince.

"Calluses. Good. My Zora says you're an artist and a writer, so I brought you a mating gift."

"You didn't have to," Sava said. Pavel barreled past him. It was as though Pavel were living in a world where Zora and Sava weren't trying to skirt around each other, where everyone was on good terms and no one needed their eardrums. His voice boomed in the quiet house.

"Here. Paints. I made them myself. Well, I followed Zora's recipe."

They weren't paints so much as they were oil-based dyes, when Victor got a closer look at them, but it was a touching gift from a man whose son would have been Sava's mate. No one could have blamed Pavel if he'd ignored Victor entirely, but he seemed to be on a different emotional ladder than everyone else, cheerfully pulling himself along while the people around him fumbled and missed rungs.

"Thank you," Victor said, but Hurricane Pavel had already swept past him, taking Sava by the arm.

"Now, show me your cellar, Snow-Walker. I want to see how you shore up your foundations."

Victor stood there for a breath, holding the paints in both hands, while Pavel disappeared with his mate.

"He's like that," Zora said. Her voice was soft, but Victor still jumped when he heard it. "My man thinks he should befriend the world. Milan thought the same. Or I thought he did."

Victor set the paints down while Pavel shouted in Sava's ear about lumber and *burrowing wolves,* which was not a phrase Victor ever wanted to learn in any language. "I know it must be hard. Sava still grieves Milan, too."

"I don't know how well those paints will work." Victor recognized Zora's tight, forced tone as grief welling too close to the surface. "I used to be a hand at them, when I was … before."

"Zora …" Victor took a breath. "Star-Finder? Have you … talked to anyone?"

Zora looked up at him. There were tears in her eyes for a moment, but she dashed them aside with her fingertips. "Ah. You've lost someone, have you?"

"Not me personally."

"Your parents, though. You said, when I found you. You didn't belong to anyone."

"Oh. Yes. It's complicated." Victor tried to explain the concept of an orphanage, and Zora stared at him in bewilderment, just as Sava had.

"If a child has no one, an adult will claim them as their hearth-child," she said. "Or an adult may become part of a loved one's hearth-family. Snow-Walker … he would have been ours, if he and Milan …" She shook her head. "This dye, here, you'll need to warm it. It will go hard in the cold."

Victor had a feeling that was as much as Zora could handle, for the time. He let her talk to him about paints—which she seemed to know a great deal about—until Pavel came back up with a hazy-eyed Sava, talking loudly about the state of the cellar.

"You have a good mate, Victor," Pavel boomed, while Sava and Zora went right back to avoiding each other in uncomfortable silence. "Enjoy your paints. Perhaps you will show us your paintings one day, eh?"

"Um. Yes," Victor said, as he reeled under one of Pavel's heavy shoulder claps.

"Good. That is good. And Snow-Walker, he will feed you more. Get you through the winter."

Victor turned helplessly to Sava, but Sava seemed about as lost as he was. Zora looked, for a moment, as though she wanted to say something to Sava, but then she turned aside and let Pavel wave her through the door.

Sava sneezed.

"What just happened?" Victor asked.

"Pavel Storm-Chaser did," Sava said. He sounded strange, muted. He sniffed and rubbed at his eyes. "He's named that because he went after a bear in the middle of a storm, got lost, and Zora Star-Finder had to see him through the winter. It's how they were mated."

"He seems nice."

Sava shrugged. "He likes people. Doesn't matter who they are or what they've done."

"You haven't done anything wrong," Victor said.

Sava didn't respond. He just ducked down to extricate Speedy from his hiding place. Speedy emerged wildly searching for the strangers who'd invaded his house, but Sava held him close, petting him until he settled into his arms with a contented purr.

# CHAPTER 10

Sava couldn't stop coughing the next morning. He tried to hide it, but Victor had grown up in a house full of kids who all caught summer colds at the exact same time, and he knew what a miserable, hacking, mind-numbing flu sounded like.

"You're sick," he said, while Sava tried to sniffle his way through stoking the fire for a bath. "You should sit down."

"I feel fine," Sava said, but his face was pink and he seemed to be having trouble catching his breath. Victor walked over to press the back of his hand to Sava's forehead.

"Liar." He smiled at Sava. "Sit down. I can make a fire."

"But ..." Sava's face contorted as he tried to hold back a cough. "I need to ..."

"Uh-huh." Victor laid a hand on Sava's chest and gently walked him backward. "I saw this at the university all the time. Professors say they don't accept late papers, so freshmen end up coughing themselves to class and snotting up the library."

"*Snotting up?*" Sava asked, sounding bewildered. "Did you just make up a word?"

"You don't want to know what it means," Victor said. He

urged Sava down to the sunken pit by the fire and grabbed a blanket off the bed. "You need to rest. Trust me. Haven't you ever been sick before?"

Sava blinked slowly, like he wasn't quite sure how he ended up sitting down with a blanket over his knees. Speedy climbed onto him, kneading his leg with sharp claws. "When I was a boy."

And Sava's mom had been around for that, Victor thought, remembering how Aunt Grace had always deployed the older kids to look after the younger ones during flu season. "You can keep Speedy company."

"I'm well enough to cook." Oh gods, Sava actually sounded *sullen*.

He wasn't well, of course. He tried twice to get up while Victor dug through their food supply and pulled out a pot for the fire, but after only a few minutes of trying to get ready to go outside to check on the animal skins in the shed, he collapsed in another miserable coughing fit. He ended up lying in bed with Speedy grooming his hair, and he looked so big and pitiful that Victor had to stop himself from laughing.

"You'll be fine," he said, filling the kettle. The Lukoi didn't have the kind of tea leaves they had in Gerakia, but Sava had bark for headaches, which Victor had used too many times to count during long nights at the Two Sisters. "Just stop *moving*."

"But I'm the dominant," Sava said, cocooned in blankets while a kitten rolled in his hair.

"No idea what *that's* supposed to mean," Victor said to himself. "Don't worry. You're about to have a real, authentic Gerakian soup, except with Lukoi noodles and no oregano."

"I don't know half of what you just said," Sava mumbled, and oh yes, he definitely *was* being sullen. Victor smiled and walked over to kiss his hot forehead.

"It's all right," he said. "I know how to handle big babies."

Sava gave him another bewildered look, and Victor grinned to himself as he turned back to the fire.

It had been a while since Victor had made Aunt Grace's tried and tested noodle bowl for anyone other than himself, but even with his limited supplies, he managed to make something that tasted close to the real thing. It was easy to fall into the old routine of warming cloths and making tea, and for a moment, the little house smelled almost like the kitchen in the Golden Street Orphanage. If he closed his eyes, he could see the bookcase of folktales from around Iperios, the wicker chair everyone hated that couldn't hold anyone bigger than a toddler without collapsing, the copper pots, and Aunt Grace's collection of dusty teacups. He opened his eyes again and looked up at the chimney Sava had made himself, the wooden chairs brought in from the porch, the bucket where Victor kept his scrap wood for carving.

"I don't think I ever told you about my people," he said.

"Gerakia," Sava said softly, rolling to the side while Speedy gnawed on his hair. "You told me some."

"Not all of Gerakia, though. Gerakia's full of different kinds of people, now." Victor poured a mug of tea and handed it to Sava, who eased himself into a sitting position to take it. "But it used to just be people like me."

Sava squinted at him, and Victor waved a hand in front of his own face.

"You know," he said. He wasn't sure how to translate the idea of a homogeneous nation. "Everyone … looked the same, and we were the first to live in Gerakia. There's a word for it, but I don't know if you have it here. But some call us the First Scholars. A long time ago, back when Lukos was empty, an empire tried to take over."

"Maybe ours," Sava said. His eyes were bright, though that might have been the fever, not Victor's meandering storytelling. "The king who exiled us? I can see him doing that."

"That's a theory." Victor flashed a grin. "You'd do well in university, Sava. That's how academic debate works, really. You guess until someone finds a piece of evidence that proves everyone wrong. But this king who tried to take over Gerakia, he was brutal. His methods were like a hammer, beating people down. And one of the Gerakians woke up one morning, hungry and tired, and heard a voice at his window saying, 'Come see.' So he climbed out the window and found a parrot on a tree branch outside. Parrots are birds that can talk like people, sometimes."

"Like a spirit in a fairy tale," Sava said.

"Eh. Close. But they can remember words and repeat them. Anyway, this parrot flew from branch to branch, and the man followed, until he saw the parrot land on the ground and start scratching marks into it, like a language. And the man memorized the marks and came back with our first alphabet. A secret one, which the man brought to his village and used to pass coded messages to other Gerakians. He said that we could defeat the king through cunning, because he wasn't really a very clever king."

"Sounds like ours," Sava said, and they smiled at each other.

"Yeah. They did defeat him, in the end, and when Gerakia was free, they made the first schools. That's why when you go to school in Gerakia, by the front door you see statues of scholars with a broken crown in one hand and a scroll in the other."

"And these scholars are your people?"

"That's what they tell me." Victor tapped his nose. "Same kind of eyes, same skin, same hair. When I went to university, they said I was *off chasing birds*. That's what they say when you're a Gerakian who becomes a scholar."

Sava looked up at Victor, and his brow furrowed. "You miss it, then. Gerakia."

Victor moved to check on the soup. "I don't know. You could say this is the most Gerakian thing I've ever done. Chasing birds all the way to Lukos."

Victor turned back to find Sava sitting with the mug in both hands, looking so dejected that Victor just stood there, staring at him.

"All my birds have flown," Sava said quietly.

"Oh. Oh, Sava." Victor stepped into the pit before the fire and took the mug from his hands. Speedy ran over to inspect it. "I'm sorry. I'm here, though."

"I wasn't enough for Milan." There were tears in Sava's eyes, and while Victor was sure some of that was the fever, Sava must have felt woeful to say it out loud. "Not enough to keep him here. And I'm not enough for you."

"What?" Victor took Sava's warm face in his hands. "That's what I think about myself half the time. I mean, look at you."

"I spend all my time building a house," Sava said, "and not enough time with the people who live there."

"Oh my gods." Victor kissed Sava's forehead and settled down in his lap, but Sava just sat there, gaze averted. "It wasn't your fault, what happened to Milan."

"It was. If I'd mated him earlier …"

"There are studies that focus on people who leave us the way Milan did," Victor said. He brushed Sava's hair off his forehead. "The thing that led him to do it, it was probably always there. He had his parents and the rest of the community here, and surely he knew you cared for him. If this was his path, there was nothing you could have done to stop him."

"Then there's nothing I can do to stop you, either," Sava whispered. "If the fox-maiden takes you, or if your people come for you."

Victor sighed. "I'm not chasing fox-maidens. But how about this, okay? We check on each other during the winter. When we're feeling low, like you are right now, we tell each other. We talk it out. Mates in Gerakia do that—or they're supposed to. Even if it's awful or embarrassing, we tell each other."

Sava gave him a desperate, feverish look. "Zora blames me for it. I know she does."

"She's grieving, and that can make people … difficult," Victor said. "It happened with kids at the orphanage. There were two sisters who *hated* each other because they blamed each other for their mother's death—but their mother died of a sickness, not because of them."

"Zora and Pavel had to …" Sava took a shuddering breath. "Had to drag him out of the sea. Pavel is scarred from the burns the ice made on his hands. No one should have to see their child like that."

"I know." Victor held Sava as he shook and tried not to cry. Sava wrapped his arms around Victor, and Victor wondered whether he'd ever really wept for Milan. If anyone had let him. "It's all right," he said. "You can let it out."

"He died alone." Sava sounded wretched, and Victor pressed Sava's head to his shoulder, watching their shadows flicker over the wall.

"I know. I'm sorry."

He held Sava while the fire crackled and the wind howled outside, thinking of how alone Sava must have felt, without a mother or his mate, in a house he'd built for two.

"I don't want you to leave," Sava said into Victor's shoulder.

Victor drew back and kissed him. It didn't matter that Sava was sick—Victor was bound to catch it anyway. "I won't leave."

"But they'll come for you. You're too precious for them to leave here."

"And maybe they'll fall in love with Lukos, too," Victor said. He thought about it: the high mountains, the thick evergreens, the rocky hills covered in snow. "The way the snow spirals in the air. The wind that sounds like a mournful howl. The thunder-snow, the cave, the way everyone here cares for each other. You." He eased Sava back onto the pillows. "But I'd stay even if I didn't love Lukos," he said, and knew, in that moment, that it was true. "Because you're here."

Sava reached for him, and Victor kissed him again, brushing the hot tears from Sava's cheeks.

"Birds have to find a place to roost sometime," Victor said. "Even odd owls like me."

Sava couldn't recall the last time he'd been sick with a fever like this. He'd had a summer cold or two, and once, when he was a child, he'd come down with a lung sickness in the worst of winter and had to sit with his head over a bucket of hot water, covered in a blanket to trap the steam. Ivan's mother made tinctures for that sort of thing, but it took a few weeks of Sava being miserable, with a crick in his neck from bending over the pail, before his father could make the trek to the other house to procure some.

"That boy, that Ivan? He told me to tell you to feel better soon," his father had reported, as Sava swallowed the bitter-tasting medicine with a precious spoonful of honey, a rare treat that was ruined by the herbal tincture. "I think he's sweet on you."

"They're six," his mother had said with a laugh, kissing his father. "I wouldn't mind him for a son-in-law, when the time comes. At least, if he gets his mother's mead recipe."

A few years later his father ran afoul of a bear while hunting in the summer. His mother was the dominant and was just as fierce a hunter; they'd thrown dice over who would go out that day, and Sava remembered his father's victory yell as he'd laughed and grabbed his bow.

When Dragan and Pavel had brought him home, Sergei had sworn he was fine, that they were being silly, that it was only a little scratch. But the wound from the bear's swipe became infected and sent him into a mumbling, feverish delirium. At the end, Ivan's mother had come round to their house with a different kind of herb. At almost ten, Sava understood that it was to ease his father into death without pain. He could still remember the strange scent, the way it made his father's last few breaths smell like moss. His mother had kept the little bottle, high up on a shelf, until three winters had passed.

He'd always wondered why his mother kept the poison bottle. Now, he figured it had been a way out in case the grief took her—one she could see and reject, a temptation to overcome.

Or maybe she'd just worried they'd need it again. His mother had been practical to a fault.

Either way, Sava had not been feverish for so long he'd forgotten what it was like to sweat and shiver at the same time, tossing the furs off one moment and wrapping himself up in them the next. For a few days, he huddled in the sunken pit and burrowed beneath every fur in the house, then lay in a bath with cooler water and sprawled out naked atop the suspended bed when the heat took him. Eventually he sweated through the worst of it and emerged dry-mouthed and stinking, exhausted from not sleeping well but pleased not to be shivering or sweating every second.

He made his way into the main room, where Victor stood at the fire, stirring something in the pot. He was talking to Speedy, who sat on the hearth, watching him with the eager stillness of a spoiled creature waiting for a treat. Sava had seen this before, with Elena's wolf pups.

"You can have a bite in a minute, Speedy," Victor said, and Sava frowned when he heard what could only be a hint of the same illness in Victor's voice. "You're smaller and not feverish."

Speedy meowed, then went up on his back paws, putting his front paws on Victor's leg and crying sadly.

"And you drink milk." Victor started to sing a song in his language that Sava couldn't translate, but it made him smile all the same.

"If he sings back, I will be worried and think my fever returned." Sava laughed as Victor startled and turned to him, looking as if he'd been caught stealing food from a cellar instead of talking to their cat.

Speedy tried to scamper over, but first he had to get his claw unstuck from Victor's pant leg, which made both men laugh, and then he fell over his own paws on a pillow and started grooming himself as if that had been his plan all along.

"You're feeling better?" Victor's face was flushed, his eyes bright behind the glasses he wore.

"Yes," Sava said. He touched Victor on the nose. "The fever is gone, I think, but I must bathe. What is this look you are giving me, eh, little owl?"

"You're so attractive," Victor said and then sneezed twice. "And you're naked."

"Yes. I will need to wash my clothes, the bedding—they stink of sweat." Sava plucked Victor's glasses off and reached for a towel on the hook near the pot. He cleaned them and placed them back on Victor's face. "There."

Victor blinked at him, then sneezed again. "Oops."

"Ah. This must be a catching sickness. You know this term? You will have a turn with it, before it leaves us." Sava narrowed his eyes. "Already you are shaking your head at me. A few days with a fever, and my submissive mate becomes the dominant, is that so?"

"I just— I'm fine," Victor assured him. He gave Sava a winning smile. "I'm only sneezing because I'm allergic to going this long without seeing you naked."

Sava crossed his arms over his chest. "That is not true, my mate. Now you are lying to me? What home have I woken up in, hmm?" He reached down and scooped up Speedy, who was going to pounce at something he shouldn't if Sava wasn't careful. He held the wriggling kitten toward Victor. "I will take a bath and clean the bedding. You have done much. You should rest."

"You went out hunting and killed a bear when you were sick. And I'm not sick, anyway," Victor added quickly, when Sava raised his eyebrows. He took Speedy from Sava, wincing only a little when Speedy clamped his needle-like teeth on one of Victor's fingers. "I'll be fine. You should clean up. I know a nice warm bath always felt great when I was on the other end of a summer flu."

Sava narrowed his eyes thoughtfully, but Victor kept smiling at him, and he really *did* want to take a bath. "All right, mate. If you insist." Sava leaned in to kiss him but thought better of it. He could use a glass of water and some of the tooth bark and the paste with the mint to freshen his breath. He paused, and Speedy tried to paw at his beard, and Victor laughed and kissed his cheek instead.

Sava went to bathe, and he couldn't deny that it felt wonderful to soak away the grime and lingering sickness. Victor had stoked the coals beneath the tub so the water was warm, and scrubbing off the sweat and general malaise was even better for his recovery than one of Ivan's herbal tinctures. By the time he'd combed out his hair and beard with softening oils, dressed in fresh clothes, and cleaned his teeth, he felt almost entirely back to normal.

When he returned to the main room, Speedy meowed at him from his favorite spot in front of the fire, where he was attacking one of the old boots Sava had finally relented and let him have as his own. He looked adorable, fluffy and half-caught in the laces, worrying at the leather with his kitten teeth and swatting at it whenever he moved and pulled it out of position. His paws, too big for his small body, held the boot down on the floor.

Victor, stirring something in the pot over the fire, smiled at Sava—and then sneezed, turning his head just in time to cover his mouth and not get germs all over their dinner.

"My mate," Sava said, when Victor gave him a sunny smile that didn't quite reach his blurry, dark brown eyes, "you have, I think, the same thing I did, yes? Sit, bundle up there before the fire, and let me take care of you."

Victor gave him a familiar mulish look and sighed. "But you *always* do that. Take care of me. I'm not just a problem you need to fix, am I?"

Sava blinked. "What? No. For the last few days, my mate, I think *I* was the problem."

"Yeah, right," Victor muttered, raking a hand through his curls. He gave Sava a sheepish smile and sneezed again. "I'm sorry. I don't like thinking that I'm this useless sack of a person who can't do anything and—" He stopped as Sava, in the name of expediency, simply placed his hand over Victor's mouth.

"You are not a problem. I am your mate. You are mine. It is my honor, Victor, to take care of you." He pulled his hand away and placed it on Victor's forehead. "And you have a fever, I think. Go, sit by the fire. Let me do for you what you've done for me. Yes? Was I a problem, when you had to take care of me?"

"No," Victor admitted. "But you do everything, Sava. All the time. I just want to—" He stopped and sneezed again, then gave a miserable sniffle and finished with, "Maybe it wouldn't be a bad idea. To, uh. Rest for a minute."

Victor settled in front of the fire, playing idly with Speedy, who thought it was great fun to leap on his feet when they moved beneath the blanket. Eventually he grew bored and curled up on Victor's chest, purring as he fell asleep.

"I didn't know they could purr," Victor said, yawning, as Sava padded over with a bowl of stewed meat and vegetables, bread, and a mug of cold water. "Wild cats like this, I mean."

"I would not have thought they could," Sava admitted. He smiled, drawing his fingers through Victor's hair. "You know more things than I do."

"About snow cats? I promise you that's not true," Victor said. "I didn't even know you had them here, until we found this one."

"No, not that, just … things of that nature. Science, facts," Sava said, feeling foolish. "You are a scholar."

"And you can build a house with your bare hands." Victor

yawned, leaning into his hand. "We're lucky I managed to keep the fire going, much less start one."

"Eat your supper," Sava ordered, threading his dominance gently into his voice, and smiled as Victor complied and lifted the carved wooden spoon to his mouth. Satisfied, Sava went to get himself some food. He ate two bowls of stew and three pieces of bread, hungry after his fever and so thirsty he finished three mugs of water. Victor didn't eat nearly as much, but enough that Sava felt a bit better when he carried their things to the kitchen to wash them.

"Just going to read over what I've written for a bit," Victor said, sounding sleepy, and Sava smiled.

By the time he was finished with the dishes, Victor was asleep and Speedy had risen to clean himself. He blinked his big yellow eyes at Sava, who settled down in front of the fire, and Sava's eyes caught on the book still resting on Victor's hand. He reached out for it, and Victor mumbled in his sleep and turned to burrow into the blankets, easily letting go of it.

The book was written half in Victor's native tongue and half in their shared language. It was nonsensical to Sava—or the parts in Victor's language were, anyway—and he thought again how clever his mate was, to know *two* languages and write in them both. He flipped through the book, glancing over at Victor now and again as he did so, feeling almost guilty, as if he were waiting for Victor to wake up and tell him he wasn't supposed to be reading it.

Instead, Victor slept on. Sava wasn't certain, but he thought the book was some kind of primer; there were illustrations of household objects with their names written carefully beneath. Some were misspelled, but in a way that made sense for someone who was learning how to speak before he learned how to write. Sava was tempted to correct them, but no. Best let Victor do that himself. As Sava turned the pages, he was delighted to see how many were given to illustrations. There were many of Speedy, despite the short time they'd had him—and they were wonderful, capturing the way he slept sprawled like a sack of beans, one paw over his eyes.

There were other drawings: of the house, which were remarkable, and of—oh. Sava's eyes widened as he saw the drawings of *himself*. There were more than a few, and in each, Victor had captured one thing as the focal point: Sava with an axe over his shoulder, Sava asleep on the bed, Sava standing up in the bath. The focus in the last one was on his cock, which made Sava grin wickedly and chuckle, even though his face heated at how *lovingly* Victor had rendered it in the pencils.

Next to one of the pictures of him was written his name, and the word *mate*, and then something he couldn't translate. One of the last pages had a drawing of Milan's parents, with a word that Sava didn't know in the corner.

Sava traced the letters of the foreign word with his fingers, wondering idly what it meant and thinking he'd have to ask Victor in the morning. Next to it, on the opposite page, was an owl with its wings spread, flying off into the hills of Lukos.

He thought about that one for a long time, as he carried Victor—along with the blanket Victor wouldn't let go of, and Speedy—to bed. The owl flying ... was that because Victor wanted to leave? Did he remember his school with the warm, sunny days and the clever people who wanted him back and think about returning? He'd been tricked into coming here, to Lukos, and—

"No, you don't have faces," Victor muttered.

Sava turned on his side and looked down at the man next to him. He reached out to touch him, then heard Victor say, "Foxes don't sing," and his blood chilled a bit.

"Victor," Sava said, shaking him slightly. The thought of the fox-maiden trying to sneak into his dreams ...

Victor didn't wake, though. He just mumbled something in his own language, turned, and climbed on top of Sava. Sava wrapped his arms around him, lost in thoughts about how much it would hurt to lose Victor, now that he knew what it was like to have him.

VICTOR SLEPT FITFULLY, shivering in the familiar throes of the flu, but when he did sleep, he dreamed of Gerakia.

He was in class, dutifully writing notes while Professor Riza scrawled charts on the board. Professor Riza's class usually took place outside, in one of the open pavilions that dotted the campus, and a few of the older students had already slipped away to lie in the grass. Victor was one of the only ones still paying attention, and when he glanced up, Professor Riza flashed him a warm smile.

"It's a shame you're so fickle." Victor jumped. David was sprawled on the bench beside him, tapping a pen on an open book. He looked just the same as when Victor last saw him, self-assured and painstakingly tidy, and he laughed when Victor gaped at him. "What? Head empty again, Golden Street?"

"You know I don't like that name," Victor said. Orphans who aged out took the name of their orphanage, but Victor rarely used it.

"If it weren't for the poor, put-upon doms you latch on to, Golden Street, you'd be reinventing yourself every season. What are you now, an artist? A mate?" David snorted. "Lovely. And what will you be when this one tires of you and you come back to Gerakia in disgrace?"

"I know what this is," Victor said. "This is my mind being an asshole."

David laughed again, and Victor glanced down to find he was standing in the ocean off the coast of Lukos, icy water sloshing over his legs. He looked back up to see David lounging on a rowboat just a few paces out, watching him.

"Go fuck yourself," Victor said.

"Come make me," David said. "But be careful, you might trip."

"Trip on what?" Victor strode forward and bumped into something hard. He peered into the gray waters, but it was hard to see through the swirling foam, so he leaned down and thrust his hands into the waves.

His hands hit something, and when he withdrew, he nearly dropped his prize in horror. It was a body, the face blurred and indistinct, skin blue with cold.

Milan. It was Milan. Ivan had said, hadn't he, that he'd seen Milan covered in ice when he was found? But no, he couldn't have, because hadn't Sava told him that Milan's parents dragged him out of the ocean on their own? Victor couldn't remember anymore, not with the chill in his lungs and Milan's body heavy in his arms.

"Look at that," David said, as Victor struggled not to sink into the waves under Milan's weight. "Your next reinvention. What will you be when you shed your feathers this time, little owl?"

Victor opened his mouth to curse and swallowed salt water. The dark closed over him, and through it, Victor could hear David's soft, mocking laughter following him.

He woke with a start to the warm touch of a hand on his chest. Sava was looking at him, a worried crease between his brows, and Victor sucked in a sharp breath only for it to catch on a cough. He turned aside, and Sava rubbed his back as Victor hacked into his elbow.

"You sounded like you were in pain, mate," Sava said. Victor tried to laugh, but it came out choppy and broken.

"Bad dream. I get them when I'm sick. When I was a boy, it was horses." Sava gave him a curious look. "Like deer, but bigger, and people ride them. At home, we call bad dreams nightmares, which is a word that means a … night horse …" He groaned. "I'm so bad at this. As a boy, I thought bad dreams were horses, that's what I mean."

"You have an active mind," Sava said, still looking baffled.

"Aunt Grace used to say the same thing." Victor rolled onto his back, then wheezed as Speedy immediately climbed up his chest. "Didn't dream of horses this time, but it was still unpleasant."

Sava pressed a warm cloth to Victor's forehead. "Well, there aren't any horses here. Just soup, if you can eat it."

The thought of eating made Victor's stomach lurch, but he let Sava help him out of bed so he could try. It didn't take, and he spent a good half hour being ill while Sava mopped sweat from his brow.

"You know," Victor said, flopping on his side in front of the fire and staring up at Sava blearily. "This is the first time I've had someone look after me like this since I was a boy."

"But the woman who took care of you," Sava said. "She didn't leave you alone, did she?"

"She had other kids to take care of. I was older. It's how things were." Victor blinked hard. "I used to wonder what it was like, when I'd visit my friends in town. They always had someone. I was fine with it. I lived with it. But I don't … I don't want to anymore."

"You're not alone here," Sava said. "I'm sorry you had to be alone for so long. It wasn't right."

"Wasn't right for you, either," Victor said, and Sava leaned down to stroke his cheek.

Victor fell into another restless dream, full of pounding horse hooves and the roar of the sea, and woke to Sava again urging him to eat. The third time he tried and ended up spitting up bile, Sava frowned at the fire, his gaze dark.

"I'm going to get you medicine," Sava said at last, and Victor pushed himself up on an elbow.

"I'll be fine," he tried to say, but he couldn't get the words out without coughing. Sava's frown deepened, and he pulled another blanket down from the bed to wrap around Victor, who was shivering again. Speedy burrowed underneath it all to press against Victor's chest, and Victor smiled as he felt the comforting rumble of his purr.

"Sleep for now," Sava said. "I will return soon."

Victor didn't have the energy to protest. He lay there before the fire, petting Speedy while the flames shifted and twisted into new shapes. They took over his dreams, turning into owls made of fire and smoke, flying high over the mountains of Lukos.

He woke alone. Victor sat up to pour himself tea from the pot Sava had left for him and flipped open one of his sketchbooks. He'd left notes in the margins, bits and pieces about the people he'd met, the stories they told around the fire, the common phrases they used. There was a drawing of Zora, sketched from memory, her gaze soft and distant.

Zora was wrong. Victor had never lost anyone. Part of that was not having any family to bury, but even in a large orphanage where illness ran rampant in the summer and kids liked to climb trees out by the lake, none of them had suffered more than the occasional bruise or broken bone. Losing a child, no matter how old they were, had to be terrible. And in a country where everyone contributed to the creation of a house, whether through carved wooden spoons or helping lay the foundation, it was no surprise that the memory of Milan made her grief go hard, had her turning against Sava like a wounded animal.

Victor crawled over to the bag where he kept his charcoal and pulled down the board Sava had set aside for him to carve. He swiped the charcoal over the wood. His first snow dream had been of owls. Owls were transformative—in Gerakia, one shed its feathers to become a girl, and in Lukos, they came in the form of a wide-eyed scholar who fell to the first winter illness.

The first owl he drew was in the top left corner, wings outspread, feathers drifting back like smoke on the wind. He turned two of the feathers into the beak of another owl and built the flock in a chain from there, all of them interconnected, a sky full of feathers. His hands were smudged with the charcoal, and he had to keep stopping to cough and fetch more water, but when he was done, he had a rough outline of what he wanted.

He sat back to look at it and jumped as something thumped near the door. He flipped the wood around—he didn't want Sava to see it yet—and was just trying to wash his hands off with water from the kettle when Sava and Ivan strode in.

"Oh, dear," Ivan said. He had a scarf wound over his mouth and nose, but the way his cheeks rose looked like he was smiling. "You do look bad."

"Thanks," Victor said. He sat back, guarded, as Ivan crouched down to click his tongue at Speedy. Speedy arched up on all fours and bounced away, fur standing on end.

"Oof, rejected again." Ivan chuckled and strode over to Victor, digging into his bag at the same time. "Hey, Victor. See, this is what happens when you don't have any meat on your bones. Where's the fever gonna go? Good thing you called me over, Snow-Walker."

"I'm not that sick," Victor said, and Ivan and Sava gave each other looks that made Victor grimace. "Not enough for a doctor."

"Not a doctor," Ivan said, "so you can't complain. That was my mom. I'm just good with herbs. Snow-Walker, can you get us more hot water?"

Sava nodded and stepped into the other room, and Ivan's bright eyes went blank, just as they had when he'd seen Victor and Sava after their mating ritual. He sat down next to Victor and pulled out a vial of green liquid.

"It'll taste awful, then it won't matter." He unwound his scarf. His smile was strangely tight, like that of a wooden puppet, soulless and fixed. "Go on, then."

"I don't think I will, just yet," Victor said.

"Oh, don't be a baby."

Victor cursed sharply as Ivan grabbed him by the back of the neck. He tried to twist around to look for Sava, but Ivan took the opportunity to tip the bottle into Victor's mouth. Victor coughed and sputtered, spraying half of it back into Ivan's face, and Ivan reared back to scrub at his eyes.

"Victor?" Sava asked.

"It's nothing," Ivan called. "Just can't take his medicine." He looked down at Victor. "Which he should. Every day until he gets better, Snow-Walker. With a mug of hot water."

"Oh, yes."

Victor sat up, grabbing at Ivan's shirt. "What was that for?" His head was swimming—he hadn't realized the fever had taken him so strongly, but it seemed even sitting up for too long was starting to be a problem. Maybe it was the drawing. "You could have just handed it to me."

"I had to make sure," Ivan said. His eyes were hard, like glass marbles. "I had to know you tried it, first."

"You need to …" Victor swayed. He couldn't seem to focus, and his vision was starting to blur. He lifted his glasses, and they fell onto the floor. "Work on your bedside manner."

"I'll remember that," Ivan said. He lowered his voice and leaned in, a hand on Victor's chest. "Just like you should have remembered to keep your promises."

"What?" Victor blinked hard. "I don't … understand."

"It could have been nice," Ivan said. His voice was low, almost too soft to hear over the crackle of the fire. "We could have been friends. But you had to take him."

"Sava?" Victor couldn't seem to form words. They came out slurred and slow, and he fumbled as Ivan gently lay him back down on the furs. "But he … wasn't yours."

"He shouldn't have been yours, either," Ivan whispered, as the world went gray and a distant roar started to build in Victor's ears. "But it doesn't matter. Not anymore."

"Sava," Victor whispered, reaching up as the last speck of light faded and the roaring rose to consume him like the crest of a breaking wave.

# CHAPTER 11

$\mathcal{V}$ictor was getting worse.

Sava sat near the nest of blankets, furs, and pillows that surrounded Victor and gripped the bowl of clear broth in his hand. "Won't you try to eat something?"

The lump under the furs made a groaning sound and shook slightly. Sava, worried and fighting back the surge of panic that *the medicine wasn't working*, put the bowl to the side and sighed. "You should at least have water, yes?" He lifted the cold mug of water, but Victor must have fallen back to sleep there beneath his pile of bedding, because he didn't stir.

Sava gritted his teeth and placed the mug on the hearth next to the bowl. He was sweating; the fire was roaring, and the heat was trapped in all the blankets that were doing nothing to keep Victor warm. He glanced at the small vial of medicine, some of which he'd added to the soup on Ivan's instructions. Maybe he could, when Victor woke, get him to take some drops before bed.

There was a soft, plaintive sound as the kitten hopped up and pawed sadly at Victor, wanting to play. A hand emerged from the blankets, patting absently, and Speedy butted at it, not yet ready to put an end to being petted … which he usually did by biting.

"Come here, little one." Sava picked up Speedy, who whined, then swiped at Sava before climbing on his chest, digging his claws into Sava's shoulder, and falling asleep.

With the sleeping kitten and his sleeping mate, and the sound of sleet against the roof and the glass windows, it should be cozy. Comforting. He had a home, a real one, with a mate … and he was losing him.

Sava was trying so hard not to let the panic take him, but it was almost impossible. All he could think about was having everything he'd wanted and losing it, watching Victor suffer and waste away here in the cold land of Lukos, far from his homeland. He belonged somewhere the snows wouldn't take him. Where he wouldn't hear the tantalizing, doomed call of the fox-maiden leading him to his end.

Sava reached out and grabbed Victor desperately, pulling him close. Speedy gave a howl of outrage and leapt away, but Sava barely noticed. He held Victor to him, face buried in his curly hair, and swore, "I will see you through this winter, my mate, and … I will return you, if you wish, to your land of sun and scholars. My owl, I will not take your feathers if you wish to fly home." He could barely get the words out, his eyes burning with tears.

Lukoi mated for life. But to save Victor, to see him safely to the spring, Sava would be willing to give him up.

"Your light is too bright for the snows to dim it," Sava told Victor, smoothing his hair back from his flushed, sweat-dampened face.

Victor didn't answer, just shivered and moved closer. Sava took a deep, shuddering breath and carried him to the bed. He piled the furs atop Victor's miserable form and climbed in after him, drawing him close. It was too warm for Sava with the fire, the furs, Victor, and then Speedy all draped over him, but he didn't care.

He fell into an uneasy sleep with the kitten stumbling around and attacking the ropes keeping the bed up and Victor tossing and mumbling, either trying to leach off Sava's body heat or escape it. He managed to get another bit of the medicine into Victor by practically forcing it into his mouth, but Victor turned away from the water Sava offered—again—and went back to thrashing in fever.

Ivan had said it might look like this when Victor took the medicine, that it would help him sweat out the sickness. But shouldn't he want water? Wouldn't that help? Sava had to trust that Ivan's medicine would work, but it was hard.

He'd just woken up from a light sleep when he heard Victor say, clearly, "Yes, Maiden, I'll visit. He won't be alone," and his blood turned to ice.

"Victor," Sava demanded, shaking him, his dominance roused despite his best efforts to keep it under control. "Victor, wake up." He should let Victor sleep, to heal, but not if he was dreaming about the fox-maiden. No. He shook him again. "Victor! Little owl."

Victor blinked his wide eyes, and they were hazy, unfocused. He reached a hand up like he was going to touch Sava's face, but it fell to the bed before it made contact. His smile was fleeting, his voice weak. "I'll say hi to him. Tell him how beautiful the house you built for him is. Milan said it was a shame, 'cause we. We could have been friends."

He was dying. Somehow, his simple illness was killing him— his body was so hot, and he had to be dehydrated, and now he was *talking about Milan.*

Sava waited until Victor's words were less nonsensical, until he could at least answer simple questions and focus on Sava instead of whatever feverish dreams had taken up residence in his head. He wiped the sweat off Victor's face, and only after Victor managed a small, sleepy smile did Sava let him drift back to sleep. Then he went into the other room with his heart thrumming hard in his chest and his own breathing as labored as

Victor's. His eyes landed on the medicine vial, and he hurried to retrieve it, barely aware of the sound of sleet on the roof having gotten even louder. He *would* give Victor this medicine, all of it, not the few drops he'd managed so far. And he would *make Victor drink water*, if it took all the dominance in Sava's soul to make him do it, and then Victor would get better. He took the mug, filled it with water, and added the rest of the medicine.

Ivan had said Victor would recover more quickly if he took the medicine over a short amount of time. So that's how it would be. Sava would be a good mate and make him drink this. He set the empty vial on the hearth, but before he could pick up the mug, he heard a soft sound and turned to see Speedy appear out of the blanket nest.

Speedy gave an enthusiastic meow, then leapt at Sava with his little paws outstretched and his ears back. Sava blinked, unused to Speedy doing his best impression of a loosed arrow, and it took his brain a moment to catch up with what he was seeing as Speedy landed on the hearth … and knocked over the mug.

The water, and the rest of the medicine, spilled onto the stones.

Sava, who was not a violent man, bellowed, "*Speedy!*" and the cat simply stared at him, then—to add insult to injury—knocked the vial on the floor next to the now-empty mug. He lifted a paw, licked it, and set to cleaning himself as if he didn't care that he'd —that the medicine—

Sava jumped to his feet and ran to the door with some half-baked idea of going to get more … but the second he opened it, he knew it wouldn't happen. The sleet had picked up, mixed with snow and the wild, swirling wind that made it almost impossible to see or walk.

Sava slammed the door and pressed his forehead to the wood. He could hear his own breathing, his choked sobs, as tears ran hot down skin chilled from even that brief exposure to the outdoors. He thought of what to do. He could try to make it to Ivan's, but if he—if something happened, if he hurt himself, Victor would be left alone, without his medicine. Even if he recovered on his own, he wouldn't survive a Lukos winter by himself. Sava couldn't risk it. The weather was the one thing every Lukoi knew to take seriously. He was a clever hunter, and they did call him *Snow-Walker*, but this was the sort of insidious storm that made walking difficult even for him. A twisted ankle, a broken leg … it would be death for them both.

Victor was sick, but Sava couldn't go out today. In two or three days, perhaps. He could make sure he left plenty of food, fresh water, a roaring fire. The snow on top of the ice would, if it fell fast enough, make it possible for him to traverse the dangerous terrain to Ivan's house. For now, he could still prepare some broth and bread for Victor. And water. Even without the medicine, it had to be better for him to have something in his body.

As he turned to go to the kitchen, he noticed a strange, mossy smell, but that wasn't important. He had to focus on keeping Victor comfortable, safe, *alive*—and giving him someone to listen to that wasn't the fox-maiden.

*Milan said it was a shame, because we could have been friends.*

*I'll tell him the house you built for him is beautiful.*

He'd built the house for his mate. He'd built the house for *Victor*, and he didn't want anyone but Victor living in it with him.

With a bowl of reheated broth in one hand and a fresh cup of water in the other, Sava headed back to the bedroom. Speedy trotted after him, and Sava bit back a snapped admonishment when the kitten meowed and hopped up on the bed. Victor blinked and gave the cat a sleepy smile, and as much as Sava felt angry at Speedy, he knew the situation was really his fault. He should have been better: better rested, steadier hands, stronger constitution. He was the dominant. The only person who had failed here was him.

"Hey," Victor croaked, patting Speedy. "I'm … thirsty?"

Sava could barely speak, still too caught up in the awful certainty of his own failures. He padded over and sat on the bed, wordlessly holding out the new, medicine-free cup.

"Thanks, I— Sava," Victor whispered. He took the water. "Are you— What's wrong?"

"It is nothing," Sava said gruffly, watching as Victor drank. His eyebrows went up. "You *are* thirsty."

"Yeah," Victor said, and maybe it was Sava's desperate hope at work, but he sounded less hazy than when he'd woken up. "Really thirsty."

Sava got him more water, and then *more,* and Victor drank some broth and even half a piece of bread that he soaked in the liquid. Speedy slept on the bed next to him, and Sava reached out to lay a careful hand on Victor's forehead. He was still warm, but nothing like last night or this morning. That was good. Perhaps the medicine in his system would keep him all right until Sava could get more.

Victor fell asleep again, but he wasn't muttering, and the tossing and turning had diminished greatly. He slept so deeply that he was snoring, and Sava felt his panic begin to recede as he watched. Speedy blinked his big yellow eyes at Sava, then put his head on his paws and settled in at Victor's side to take his seventh or eighth nap of the day. Sava smiled, then went to the kitchen to make another pot of stew. He was hungry, and he needed more than the broth he'd been trying to shovel into Victor. He himself was still recovering from his cold.

By the time he finished doing his chores for the day, he was cautiously optimistic that maybe things were going to be all right. Victor, every time he peeked in on him, was sleeping soundly and calmly.

Sava was halfway through cutting up some root vegetables for the stew when he felt a pair of arms wrap around his middle. He jumped, then placed the knife down before turning around in

Victor's arms. "You should watch out, sneaking up on a man with a knife, eh?"

"Probably. Sava, I feel a lot better." Victor looked better, even more so than before he fell asleep. "It's strange, but that nap I just took was the best sleep I feel like I've had in days. Also, I'm thirsty again."

"Good." Sava swept Victor into a relieved hug. "That is how you get better. Drink water, sleep, eat well. And a hot bath. You will have that, and I will finish making this stew, and tonight I will show you some easy ways to cook things, eh? You will write them in your clever book, in case you … need to know them, for some reason."

Victor narrowed his eyes. "That sounds suspicious. Even you aren't a sweet enough man to lie about my attempts to cook being anything other than terrible."

"I have to, tomorrow, or as soon as I can, go and find more of your medicine. Visit Ivan. I could not go today, because we have the—ah, we call it the *invisible ice*. It falls, and you cannot see that it is dangerous, and it can make you slip. Break limbs." Sava pushed Victor's hair off his brow, amazed at how much cooler his skin felt. "It is what happens before the snow comes. And you'll need more— What is this face, little owl?"

Victor was wrinkling his nose. "Honestly, that medicine might have made me feel worse. I think something in it didn't agree with me. But I'm fine, Sava. Or, not yet, but I will be. I just had a fever. I wasn't dying or anything."

But he *was*. Or he had been. That fever, his refusal to drink water … Perhaps Sava had gotten a bit caught up in his head about it, but it had seemed as if Victor was sicker than he should be from a normal cold. How could he have gotten better so quickly?

But Victor was talking and smiling, and while he still needed Sava's help to make it to the bath, his fever stayed gone. He ate well, two bowls of soup, and by the time the sun set and the wind picked up, the sounds of sleet fading as the snow moved in … Sava forgot all about anything but Victor, in his arms, alive and no longer burning up with fever. Speedy was content to lie in front of the fire, looking for all the world as if he were smiling in his sleep.

IN THE MORNING, Victor woke from muddled, hazy dreams of horses, owls, and icy waters to find Sava lacing his boots to go out. The windows were already blocked with snow and reinforced with wooden shutters, and the fire was high, casting an orange glow over the little house. Victor rolled to his side, watching Sava while Speedy purred like thunder in his ear.

"You should stay," Victor said. Sava paused in the act of putting on his coat. "Don't go to Ivan's."

"You need to recover, my mate." Sava walked over to press a hand to his cheek. Victor grabbed his hand, holding him there. "I can get you another medicine, perhaps, if the last one didn't work."

Victor frowned. He couldn't remember much of the worst of his fever—it was all hazy, a jumbled mess of dreams and fear—but something made him shiver at the thought of Sava being alone with Ivan. He could have sworn that Ivan had … said something. He couldn't remember what it was, but he could remember Ivan's eyes, blank and expressionless, and that was enough. "What I need right now is you," Victor said, and Sava sighed, kissed his forehead, and went to take off his boots.

Sava stayed by the fire with Victor, who wrote down old recipes Sava had picked up from his mother, mixed in with frantic notes about farming and agriculture as they inevitably went down a sidetrack about how Sava had the grain to make bread in the first place. That led to Sava awkwardly recounting a folktale about a snow cat with seeds in his fur, and Victor spent so long translating it that he forgot all about the recipe for a meat pie.

"I think this was supposed to be the part about the jelly," he admitted, looking down at three pages of notes. Sava held out a hand, and Victor passed it over.

"Your writing is so small," Sava said. "I have the smartest mate in Lukos, to be able to write this much while he's sick."

"I don't even feel it anymore," Victor said, and sneezed. Speedy jumped from his spot by the fire, and Sava gave a startled laugh.

The snow kept falling. It blanketed the house, making the world go quiet and dark, and Victor took notes while Sava showed him how to check for weakness in the roof and walls. He started carving his owls, spending so long hunched over the wood that Sava would pluck off his glasses to clean them for him, and even managed to make a dinner of fried venison that didn't taste horrible.

"Admit it," Victor said that night, as he lay in the bed with the blankets draped half over him. "I'm better."

"Yes, I noticed." Sava kissed him softly.

"Which means you can stop staring at me like I'm going to turn into smoke," Victor said.

Sava looked down at him. "You don't think I'm not staring because you're beautiful?"

Victor opened his mouth to contradict him, then stopped himself. David was the one who liked Victor to make himself small. "Are you?"

Sava kissed him again. "Yes. Because you are. You'll be prettier still, I think, soon enough."

"Really? Why's tha—" Victor yelped as Sava wrapped him in his arms, kissing him so thoroughly that Victor couldn't even draw breath to speak. He kissed Victor's temples, his forehead, his palm, and he gazed into Victor's eyes and lifted the glasses not to take them away, but to wipe the fog off and give them back.

David had always hated Victor's glasses. He'd thought of imperfections of the body as reflections of imperfections of the soul—but he didn't deserve Victor, anyway. Not the Victor who was Sava's mate—Sava, who kissed him like he was dying for it and called him beautiful.

Sava climbed atop Victor, preparing himself while Victor stared up at him with his arms over his head. When Sava lowered himself onto Victor's cock, Victor almost came just from the tight heat, the sight of Sava's face flushed and his lips slightly parted with pleasure.

"And you call me beautiful," Victor said. Sava flashed a smile and leaned over him, pulling him into a harsh kiss.

He rode Victor until Victor was sobbing to come, thighs tense and toes curling on the sheets. But Sava didn't let him, not until he'd come over Victor's chest and tugged on his curls until Victor was shaking with need. When he came at last, Victor wept with relief into Sava's shoulder and went boneless as Sava carried him to the bath.

"We should do that again," Victor said, while Sava kissed him and ran soap over his body. "Was that your first time? You know. Being … taking a …"

"No, but it was my first time with my mate, and that means more."

"Charmer," Victor said. He leaned back in the water and ran a hand up Sava's chest. "I love you, do you know that? I wanted to when I first met you, I think. I took one look at you and thought, I want that man to be my friend."

"Just your friend?"

"I couldn't imagine deserving more." Victor teased his fingers through Sava's hair. "But I do deserve it, I think. So do you." Sava glanced away, and Victor sat up to kiss him. "You do. Maybe I'll convince you by the time spring comes."

Sava just sighed.

"How long does the snow last?" Victor asked, as he and Sava

warmed themselves before the fire. Speedy, disdainful as always of their actions in bed, stalked over to pointedly ignore them from a distance, and Victor smiled.

"Weeks. At times a month or more. Then there will be a few weeks of only wind, before more ice, more snow, and then what we call the false spring, because it seems as if winter is over and then the sleet comes again. We will see the others during that respite, make sure everyone weathered the long snowfall safely."

"Lukos is amazing that way," Victor said, and Sava stared. "It is. I mean, in Gerakia we have something similar, in that if someone's house falls in a storm or there's an accident of some kind, the whole town gets together to raise money for them. Or rebuild their house. If someone's mate dies and they don't have children old enough to look after them, everyone comes by to take care of them. I used to ride my bicycle—it's a relatively new machine, two wheels on a frame—to the widowers and widows with pies from the orphanage once a week."

"Yes, I can see you caring about a person who is left alone," Sava said, eyeing Speedy.

"Well." Victor blushed. "I guess. But everyone did that. And they do that here, too. It just goes to show that there are good people wherever you go, I suppose."

"That's not what you said earlier," Sava pointed out. "Your opinion of people, perhaps it is changing."

"I'm not saying everyone is good, just that ... you know. Ugh." Victor snuggled closer to Sava's side. "I'm saying it's fascinating that two countries that are so far apart can be so similar, that's all."

Sava swung an arm around Victor. "Maybe I was fated to have a Gerakian mate, then. You come from a country that ousted a king. Lukos outlived the one that exiled us. But we don't have bicycles, here, or your long summers. What does a bicycle look like?"

"Let me show you." Victor scrambled for his books and a pen, and they spent the rest of the evening mapping out imaginary bicycle paths across Lukos, bringing a piece of the Gerakian summer into their snowy cabin at the far end of the world.

That night, Victor dreamed of Milan.

They were both sitting on the porch, rocking in the chairs Sava had carved and watching the snow melt over the hills of Lukos. Milan's face was covered in a sheer veil that made his features indistinct, and his skin was pale blue with the cold, but Victor had a feeling that he was smiling.

"The fox-maiden isn't the one who draws people out," Milan said. "Or she wasn't always, anyway." A bird lighted on a tree branch in the distance, ruffling its feathers. An owl, white and wide-eyed, watching them. "She used to be a comfort. Someone who found the dead and brought them to what comes after. But maybe she became something else."

Victor sat there, watching the owl. The chair beside him creaked as Milan pushed it back and forth with a foot.

"I don't mind you being with him." His voice was mellow, quiet. "I loved him. Why would I want him to be alone?"

"Is this actually you?" Victor asked. The owl flew to earth, wings outspread, and disappeared into the snow. "Or are you just a leftover piece of the fever?"

"Don't think that matters, really." Milan swung his foot hard and laughed as the chair rocked. "Oh, I would have loved this. Love it for me, okay?"

"I'll try," Victor said. The veil over Milan's face fluttered in a breeze he couldn't feel.

"Good. Everyone got it wrong. You know that, don't you? You almost figured it out."

"Got what wrong?"

Milan lifted the veil, and Victor turned away rather than look at the dead eyes staring at him from beneath the folds. "I wasn't alone."

"When?" Victor asked, but Milan just stood, letting the veil fall again. The owl emerged from the snow, only it wasn't an owl at all but a woman with black hair and a blood-red gown under her white robes, beckoning him.

"Good luck, Victor." Milan stepped down off the porch, into the snow. "You'll need to be owl-eyed to see this through."

Milan reached out a hand for the fox-maiden, and then they both disappeared, the snow flying in a spray like the sea in a storm.

Victor woke in the dark next to Sava and sat up, dislodging Speedy from his spot on Victor's chest. It had felt so real. Victor didn't believe in ghosts, not really, but how, then, did Milan seem to know so much? And what did he mean, *Good luck*? Victor sighed and rubbed his face. Ghost or no, dreams weren't supposed to make sense.

Still, Victor couldn't sleep after that, so he got up and went to the fire with his board, where he spent the rest of the night carving feathers. He lost himself in it, brushing off bits of wood dust and carving out eyes for the owls, and almost missed the sound of Sava getting up from the bed. He turned, smiling at the dark shape looming over him, and blew off the last of his carving.

"I was going to give it to you when you woke up," he said. "Look."

He held the carving up to the firelight. Dozens of owls flew across the wood, feathers blending into each other, a wall of claws and eyes and beaks that looked like a storm cloud until the light cast shadows over the intricately carved feathers. They seemed alive in the half light, their wings moving slightly as Victor tilted the wood, and Sava leaned down to take the carving in his hands.

"There," Victor said. "My first snow dream, for you. What do you think?"

"I've never seen anything like this before," Sava said. "It's … like there's something … changing in my mind, when I look at it."

Victor held his breath. That was how he had felt as a boy, the first time he saw the Kallistoi painters in the market square. The thought that someone else would see his own art and feel that way made his chest go tight and his eyes burn. "Really?"

Sava stared at the carving for another long minute, then walked over to place it on the mantel over the fireplace. "It's perfect." There were tears in his eyes as he leaned down to kiss Victor. "Now this truly is the best house in Lukos."

# CHAPTER 12

*E*ven though Sava had seen it before, the way the snow transformed Lukos amazed him every time. Like there should be no way the world could change that completely, the landscape covered in an icy white blanket that clung to trees and turned the hills into softly rounded slopes.

"It's, ah. A lot of snow," Victor said, eyes wide, standing half-behind Sava just outside the front door of their house. Speedy was frolicking about on the porch, looking adorable and warmer than a small kitten should. "It looks fluffy, and still terrible and *cold.*"

"It's not fluffy, but it *is* cold," Sava said, amused, as Victor pressed next to him. They were both dressed in furs, but the wind was biting and the snow was blowing wildly, stinging their faces. "You can go and see, if you do not believe me."

"I believe you," Victor said, and they both laughed as Speedy— apparently eager to show off his superior snow attire—leapt off the porch and landed in a snowbank so deep the only thing visible was his tail. He managed to dig himself out, meowed loudly at them, and marched back into the house as if he were making some kind of point.

The snow kept coming, and Victor kept watching, like he couldn't quite believe it. "How do we know this is the, you know, real thing?"

"The snow is real, mate. If you do not believe me—"

"Stop, no." Victor punched him on the arm, grinning. His eyes were bright, happy, free of fever … but Sava still felt a chill when he thought of how he'd believed Victor was dying. "Just, when does it …" He waved his hands.

Sava blinked. "When does the snow … what?"

"Keep coming," Victor said.

Sava glanced at him. "It is doing that now. The key to surviving the winter, my mate, is to take the snow as it comes and let it be what it is."

"Oh, that's the key, is it?" Victor sidled close, warm and bright-eyed, and wrapped his arms around Sava's neck as Sava walked them both back inside. "I thought the key was to have a strong dominant who can build houses, start a fire, and get food. Pretty sure *you're* the key to surviving the winter, big guy."

"And yet, before the snow truly came, I almost lost you," Sava said, before he could stop himself.

Victor's smile faded a bit. "Of course you didn't. And in any case, it wasn't your fault I caught the flu."

That hadn't been a simple illness. It had descended too rapidly into fever and confusion, the sort that would disorient a man, make him think he heard a fox goddess singing in the frigid, ice-capped waters of the sea.

"Okay," Victor said slowly, touching the side of Sava's face and rubbing his beard. He sounded as if he'd arrived at some sort of conclusion, or the solution to a problem. "I might not know about life here in the winter, but I know a dominant who's feeling out of sorts when I see one. What do you need to stop worrying about this?"

Sava would not have thought he was out of sorts, exactly, but it made sense: his natural dominance perhaps was chafing at the idea he'd failed somehow. Even though Victor was healthy again, Sava couldn't shake the feeling *he* wasn't good enough, strong enough, to be the mate Victor needed. The mate Victor *deserved*.

But he didn't know the answer to Victor's question, either. Well, no, he did—but it seemed as if it wasn't something he should ask for. Except that if it were Victor needing something, he'd want to know. He drew in a slow breath. "What I want is to believe that I am enough for you. To keep you safe, to make you happy."

"Sava, you're—" Victor gave a little laugh and shook his head. "If you had any idea how ridiculous the thought you *wouldn't* be is … but I don't think it makes much sense to go back and forth about how neither of us feels we're good enough for the other."

Immediately, Sava said, "No, you are perfect as you are—"

"Sava," Victor interrupted. "Let's make this about you. I'm a submissive—I'm *your* submissive. And if you're right, if—as you've told me before—this is a partnership, then I should give you what you need. What your dominance needs. It's a way I can take care of you. We take care of each other, yeah? So, let me do that. Tell me what you need."

Sava said it before he could think it through. "I want to tie you down and make you beg for me, show you that you're mine."

Victor gasped. "I can't tell you how much I want you to do that. Wow." Before Sava could say anything more, Victor went to his knees. He put his hands behind his back, tipped his face up, and showed his throat. "I'm all yours. Take me any way you want. Make me fall apart for you."

Lust and dominance rose in tandem, taking Sava's own breath and making him reach out to tangle his fingers in Victor's curls before he was aware he was doing it. He tugged, firm but not too hard, and watched Victor shiver. "I want to gag you, if you can breathe that way. I won't hurt you. But I want all of you at my mercy."

"Fuck," Victor breathed, face flushed. "Yes, please. I'm fine. I can breathe. Please do that, *please*."

That was all Sava needed to hear. He pulled Victor's hair again, then said, "Crawl." For a moment he worried it was too much, somehow debasing, to make Victor do such a thing. But Victor *grinned* and went to all fours, and he didn't seem to mind the instruction in the slightest as he followed Sava toward the bed.

"Strip and lie on your back, and do not speak unless I ask you to." Sava went over to a wooden chest by the bed and opened it; there were things he'd been keeping for the time he had a mate, things he'd fashioned and put away for when it was time to use them. One was a strip of leather, and there were soft cuffs lined with bear fur, and a bar of wood he'd carved and whittled and polished until it was smooth, with another pair of cuffs affixed on the ends. He carried it all to the bed, where Victor was already spread out naked and half-hard, and stared down at him for a long moment.

"You are beautiful," he said, and when Victor opened his mouth, he held up the strip of leather, his dominance heavy when he added, "and you will not argue with me. I want to have all of you, and you will let me. Yes?"

"Yes," Victor said, his cock growing harder as Sava reached down to gently place the leather strip in his mouth, tying it behind his head.

"If you need to stop, you will do this." Sava held up his hand and showed three fingers. "And I will stop. Nod so that I know you understand."

Victor nodded, eyes already going hazy and unfocused, and Sava gave a sigh of satisfaction as he put the cuffs around Victor's wrists and attached them to the ropes that held the bed off the floor. He secured Victor's ankles in the spreader bar so that he was open, vulnerable and gorgeous and all *his*.

Sava did not enjoy inflicting—or receiving—pain, though he

knew there were dominants who were sadists, and even some submissives, though that was said to be rare. What he wanted was control, and it went a long way toward satisfying his urges to see Victor so beautifully laid out and waiting.

"Your David was a foolish man," he said quietly. "I do not want to speak of him, for he is worthless and never deserved you, but you should know that you are remarkable. Your clever mind, the way you came here and became one of us. How you look at me, as if I am worthy of you. You should understand, little owl. You deserve to have someone *want* to be worthy of you."

Victor was squirming, red-faced, but he didn't hold up his fingers, so Sava continued. "I want you to stop thinking about anything that isn't how good it feels to be taken." He reached out and started to stroke Victor's cock, lightly enough that Victor whined and bucked his hips up as much as he could in the restraints.

"Ah, you would already like to come, yes?" Sava smiled, taking Victor more firmly in hand. "Look at you, so needy. Already so hard for me." He twisted his hand around the tip of Victor's cock, and Victor made a delicious, desperate sound and his eyes rolled back in his head.

Sava stroked him, firm and fast, until Victor's breath was strangled and he was writhing in the restraints. Sava knew, by now, what Victor looked like when he was near the edge. He kept going, waiting until the tip of Victor's cock was slick and wet, and then drew his hand away and thrilled at the sound that pulled from Victor, a whining moan that was caught behind the leather of his gag.

Sava did it again, and then again. Victor's face was damp with sweat and his eyes were bright, but even though he chased the pleasure Sava gave him with fierce determination and made such lovely sounds when he was denied, he never once held up his fingers for Sava to stop. He drew away once more and let Victor shudder in unfulfilled want for several long seconds, then moved to the end of the bed. It took a moment to get situated, lifting Victor's hips so that his calves were resting on Sava's shoulders and the spreader bar was up in the air. Victor was flexible enough that Sava knew he could hold the position without undue stress, and the sound Victor made when Sava licked a hot stripe over Victor's balls and moved *lower* was loud and almost shocked.

"I said you are worthy of being adored, and I meant it. And you should be adored everywhere, little owl, yes?" Sava didn't wait for a response, licking at Victor's hole and relishing the resulting sounds and the way Victor's calves were tensing on his shoulders. Sava had never done this before, but he loved the way it made Victor react, and he spread him open and buried his face between Victor's parted thighs, losing himself in the act as Victor sobbed so prettily for him.

"Mmph, mmph," Victor moaned, and Sava glanced up to make sure that wasn't a sign to stop … and was caught by how gorgeous Victor looked, tense and trembling, head tipped back as he pulled on the restraints anchored to the ropes.

Pleased, Sava lowered his head and went back to it, licking and sucking at Victor's hole. By the time he pulled away, gently lowering Victor's hips back to the bed, Victor was nearly sobbing with pent-up need.

"There is no part of you I would not take care of, my mate," Sava told him, his own cock hard inside his pants. His hand moved to curl around Victor's throat, squeezing lightly, his dominance so roused it was hard to think. Victor didn't fight his air being constricted—instead, he went boneless, limp, submitting utterly in a way that made Sava bite him, hard, on the shoulder. Victor's cock was flushed, hard and wet as it lay on his stomach, and Sava could see it twitch as he continued to choke him.

Finally, Sava's body made demands of its own. He settled mostly dressed on top of Victor, and it wasn't until he'd slicked himself up and pressed inside that he felt his dominance even out, as the desire to come took over everything else. He fucked

Victor hard and fast, the bed shaking as he took him, one hand on the wall above Victor's head. He couldn't look away from Victor's tear-streaked face, his bared throat, his sweat-damp, flushed skin.

"I am going to come inside you, so that you know you are *mine*," Sava growled, and he felt Victor shift and tense beneath him, like he was trying to urge him on. He could hear something that sounded like *Yes, yes*, and Victor's hands were clenched, no fingers held up … no reason to stop, or slow, or not give in to his fierce need to *possess*.

All his fears of losing Victor, his worries that he was not the right mate for such a clever submissive, fell away as he fucked Victor hard. He could only just make out the wind howling outside, the tense trembling of Victor's body beneath him, the tears on his face that made him look so beautiful. Sava wished he were half as good with words as Victor was, so that he could tell him.

"Do you want to come for me, my owl?" Sava's teeth bared in a feral grin as Victor nodded so emphatically the pillow fell off the bed. "On my cock, then. Let me see how you are mine."

It only took three strokes of Sava's hand before Victor came, his shout barely muffled by the leather of the gag. He felt Victor tense around his cock, and Sava thrust in hard, grinding himself into Victor's tight heat. He bit Victor on the shoulder again when he came, his own moan just as loud. Pleasure ran through him in delicious pulses as he shuddered, until the last shock eased and left him lying on top of Victor, panting, his mouth still pressed to the bite mark on Victor's shoulder.

Sava raised his head and saw Victor—eyes closed, blissful, under. This was how it was supposed to be. This was *right*.

"I love you," Sava said, as the words settled warm and easy in his soul, down to his bones. "And I will always keep you safe."

Victor made a little noise and blinked up at Sava. He wasn't trying to speak, but Sava could see the feelings there, in his eyes.

Trust, love, submission. Sava's cock was softening, but he didn't draw away, just fumbled for the leather gag and removed it.

Sava rubbed his fingers through the mess on Victor's face, sweat and tears and spit, then brought his hand to his mouth and licked the moisture away. Victor gave a weak laugh and smiled like a man who'd had too much cider. Sava smiled back.

"I love you, too," Victor said, slurring his words. "And that. Anytime. Yeah."

Sava laughed, pleased and sated, and went to move so he could undo the rest of the restraints.

"Not—not yet," Victor asked, voice still a little shaky. "Just a few more. Minutes. I like how you feel on top of me."

Sava would not say no to that, so he rested against Victor again, though he shifted to relieve Victor of some of his weight. They lay together, breathing quietly, and Sava felt Victor's heartbeat against his as it returned to a slow, steady rhythm.

Outside, the snow fell and the wind howled. Whatever the winter would bring, they had this. They had each other. And it was everything Sava had ever wanted.

*WHILE SNOW MAY FALL over Lukos often in the early months of winter, the true First Snowfall is impossible to mistake for a simple storm. Any Lukoi foolish enough to leave their home during the First Snowfall is bound to lose themselves in endless curtains of snow, which can bury houses and wanderers alike. Forced to remain indoors for weeks on end, the Lukoi resort to games of fire dice (see fig. 34), bone-breaker (see fig. 35), and the popular craft of woodworking—among other pursuits.*

"WHAT DOES THAT MEAN?" Sava asked.

Victor looked up from his book. His fingers were smudged with ink, his hand was cramped from writing, and his glasses were starting to slide down his nose again. Sava leaned down to fix them, and Victor flashed him a smile.

"Other pursuits." Victor pointed to the words. He'd been teaching some of the language to Sava while the snow fell outside, the two of them tossing words back and forth between their native tongues until the house sounded like it was haunted by a pair of very befuddled parrots. "I'm writing about Lukos. I think it's turning into something. This part is about what, uh, what the Lukoi do when it's snowing."

"Really?" Sava tapped on the illustration Victor had made of two children playing bone-breaker, a game that involved one child making a tower of sticks while the other tried to pull out the pieces. "That's what we do, is it?"

Victor shrugged and rolled over on his side. Speedy, who'd been stretched out there, made a trill of disgust and padded over to the fire. "You showed me once."

"Yes. And what else do we do?" Sava climbed over Victor and kissed him, smiling. Victor only just managed to push the book to safety before Sava rolled him into the pit of furs, where an outraged Speedy grumbled so loudly that Sava startled both Victor and the cat with a booming laugh.

*ON THE SUBJECT OF COURTSHIP.*

*Societal standards for those with the biological bent for dominance are such that [illegible]*

"SAVA." Victor laughed as Sava picked his glasses up off the floor, where they'd fallen when he sneezed. "Sava, I need those to see."

"Yes, mate, be patient." The house was dark save for the fire in the fireplace, the snow so high up the outside walls that the windows had to be shuttered and vents opened near the roof.

Sava was a silhouette against the fire, and Victor could only just make out the flash of his glasses in Sava's hands.

"Fine," Victor said. "I'll write without them."

[ILLEGIBLE]

"Huh," Victor said, looking down at the blurry smudges on the page. That had gone about as well as expected.

"Patience, I said. This is a new word I should teach you later, hmm?"

"Ha, ha." Victor sat up, blinking, and Sava handed his glasses back to him. There was a small ribbon connecting the ends of the glasses, soft to the touch and tied expertly. Victor put them on and smiled at Sava's nervous look.

"You always curse when they fall," Sava said.

Victor stared at him. It was such a simple thing, really. Just a piece of ribbon and a few seconds to tie it. But Victor's face heated, and perhaps the book slipped under a pillow when Victor surged up to wrap his arms around Sava's shoulders.

It was still snowing, and the next time they left the house, it was through a hatch above the door. Speedy was left crying on the rug, a lanky, fluffy kitten with the widest, saddest eyes Victor had ever seen.

"Trust me," Victor said, closing the hatch after him. "You don't want what's out here."

They spent all day shoveling snow off the roof and digging a path to the door. Afterward, Victor drew an illustration of Speedy sitting in the doorway, looking at the walls of snow with his ears perked up as though something might leap out at any moment. Which, given the stories Sava had told Victor of creatures tunneling through the snow, might actually have been possible.

Victor hadn't walked ten paces from the house in weeks. He'd painted three canvases and filled almost every page of his journals, and he realized, when the snow finally stopped falling and he woke to find Sava rolling a wooden toy he'd made for Speedy across the floor, that he was happy.

He'd been happy before. Perhaps the owl girl in the Gerakian fairy tale had been happy, too, in the temporary homes she left behind. Perhaps she enjoyed the thrill of flight and the warmth of the sun on her feathers. Perhaps she liked the way the giants sang in the mornings, their heavy voices booming over the forests, and the way the light curved along the bars of a golden cage. But she couldn't shed her feathers until she came home to a place where she was loved.

"My little owl," Aunt Grace used to say, petting Victor's hair as yet another prospective family walked out the door. "They weren't right for you, that's all."

"Maybe I'm not your boy," Victor, young and desperate for a friend, had said to the dog in the street. "But I could be."

But the dog hadn't come home with him. The owl girl kept flying. Victor hadn't left with the adults who stared at him like he was a doll on the shelf. And maybe it was because his home wasn't meant to be in the long, vibrant summers of Gerakia, but in Lukos, where snow swallowed houses and the wind sounded like a ghost at the door.

"I'm glad it happened, you know," Victor said. Sava looked up. Speedy was trying to gnaw on Sava's hand, smacking him with his fuzzy back paws.

"What?"

"This," Victor said. "Ending up here. I'm glad."

Sava smiled. "So am I, my mate."

Outside, the snow was piled to the windows. The world was quiet and cold while winter maintained its hold over Lukos, but Victor was warm in the home his mate had made.

# CHAPTER 13

There was someone outside the house.

Victor jolted awake when he heard a voice calling out from beyond the door and the walls of snow. He couldn't say why it alarmed him—only that, for a moment, he couldn't breathe, and he felt as though a person were holding him down, a hand pressed to the hollow of his throat.

"Someone's here." His voice came out choked, tight, but Sava was still asleep at his side, and the wind howling over the roof was louder than Victor's panicked whisper.

"Sava?"

The voice outside sounded mournful, only half real. Sava stirred in his sleep. Speedy was stretched out between them, paws extended, and Sava gently shifted so that he didn't roll over on Speedy's tail.

Victor looked up at the hatch above the door. A shadow passed over it, and something scratched at the snow by the window.

"Sava." It was Ivan. Victor tensed, and Sava mumbled in his sleep, reaching out for him. Victor set his hand back down, heart hammering. He couldn't explain why, but he didn't want Sava to speak to Ivan. It was like when Victor thought about David—there was a yawning pit there, at the edge of Victor's mind. Something wasn't right. Why would Ivan show up when another snowstorm was brewing, well before the false spring?

Victor climbed out of bed and slipped on his coat and boots. Outside, Ivan was digging, like he was trying to unearth the house with his bare hands. He stopped when Victor put a foot on the first rung of the ladder, and Victor's gloved hands felt clammy as he wrestled with the hatch.

His hair was covered with a hat Sava had made for him, and only the top half of his face was visible over his coat, but there was no reason for Ivan to jump the way he did when Victor emerged. Ivan's mouth was a dark O in his blurry face, and Victor realized he'd been so sleepy that he forgot to grab his glasses. When Ivan stepped back, his features sharpened enough for Victor to see the clear dismay written there. Ivan was rocking back and forth on the balls of his feet and fumbling with something in his coat.

"Oh." Ivan laughed. It sounded forced, too high. "Victor. Good to see you're feeling better."

"You shouldn't be out right now," Victor said. Light hail was starting to fall, tossed about in the wind. He tugged at his collar. "What happened?"

"I … I wanted to check on you." Ivan took another step back. It was hard to hear him over the wind, so Victor took an uneasy step across the snow. "You seemed delirious the last time I saw you. Acting like I was trying to force the medicine on you." Ivan tried another smile, but it didn't reach his eyes.

Victor thought of the medicine, the long hours of fever dreams and misery, the fear in Sava's eyes when Victor recovered enough to speak. "I almost died."

"Well, a foreigner like you, it's expected." Ivan waved a hand. "Come over here. Help me with this."

Victor didn't want to help. He wanted to turn around and

leave Ivan outside, but that didn't seem like the Lukoi thing to do, and the storm was getting worse.

"You might as well come in," he said, coming closer. Ivan reached out and grabbed him by the wrist, pulling him forward. Hail drummed on Victor's shoulders, but Ivan's grip was far more painful, tight as a claw.

"You couldn't just take your medicine, could you?" Ivan's voice was a low wail, the kind Victor used to hear from unhappy toddlers who had to go to bed without dessert. "I put enough of the yellow poppy in that potion to have you talking to the *stars,* but you probably spat it out and complained about the taste and let *him* baby you, didn't you?"

Victor yanked on Ivan's hand. "What do you … the yellow poppy? What was the medicine supposed to do, Ivan?"

"You ruined *everything,*" Ivan howled.

"What the fuck was the yellow poppy supposed to do?"

Ivan pressed something to Victor's stomach, and Victor looked down. The glimmer of a blade shone there, clenched in a tight fist.

And, just like that, Victor looked into the pit in his mind and stepped in. "Milan died alone," he said.

"Shut *up,*" Ivan said. He was crying, breath coming hot and fast. "Just shut up."

"If Milan died alone, and his parents were the ones who took him out of the water," Victor said, wincing at the pain in his wrist, "then how did you see him covered in ice?"

He waited for Ivan to deny it, but he just stood there, the wind whistling between them.

"You don't get it," Ivan said. He lurched backward, dragging Victor with him in an awkward, hobbling march. He kept the knife firmly pressed to Victor's stomach. "You don't deserve Sava. Neither of you did. You don't understand him the way I do. You didn't *earn* him the way I did. You just stood there and looked pretty, and he fell all over you and your, your softness and your weakness, your big eyes and your fucking *sympathy.* You think you're nice? You think you want to be my friend, when you're just, just another fucking slut batting your eyes at the first big—"

Victor wasn't a strong man. He'd never thrown a punch in his life. This one, though, struck Ivan straight in the nose, and Ivan went down like a sack of bricks.

"That was for both of us," Victor said, and turned to run.

He didn't make it more than a few paces. Ivan tackled him from behind, and Victor cried out as he went down. Ivan got the knife wedged under his chin this time, and Victor looked up into bared teeth and a wild, desperate face.

"Get up, whore," Ivan snarled. He was still crying, blood and tears making a ruin of his face. "We're going for a walk."

SOMETHING WAS PAWING at his face.

Sava turned his head, trying to escape the relentless *poke poke tap poke tap,* but it wouldn't stop. He blinked his eyes open to see Speedy standing on his chest, meowing.

"Speedy," Sava said, voice still rough with sleep as he gently relocated the cat from his chest, "this is not how you behave when you want something."

Except it was, and Sava sighed, turning to the side. Victor wasn't in bed, which wasn't in itself alarming, even if Sava was usually the earlier riser. He pushed the furs aside and then frowned; it was unreasonably cold in the cabin, and he heard something that sounded like hail—not outside the house, but *inside.*

Victor's glasses were still on the table. He always put those on first thing when he left the bed, even when he had to get up and go the bathroom in the middle of the night.

Sava's stomach fluttered. "Victor?" He padded out into the main room and stopped dead as a blast of icy air swept over him.

The roof hatch was open, and a steady stream of hail was striking the ladder and bouncing across the floor.

Speedy paced, meowing and batting at the hail as he circled the ladder. He gave Sava a plaintive look.

Sava barely managed to remember he would need his boots before shooting up the ladder. A cursory glance showed Victor was not in the house or the cellar, but Sava had no idea why he would have gone outside, now, in the worst of the winter. His anxiety grew as he dressed hastily in his outerwear, and his breathing was too fast as he exited through the hatch, pulling it firmly shut behind him.

There were footprints on the snow, and for a horrifying moment Sava pictured Victor wandering lost amid the hail, which obscured the landscape so completely it was almost impossible to navigate when you *knew* the territory, much less when you didn't. The winter sun was dim and weak in the overcast sky, but the chill that took hold of him was born more from fear than cold.

Victor, alone and wandering in the frigid, dangerous conditions and heading—

That's when Sava realized he was seeing not one set of footprints, but two.

And there was blood on the snow. Not a great deal, but enough to know someone was hurt.

Someone was hurt, and the footprints were heading toward the sea.

"No," Sava said. "*No.*"

With that, he began to run.

The footprints continued, and Sava sent up a thank-you to the weather, which was, shockingly, cooperating with his tracking. The hail was the kind that was half the size of a small pebble, and it hadn't yet filled in the impressions the boots had left in the snow. The size was increasing even now, though, and if he'd slept much later—

He would have to make sure Speedy had all the toys he wanted, forever and always, and Sava would let him sleep on his *face* without comment.

Victor was in trouble; there was no doubt about that. Sava knew Victor wouldn't go out into the snow, but more than that, he wouldn't leave the hatch open, knowing how dangerous it could be to their home and their continued survival if he did.

*Unless the fox-maiden called, and his mind was too weak to resist her.*

No. That wasn't it. Victor might not know how to skin a deer or build a house, and his cooking was only just becoming passable at best, but Sava's mate was *clever*, the cleverest man in Lukos, probably. He'd learned their language. He'd carefully copied the carvings from the cave into the book he was writing —*the book he was writing*. Victor was strong, and the fox-maiden, if she'd sung to him … he would know better than to do what she wanted, even if he *did* listen to her song.

Victor was strong. If he had left their home, it was because someone was dragging him away … and the blood was because he'd *fought*. Fierce pride, love, and determination swept through Sava, and he ran so fast he skidded twice on the ice, nearly toppling over into a snowbank but righting himself at the last minute. Snow-Walker he was not, at the moment. Snow-Slider, Snow-Runner, Snow-Panicked. Any of those fit better than his sobriquet.

The hail slammed into his face, stinging and obscuring his vision as the wind picked up. Sava swore under his breath, but he didn't stop—even though his heart almost did, every time he saw the footprints change so it was clear one person was dragging the other.

Was it David? Had he come to Lukos to take Victor back? Victor would not want to go. Sava might have worried before that Victor would yearn for the warm summers of Gerakia, but Victor loved him. They were mates, and Victor was Lukoi now.

He knew what that meant. Sava trusted him completely. More than that … If Victor wanted to leave, if the footprints were him walking to meet a boat to take him home, Sava would not stop him. He loved Victor too much to keep him somewhere he didn't want to be. But he also knew in his bones that Victor did not want to leave. Victor had told him so, and Sava's clever mate did not lie.

Victor was in trouble, and Sava had promised to keep him safe. He could see this as a failing, maybe, that someone had dragged Victor away … or he could do what he'd promised and bring Victor home.

His mind cleared, and his feet stayed on solid—if slippery— ground as he ran. Along with the wind and the hail, he could hear something else. Waves. The ocean was just ahead, and along with that came the muffled sound of someone shouting.

The beach was windswept and less snow-covered than the rest of the island. The icebergs in the distance stood stark and violet-blue against the waves and the dreary sky. And there, perilously close to the water's edge, stood Victor … with Ivan behind him, holding a knife to his throat.

Sava skidded to a stop just as his heart began to race even faster. He couldn't understand what he was seeing … but then he remembered Victor saying, so many weeks before, that something was wrong with Ivan. Sava hadn't listened, and he should have. Should have trusted that his mate might know something he didn't. That Victor's keen mind was as sharp as any of Sava's knives, that he knew people like Sava knew the forests and the game that hid there.

"—ruined *everything*," Ivan shouted. "You could have just *died* like you were supposed to, and then I wouldn't have to do this!"

"Ivan, you don't have to do it *now*," Victor said, and Sava's heart clenched at the desperate, pleading tone in his voice.

"Your life is over, you worthless whore," Ivan snarled. He clearly hadn't seen Sava yet. "He's mine. He was always supposed to be mine. And after I put you in the water, just like I did to his *fucking precious Milan,* no one will want him except me. And there'll be no one left to take him away from me!"

Sava stood, hail battering him and stinging his eyes, tears falling and freezing on his face. What—what was Ivan saying?

"He'll know I would never do this," Victor said, struggling as Ivan dragged him closer to the water. It was low tide, which was a blessing, because Victor was clearly trying to slow Ivan's implacable death march. "He'll know, Ivan."

Somehow, Sava made himself walk forward slowly, his hands raised. "He is right, Ivan Spring-Singer. I would know. And this is not going to happen."

"Oh, I'm sorry, Sava, but it *is*," Ivan snarled, after a momentary hesitation. "He's worthless. What do you even want him for? He's some foreigner who can't start a fire, and you think he's your *mate*? I'm doing you a favor, just like—just like the fox goddess did when she called Milan away from you."

"He lies, Sava. Milan never wanted to leave you. Ivan killed him—" Victor cried out as Ivan wrenched at him, pulling him farther toward where the water waited, ice-cold and deadly.

"You can't do anything, you're useless, and you're not *meant for him*." Ivan looked up as Sava moved closer, stalking like he would a bear at the height of spring, when the animals were restless and hungry. "Sava, you don't understand. We're the same! We both lost our mothers, and this one never even *had* a mother to lose."

"The yellow poppy!" Victor shouted. "Sava, he—he tried to poison me, and I'm guessing he did the same to his mom."

"Stop this," Sava demanded, his dominance rising like the waves behind Ivan. He held up his hands again. "Ivan. We will talk about this somewhere else. Let Victor go. Come with us and tell me plainly what the problem is—"

"The problem is this one, living, breathing, standing here like he thinks he can have you!" Ivan's voice carried on the wind, and

Sava knew he was going to have to do something drastic. He was close enough now to see the wildness in Ivan's eyes. The knife pressed up against Victor's throat. Victor, shivering in the wind and the hail that was even now falling harder, the stones larger, making him feel as if he were being punched in the head every second.

Sava ignored it all, inching closer, slow and easy. Panic would not help Victor. "He is my mate, Ivan. The laws of Lukos are clear."

"The laws are for the *Lukoi,* not bastard sons no one wants who are thrown away like trash. Is that what you think you deserve, Sava? Trash? You should have better. You should have *me.*"

"You never even spoke to me of this," Sava said, though maybe he shouldn't. "Not once, Spring-Singer."

"Because you couldn't stop looking at *Milan,*" Ivan spat, like the name was a curse. "Oh, he was so happy to tell me how you were going to be mates. *If he doesn't ask me soon, Spring-Singer, I'm going to go to his cabin and offer myself.* You should have heard him, the slut, as if that's what you needed. You're a hunter; you should *hunt.* Not have some—some useless creature tossed at your feet like they do across the sea, where they don't know what it's like to be one of us!"

"Ivan, let Victor go," Sava said, ignoring—for the moment— his horror at understanding that Milan hadn't left him willingly. "You have heard the fox-maiden, and you are listening to her. Do not do this. Listen to me, instead."

It didn't matter. No matter how much dominance he infused into his voice, it wasn't making Ivan let Victor go. Ivan was clearly affected by it, swaying a bit, but his hand on the knife didn't lower, and he kept Victor's arm wrenched behind his back.

"No," Ivan snarled. "No. Not this time. I was going to push him into the sea like I did that useless Milan—it didn't matter how much bigger than me he was, not when I had the drugs to make him weak, disoriented. Drugs that should have killed your false mate, too. I tried to be kind! I tried to send them to death without pain. Milan drowned before he even knew I was there, and I was going to do the same with this one, but now that you're here…"

"I love you," Victor said to Sava. His voice was trembling but loud, and the smile on his face made Sava want to weep. "And you know I didn't want this. I want to stay with you. Always."

"You'll fucking die here, and he'll watch," Ivan shouted. "And then I'll be here to pick up the pieces. I'll heal his heart. It won't take long. He can't love you; he *can't*. You're too … too eager. You just—you're not—you're not for him. You're nothing, you're no one, and everyone would have believed me if I'd told them you walked out here and drowned. Just like they would have believed you stepped in one of the traps I set for you. Of course Sava carried you everywhere, so even that didn't work, but it wasn't because of *you*. You're *weak*. They would have believed me, just like with Milan. I'm not weak. I'm a submissive, but I learned how to hunt, unlike this useless whore. I learned how to *kill*. He won't feel it all that much. The knife is sharp, Snow-Walker. And then I'll be yours, like I was always meant to be."

Hail and tears flooded Sava's eyes. He couldn't get to Ivan fast enough. It would take no time at all for Ivan to draw the knife across Victor's throat. The second Sava moved like he was going to do it, Ivan would make the kill. And Sava would watch Victor die in the surf, and then he would tear Ivan apart with his own bare hands … but it wouldn't matter.

He would still be alone. His house would never be a home, not without Victor there to share it with him.

"Snow-Walker," a voice behind him said softly, "tell your mate to kick him in the knee and run."

Zora Star-Finder. Milan's mother. Sava did not question why she was there, but as it turned out, he didn't need to say anything —Victor must have known, too, that he had only one chance to attempt an escape. He kicked out, trying to get free of Ivan, and it took Ivan by surprise enough that Victor could pull away slightly.

There was a whistle of a different wind past Sava's ear, and then an arrow struck Ivan in the shoulder. He cursed and dropped the knife, and Sava was already moving toward Victor as another arrow struck Ivan's other arm.

Zora moved from the dunes like a ghost, walking with her bow drawn. That she'd managed to hit a target, twice, in the hail was a testament to just how good an archer she was.

"You killed my son," Zora said, her eyes on Ivan as he staggered and tried to pull the arrows from his flesh. "The law says your life is mine. And now I will take it as you took his. Without mercy. The sea took my unwilling son." She fired another arrow, and Ivan howled in pain as it struck his thigh. "The same death will do for you." She fired again, struck Ivan in his other thigh, and kept walking toward him like death come calling.

Sava drew Victor close, enfolding him in his arms, and pressed Victor's face to his racing heart. "Don't watch," he choked out, as Victor clung to him and shook in his arms, safe now, where he belonged.

Victor didn't watch, but Sava did, as Zora pushed Ivan backward into the water, his pleading falling on unhearing ears. Zora raised the bow again, and Sava knew the last shot would end it. Ivan managed half of a scream before she loosed the arrow, and it struck him in the heart, sending him toppling into the sea.

The beach went quiet, the waves and the wind the only sounds.

Zora stood watching for a long moment as Ivan's lifeless body bobbed in the frigid water, as it was carried out into the cold sea.

Eventually, she turned and walked back to them, bow settled once more on her back. She stared at Sava, grief in her eyes: killing Ivan hadn't brought back her son. But she said, in an even voice, "Come, Snow-Walker. My husband has made stew; there is a fire to warm you. You and your mate will weather this storm with us. And there are things we should speak of, before you and your Victor go home."

With that, she began walking toward her house. Sava wrapped his arm around Victor, then decided there was an easier way … and picked him up. Victor wrapped his arms around Sava's neck, his breath warm on Sava's skin, limbs shaking though he held on tight. "I knew you'd find me. And even if you didn't, I knew you'd never believe I left you on purpose."

Sava couldn't speak, still too distraught over what he'd learned, over the sight of Ivan falling dead into the water. He walked on, just as he always did, the snow beneath his feet and the unrelenting winter sky stark above.

VICTOR AND SAVA changed into Pavel's spare clothes while their own steamed in front of the fire, and Pavel and Zora sat on the floor with mugs of hot tea, staring into the middle distance.

Sava was quiet, but Victor knew he was shaken. Ivan had never shown his true self to Sava before, and Sava always thought the best of people. This wasn't just a pit opening up in his mind, it was being brought to the edge of it and shoved in. Victor sat pressed up against him, and when Victor reached for Sava's hand, Sava threaded their fingers together and held on tight.

"My Pavel tried to warn me that I was turning my grief on you," Zora said, at last. She didn't look at Sava. "But Milan … I knew he had a strong heart. I thought you must have done something terrible to break it. It was wrong of me. And now we are here."

"You couldn't have known," Pavel said.

Sava took a shaky breath. Victor looked into the fire. He thought of David, of all the warning signs Victor had ignored or overlooked. Even his college had discarded the obvious explanation to blame Victor, because it was easier to place the blame on a student than to admit that one of their professors was corrupt.

"Victor saw it," Sava said. "He saw it in Ivan before anyone else did."

"Sometimes it takes another perspective," Victor said. "The rest of you were too close to the situation to see it."

Sava squeezed Victor's hand. "I understand, I think, what you said before. About not seeing the forest because of the trees."

Zora sat back, looking them over, while Pavel stoked the fire. "I should have seen it, Snow-Walker. I shouldn't have placed that burden on you. Milan would be ashamed, I think."

Sava met her eyes. "He would have stolen your bow in revenge."

Zora smiled, and Victor's chest tightened as Sava smiled back. It was small, and sad, but it was there. Victor sat up, still holding Sava's hand. "Can you tell me about him?"

"He never wanted to skin his kills," Pavel said. "And he made this awful joke about a bear and a tree …"

"He told me that one," Sava said. Zora chuckled softly, and they all started talking at once, even Sava, trying to remember Milan's favorite terrible joke. Then Pavel brought out the guitar they'd made together, and the little house filled with enough sound to muffle the storm outside. Between Pavel cursing while he tried to tune the guitar and Zora showing Victor the last sweater she had made, the morning's horrible events were pushed to the back of his mind. He would process it later—his terror, the realization that he was about to die, the sound of arrows striking flesh—but for now, he could handle it.

Zora came to him later, while Pavel was trying to show Sava how to put his fingers on the neck of the guitar. She sat next to Victor and handed him a tangle of yarn.

"Your hands were shaking," she said. Her own hands were steady as she took out a half-made length of knitting. It was hard to tell what it was meant to be, but it had a pattern like waves, and the colors were soft and muted, blue as the ice at sea.

Victor untangled the yarn while Zora knitted, focusing on his hands and the movement of the wool. As he worked, the tension slowly fell from him, draining from his shoulders and his tight jaw. Eventually, his fingers stopped shaking and his movements grew more certain, and Zora glanced at him out of the corner of her eye.

"Thank you," he said, his voice soft.

"It will be a sweater," Zora said. The needles moved quickly, flashing in her hands. "I'll give it to your mate, I think. And a thicker one for you, yes?"

"That would be nice," Victor said. "And what would you want?"

Zora finished a row of stitches and started another. "I would want you to visit in the spring," she said. "Both of you. You can bring me a painting for the wall. Something bright, perhaps. A painting of the mountains in the sun."

Victor unwound another length of yarn for her. "I think I could do that."

They stayed in the main room while the storm raged outside. Victor slept, eventually, tucked up in Sava's arms near the fire, and woke in the night to find Sava holding him close, his hands clenched tight in Victor's shirt. Victor stroked his hair and murmured in his ear until Sava relaxed. He wondered whether the tide had taken Ivan's body, or if he was left frozen on the shore. Wondered where it had all gone wrong for Ivan, and for David, for those who believed themselves princes of the world.

Then it was morning, and the storm had washed it all away. The footprints leading to and from Zora's house were gone. The terrifying path Victor and Ivan had taken had been erased by hail and snow, and the ground shimmered like stardust as Victor and Sava made their way outside.

"We'll tell the kuvar, when the spring comes," Zora said. She lay a hand on Sava's arm; then, after a moment of hesitation, cupped his cheek. "Be safe, Sava."

Sava nodded, and Zora stepped back.

The walk home was slow. They went carefully, holding on to each other like a mutual lifeline. When the roof of the house came into view, Victor let out a heavy sigh. "I never want to leave again."

"I know someone who will be happy to hear that," Sava said, opening the hatch. The air immediately filled with the cries of a thoroughly unimpressed Speedy, who attacked Victor as soon as he climbed down the stepladder.

"I know," he said, as Speedy pounced and batted at his legs. "I'm sorry. We'll feed you right away."

"We'll feed you as much as you want," Sava said, picking the cat up. Speedy grumbled at him. "He saved your life twice, now. He knocked over the poisoned medicine before I could give you more of it. And I wouldn't have found you yesterday if he hadn't woken me."

Victor scratched Speedy's cheeks. "I won't glare at you for playing with my brushes ever again."

Speedy blinked at him like, *Yeah, yeah, just wait and see, human.*

Victor lit the fire while Sava prepared a feast for Speedy, who was as ungrateful as a spoiled child and made little muttering sounds as he ate. Clearly, being left alone for so long was a grave transgression, because he insisted on being lifted onto the mantel so he could stare at them while he slowly fell asleep.

Victor was just about to comment on how people, as a whole, didn't deserve cats, when Sava gathered him in his arms. The air left Victor with a soft *oof*, and he grabbed Sava around the shoulders. "Hey," he said. "Hey, it's okay."

"I need to know you're here." Sava kissed him, backing him up against the bed. "With me."

"I am," Victor said. "No more answering the door without you."

Sava didn't reply. He just lifted Victor onto the bed and climbed up after him, threaded his fingers through Victor's curls, and kissed him breathless.

"It's okay," Victor said again. "I'm here."

"Tell me one of your stories from far away," Sava said. Victor looked at him in surprise. "I want to hear your voice."

"Oh." Victor smiled, reaching up to stroke Sava's cheek. "All right. Let me tell you about … this old Senex book I read, about a man who went missing in Arktos and came back to lead an army."

He spoke while the clouds built outside, murmuring between Sava's frantic kisses, and brushed the tears from Sava's cheeks when they came. Then, when the story was done, Sava tugged at Victor's clothes and kissed every inch of skin he uncovered, making Victor writhe and gasp on the furs.

"No one will take you from me." Sava settled over him, stroking Victor's thighs. "You are so clever, my mate. So strong. You have always been worthy of me. You know this."

"Yes." Victor was surprised to find he believed it. Ivan had voiced all the ugly thoughts that had made Victor feel small over the years, and it was easy, now, to see that they were lies. He had never been weak or useless. He was always worthy.

"I love you," Sava said, and Victor smiled, letting his head fall back on the pillow.

They barely noticed when the storm started up again. The wind was wailing over the snow when Victor remembered that there was more to the world than Sava, and he lay sated and exhausted on the furs while Sava kissed marks down his neck and whispered praises into his skin.

"I love you, too, you know," Victor said, and Sava kissed his knuckles. Then Sava startled, and Victor barked out a laugh as Speedy came walking up over his shoulder, crying plaintively.

"He's spoiled," Sava said, while Speedy hopped down to knead Victor's bare chest. Sava picked him up before his claws could dig in too deep, and Speedy cried in protest. "There is such a thing as privacy, cat."

Speedy meowed.

"'What are you doing, human?'" Victor said in a small voice, such as he imagined Speedy would have. "'I was helping!'"

Sava smiled. "No, you were not. Back down you go."

"'Nooo,'" Victor made Speedy say as Sava set him down. "'Cruel human! Betrayal!'"

Sava laughed, and the last remaining knots of tension from the day's events started to unravel in Victor's heart.

Speedy remained underfoot while they cleaned up and warmed the house, and Sava and Victor provided commentary to translate Speedy's insistent meows and trills. When they were done, they curled up by the fire with Speedy walking between them as though trying to assure himself that they were both safe and accounted for.

"I never knew," Sava said, staring into the flames while Speedy purred and slitted his eyes at them like a sentinel. "Ivan never said he was interested in me. He never seemed like someone who would ... do those things."

"I'm surprised you aren't angry," Victor said. He took Sava's hand. "I was. I might have, um. Punched him, when I found out."

"You did? Of course." Sava kissed his cheek. "I don't know if I'm angry. I'm just ... hurt. I'm not good at words like you are."

"Take that back."

Sava smiled at Victor and squeezed his hand. "But it feels like ... when the snow thaws and the land seems different than it was. Like everything you knew before was wrong, and now owy have to learn the land again."

"That's how it felt with David," Victor said. "I know this isn't the same situation, but it does change things, doesn't it?"

Sava nodded. "I still don't understand. He never acted like he loved me."

"Because he didn't. He didn't know you, Sava. He loved the idea of you. He was obsessed with a dream."

"And he killed for that dream." Sava scratched Speedy between the ears. "Murder is a terrible crime in Lukos. Zora will be forgiven—she was right, the laws gave control of Ivan's fate to her—but the kuvar will be pained to know these things happened under his eye. But maybe Milan's spirit is at peace, knowing the truth is out."

"And Ivan's mother. I … think maybe he killed her, too. I don't have any evidence, really," he said, when Sava stared at him. "But it seems likely. I don't know; maybe I'm wrong."

"You do have good intuition about these things," Sava said after a moment. "We might never know what happened, but perhaps her spirit can find peace, now."

They were silent for a while, watching the fire while Speedy tried to decide which one to lie on before oozing between them like a furry puddle.

"Lukos is not welcoming," Sava said, his voice careful and slow. "But I thought its people were."

"They are." Victor turned to him, upsetting Speedy, who trilled and batted at him. "You're part of Lukos, too, you know." He gestured to his book, the paintings propped against the wall. "Why would I write and paint about somewhere that didn't welcome me?"

Sava smiled again, the soft, perfect smile Victor loved so much, and pulled Victor into his lap. "You are right, my mate. So clever, so beautiful, so fearless, to look at Lukos and find something to love."

"It's not like I have to look too hard," Victor said, and kissed him, warm and happy and safe.

# CHAPTER 14

True spring came gradually to Lukos, bringing first cold rain, then mist. Melting snow turned the fields to mud, and pops of blue peeked through thick clouds. The most beautiful weather was still to come, when summer—all four or five weeks of it—would turn the valleys into bright green jewels dotted with thick, full trees, the forests full of game and wildlife.

The year's first gathering of the Lukoi was held a couple of weeks after the ground emerged from beneath its blanket of snow and ice. Victor made a face as they trudged through the sludge, while Speedy bounded along like it was the best thing he'd ever seen.

"How do you wash a snow cat?" Victor asked, sighing when Speedy splashed in yet another puddle.

"Carefully." Sava smiled as Victor laughed—though it hadn't been a joke.

The first fire of spring was a joyful affair, the community coming back together after long months of isolation. But there were somber moments as well, when people had to break the news of a loved one's passing or learn of it months later. Funeral pyres would be planned, the sacred ceremony held on the beach, but none of that changed the simple happiness to be found in seeing those who had, once more, survived the worst of a Lukoi winter.

As they rounded the bend toward the fire pit, Sava took Victor's hand and smiled down at him. The pain from Ivan's betrayal hadn't fully faded, but like the winter, it had eased enough to let the sun shine through and warm him. He didn't think he would ever understand Ivan, why he'd chosen to kill instead of simply *talking* to Sava about his feelings. Though if he'd asked, made advances, Sava would have turned him down. He'd never had any impression that Ivan would make him a good mate, but there'd been nothing unkind or disturbing about him.

Now, of course, Sava felt guilty that he hadn't seen it, because if it would have saved lives, who could say he *wouldn't* have taken Ivan as a mate? But how could he have known that Ivan was capable of such violence? That was no way to make a home, in any case. Still, as happy as he was with Victor, their joy came only because Milan was dead. Sava liked to think that if he and Milan were mates and Victor had shown up, they'd have taken him in together, perhaps kept him as their third. It wasn't unheard of in Lukos. But the truth was, if he and Milan were newly mated, Victor wouldn't have had a place there—simply because Sava wouldn't have had enough supplies for three of them to last the winter.

It was a foolish thing to worry over, and he knew it. The stark reality was that Ivan had killed his own mother and Milan, and he would have dragged Victor into death as well if not for Zora hearing him on the beach that day. All the small threads that wove the tapestry of Sava's life seemed fragile and far too easy to cut, and he was worried that being happy was somehow disloyal to Milan.

"It's called survivor's guilt," Victor had told him, when Sava managed a somewhat bungled explanation of his conflicting feelings. "And it's normal. I'm a little sad about being so happy with you, when I know you loved Milan. I think it's just how we'll feel for a while."

Victor was very smart. There *was* an ease of an old ache, knowing that Milan hadn't wanted to leave him. That Sava had been enough for him. Sava was grateful Victor understood that, instead of feeling as if Sava had somehow settled for him.

"Brace yourself, my mate," Sava said, as they approached the gathering. "This involves a lot of hugging, pounding on the back, and loud voices."

"Snow-Walker!" Elena hurried over, beaming, her wolf pups yipping and scampering after her. They were bigger now but were still mostly paws and ears. Speedy, muddy but lording it over them as cats tended to do, flicked his tail and hissed. That lasted until one of the pups barked and pounced, and the other joined in the chase as Speedy, highly offended that *dogs* were trying to *play* with him, went running up a tree.

"Elena," Sava said, and accepted the traditional greeting. "The spring finds you well, then?"

"My porches are uncovered," she answered, then turned to Victor. "So, I hear you survived and earned a name!"

"Um," Victor blinked at her, then said, "I already had one?"

"You're funny," Elena said. "I mean a Lukoi name. You get one when you winter on your own or with your dominant. So? What will we call you around the fire, eh?"

"Victor Owl-Eyed," Sava said. "For he is clever, and he sees many things that others do not. You like that, yes, Victor?"

"Oh." Victor beamed. "Yes. I like it very much."

"Victor Owl-Eyed." Elena nodded. "It suits you. Already you speak Lukoi much better than when you first arrived. Come, we should rescue your cat from the tree."

Elena pulled Victor off toward where their pets were frolicking (or where Speedy was yowling down at the eager pups from his perch on a branch), and Sava saw the kuvar heading toward him.

Dragan looked mostly the same as he had before the snows came. His beard was fuller and his hair longer, but that was true for most of them. His pale, wolf-blue eyes were as shrewd as ever, and his dominance was so strong that Sava could feel it from where he was standing. It must be difficult, living with another dominant through the winter, even—perhaps especially—when that dominant was your own daughter. Sava was older than Elena, but he knew her to be stubborn, and she likely didn't let her father get away with throwing his dominance around … at least, not without throwing some of her own right back.

He remembered Ivan hinting about wanting Dragan as a possible mate and tried not to shudder. Who knew whether Ivan had meant it, but it was still a chilling thought.

"Snow-Walker." Dragan nodded, his face serious, as they embraced and exchanged the traditional spring greeting. Dragan didn't waste any time on pleasantries afterward, though, saying, "I heard about Ivan and the truth of what happened to Milan. Zora Star-Finder came to me with the news and told me that she has not seen the body. Not that it matters. A murderer is not given to the sacred pyre. Let the cold waves have him."

The words were harsh, but Sava couldn't blame him. Dragan would take this personally. "My mate knew," Sava said quietly. "He alone saw the truth we could not."

Dragan nodded. "My failure to recognize the danger weighs heavy on me, Snow-Walker. You are an honorable man and did not deserve to have your desired mate taken before the bonds were made. But you have a good mate now, a strong, intelligent man who sees truth where it is hidden."

Sava thought Victor would like hearing that, how the kuvar recognized his strengths for what they were. Sava, too, was glad. "I love Victor. He is the best of mates. I am glad he is here, and his cleverness will be a boon for the Lukoi."

"Yes." Dragan gave a heavy sigh. "But this must not happen again. You will tell your mate that if he finds this darkness in others here, I want to know about it. Ivan's mother, Vara Breath-Bringer, assisted my mate when Elena was born. She was a good woman. She did not deserve death at her son's hand if your Owl-Eyed is right about what happened. Nor did Star-Finder's son or your mate deserve to die. It is good Ivan's poison is among us no longer."

"It is," Sava agreed, and yet he wondered whether he would ever fully recover from the terror of finding Victor gone that morning, the blood on the snow, Ivan with the knife to Victor's throat. If Speedy hadn't knocked over the medicine, the medicine *Sava insisted Victor take*, then Victor would be one of those on the pyre, and Ivan would be alive instead, with his false sympathies and wild-eyed stare.

"Do not blame yourself," Dragan said gruffly. "Try to put this behind you. Betrayal is how we came to be here, Snow-Walker. We have weathered it before, and we will again." He reached a hand out, and Sava clasped it and nodded. He wasn't sure it was accurate to compare the long-ago exile of the Lukoi to such fresh, new pain. But perhaps it wasn't all that far from the truth. In time, this, too, would fade. And he and Victor would greet each winter, and the spring that came after, together.

Victor was holding a mug by the fire, laughing as Speedy—who had apparently learned that mud was, in fact, very aggravating to get off one's fur—wound around his legs and meowed unhappily. Victor looked lovely in the firelight, smiling, a part of the Lukoi now and named as one of them. *Owl-Eyed.* It suited him.

"You look appropriately lovestruck," Zora said, materializing next to him. She was wrapped in furs, as the spring wasn't *that* warm and her walk to the beach was long, and she sipped what smelled like cider from her own mug. She smiled, tentative, and Sava smiled back immediately.

He had always liked Zora, and it had hurt when she'd turned so cold to him. He'd understood, because he, too, had blamed himself for Milan's death. But he was glad that could ease, as Milan would never have wanted them to be distant with each other.

"I am," he said, hoping she would not be pained by his affection for his mate.

But she was a Lukoi, and they were strong people, fierce and brave. Her chin went up. "I have learned your mate was—ah, the word, he taught me. *Orphan.*" She said it slowly, carefully. "It means to not have parents, to have been given to a house full of children no one wanted. Can you imagine this, Snow-Walker?"

Children were a blessing in a land with so few people. "No. It seems as strange to me as their endless summers and the contraptions of two wheels one can ride down streets of smooth stone."

"I think your mate was having you on about that," Zora said, sounding suspicious. She waved a hand. "But he was this, this *orphan*, and I have decided that is not how it should be, for one of the Lukoi. So. Victor Owl-Eyed is my son, and Pavel's. And you are also ours."

Sava felt his heart clench, and his voice was rough when he spoke. "It is an honor to be considered such, Star-Finder." He couldn't help asking, "But does he know this, my mate?"

Zora was rather headstrong. It was entirely possible she thought Victor would just pick up on it.

"Owl-Eyed is intelligent, is he not? He should know. But I will tell him. Here." She shoved something at Sava, a soft bundle of fabric carefully rolled up and secured with twine. "I have made these. One for you, one for him. You will wear them when you come to our home to share cider with us."

Sava smiled and nodded at her, holding the warm bundle close. "We will. Thank you, Star-Finder."

"Zora, dear. We're family now." Her eyes went misty. "As we always should have been. And my Milan would have loved your Victor. Do not let your heart hurt, Sava, over what might have been. Celebrate that my son loved you and that your mate loves you. That is enough. There are no orphans here. No parents who cannot find children to care for."

Sava drew her close and hugged her tight. "Thank you, Zora. We will be happy to be known as your hearth-family."

She beamed, then wiped her eyes and looked around. "Well, there's no point in crying over our feelings any longer. Let's go make sure that sweater fits your mate, and celebrate that spring is here again."

It was at this same fire, last spring, that Zora had wept for her son's body on the pyre. That spring had not been joyful for Sava or for Milan's family. But like the seasons, this too had turned. And Sava had his Victor to thank for that, his mate who was clever and brave and wonderful in a way Sava finally began to accept that he deserved.

Victor's sweater was slightly too big for him, and Sava's was a little too tight. But they were warm, and they smelled like hearth smoke and other things that made Sava think of home. He caught Victor up and kissed him, hard, while the assembled Lukoi laughed and cheered for them.

"I am glad you will take your feathers off, here," Sava said when he returned a furiously blushing Victor to his feet. "I promise you will not need a false cloak to hide behind, when you have me to keep you warm."

"If I wrote that in a book, no one would believe a real person said it." Victor laughed and kissed Sava again, a hand curled around the back of his neck. "Thank you for giving me a safe place to cast them off."

They enjoyed a pleasant evening sipping cider and talking by the fire, and it was a relief to learn the only others who had passed from this life during the winter were several of their elders, who met their deaths with the bravery the Lukoi were known for. Only Ivan had been lost in his youth, and for his crimes he would not be spoken of, or missed, by the people who'd never really known him at all. Perhaps his broken soul had found some peace in the cold dark. Perhaps not. Sava was no longer going to think on it.

Speedy, muddy and apparently not resigned to that or to the fact that it was his own fault, was inspecting Victor's new sweater with mischief in his golden eyes. Elena's wolf puppies, not as picky about the mud as Speedy, had tired themselves out and were asleep at her feet, their paws twitching as they dreamed. When the chill began to grow a bit too pronounced, everyone took their leave, lingering over farewells because it was good to see other Lukoi, to share stories and promise to trade leftover goods and supplies for those they might need.

Sava had just agreed to bring dried meat for the wolf pups to Elena—in exchange for some yarn to make a toy for Speedy, so their sweaters would be safe—when someone came crashing through the woods, still-bare branches snapping in their wake.

It was Aleks, who'd left ten or so minutes before, shouting as he approached. "—saw it!" He stopped, put his hands on his knees, and gasped. "A. Masts. Those things, it's. Um." He waved a hand, saw Elena, and turned red as a summer apple. "A ship. There's a ship. Heading this way!"

A murmur ran through the assembled group. Dragan walked up and took Aleks's shoulder in one hand. "A deep breath, boy. Tell us about this ship."

"It's, um, pretty far away, still? I only saw it because of the moon. It's so bright since it's full, and you can see past the—"

"I am aware," Dragan interrupted, his dominance so heavy that Aleks went to his knees there in the mud, "of what the moon does, Aleks. Will this ship make landfall soon?"

"No, Kuvar. By dawn, perhaps, or after … They'll need the sun to navigate through the icebergs. You know, they're as big as mountains underneath the water sometimes, and—mmph."

Dragan had placed a hand over the talkative submissive's mouth. Elena giggled, and Sava and Victor exchanged grins as

Aleks looked like he wanted to die that Elena was seeing her father quiet him like an errant puppy.

"Then we will greet this ship at dawn and see what it has brought to our coast." Dragan took his hand from Aleks's mouth.

"It has the same sails as the one that came before the winter," Aleks added.

"Oh," someone said. "Maybe another scholar. I would like a clever mate like Sava's."

Sava looked at Victor, who looked back at him with wide eyes. "I didn't— Why would they come back for me?"

"You are clever and wise," Dragan said. "Maybe they realize they made a mistake, sending you away, when you are smarter than they are."

Victor's grin was sharp. "I doubt that, but thank you. If it really *is* here for me—"

"You won't go," Sava said, with conviction. "I know. Your place is here."

"That's right." Victor's eyes gleamed. "They can take one thing back, though. *My book.*" He took Sava's hand, and Speedy bounded alongside them as they headed to the cabin.

And Sava realized he was not at all worried that Victor would leave with the boat, even if the opportunity were offered to him. He was enough for Victor, and Victor loved him even more than he loved the warm sun and strange contraptions of his homeland.

"Yes." Sava squeezed his hand. "They may have your book."

SPEEDY CAME with them to the beach in the morning, racing about underfoot as Victor and Sava strode across the grass. Rocks and uneven ground that would have felled Victor a few months before were commonplace to him now, and he looked out over the low hills and valleys, admiring the way the snowmelt made little streams through the grass. Lukos truly was a beautiful country, harsh and dangerous but full of life.

He wasn't sure how he felt about the ship. If by some chance someone at the Two Sisters had enough funds to stage a rescue, surely they wouldn't try now, when blocks of ice still drifted in the waves. And he couldn't shake the strange feeling that this was a novelty, that he wasn't greeting someone from home but going out to see strangers arrive on his shore.

"Look," Sava said, as they reached the dunes. Zora and Pavel's house was on a hill nearby, with colorful curtains at the window, and on the blue-gray water was a ship, white sails stark against the clear sky.

"That's not the same ship I came on." Victor let out a sigh. The ship was a darker color than the one Victor had boarded all those months ago. It had a different figurehead, too, a horse of some kind with wings like a bat's. "It looks Starian. See the wings on the figurehead, there? Ships in the Starian navy always have wings somewhere. I don't remember why—something about how fast they are, probably."

"Why would a Starian ship come to Lukos?" Sava squinted at the high masts. "The last one that passed us nearly ran into the ice and sank."

"Maybe they're lost?" But that made no sense. Starian ships were the best on the sea. He knew some people in university who were training to be navigators, and the competition to secure a post on a Starian ship was cutthroat.

A crowd had already gathered when they neared the shore. Zora was there with Pavel, wrapped in what looked like a quilt. She smiled at Victor, who smiled back. He was still reeling from the fact that she and Pavel had just decided, with little fanfare and no warning, to take Victor and Sava under their wing. But Victor supposed that they'd gone through enough together. They were all bound, now, by what had happened that winter.

"They're on the beach," Zora said as Sava and Victor

approached. "A woman and some men, on a little boat. They need someone to translate, I think."

"They can't all be as clever as our Victor, I suppose." Pavel shrugged.

Sava smiled. "No, they can't."

Victor's cheeks warmed, and Sava wrapped an arm around his waist. He saw Aleks and Elena, a small family with a little boy who kept trying to leap out of his mother's arms, and Dragan, who was standing with his hands on his hips, staring down at a small group of people crowding around a rowboat.

One of the people by the boat was a woman with the same brown skin as Victor's, her hair wrapped in red and gold silk. She was trying to speak to Dragan, gesturing with both hands, and Victor stumbled over his own feet when he saw her wide-set eyes and the gold piercing in her brow.

"Aurelia?" David's ex-fiancée and humanities professor at the Two Sisters turned at the sound of Victor's voice. So did the others, but Victor wasn't looking at them. He stepped forward, and Sava followed, his hand on Victor's back. "What are you doing in Lukos?"

"Oh, thank the gods." Aurelia broke away from Dragan and marched across the sand. "Victor? Are you okay? What was that you said, just now?"

It took Victor a moment to realize that he'd addressed her in the language of the Lukoi. He spoke in his native tongue instead. "I asked what you're doing here. Did something happen?"

"Yes, of course. *You* happened." Aurelia sighed and reached for his hands, and Victor, bewildered, took hers. "I was furious when I heard what the university board did to you. What *David* did to you. They had no right. When I heard you were sent here, I was determined to find you. Even if there was a chance you were … that he made them … I'm just glad you weren't tossed into the sea."

Victor stared at her. Not once had he thought that Aurelia

would be the one to look for him. But it made sense—she'd seen it, hadn't she? She knew precisely what kind of man David was the moment she saw him with Victor. Victor realized sheepishly that if he'd been a wiser man in university, he would have befriended Aurelia, instead.

"I'm fine," he said. "Thank you."

Aurelia looked into his eyes, her own narrowed. "You look different, Victor."

"Better, I hope."

She smiled. "Yes. I think so. You definitely look better."

"Victor?"

Victor startled as one of the men by the boat staggered forward. He wasn't nearly as well put-together as Aurelia—he had dark circles under his eyes, his hair was a mess, and his clothes were disheveled and far too light for the weather. One of the other men reached for him, but he dodged out of the way and came stumbling over. Aurelia turned to him, eyes flashing, and he dropped to his knees in the sand.

"Oh," Victor said. "David."

"I brought him to make him own up to his actions," Aurelia said, as David stared up at Victor like he was a ghost. "I can make him leave, if you want."

"David?" Sava's voice was tense. "Is this the David who sent you here?"

Victor stared at the shaking, bedraggled man on the sand and nodded. Sava stepped forward.

"You," he said, in Victor's language. His accent was thick, but the word was clear, and Victor's heart swelled at the sound of it. Sava was not the only one with a clever mate. "You left Victor to die."

"Oh, gods." David struggled to stand.

"Stay where you are," Aurelia said, dominance heavy in her voice.

"I thought you didn't believe in gods," Victor said. "I thought you believed the individual could surpass the need for gods. Or is it different when you're the one on your knees?"

"Victor," David said, as Sava approached. "Please. You don't know what my life has been like since you left me."

"Since *he* left *you?*" Aurelia's eyes blazed. Sava looked equally furious, and Victor laid a hand on his arm.

"Wait," Victor said. "The laws of Lukos are clear. I'm the one he tried to kill. His fate is up to me."

Sava didn't look pleased, but he stopped, glaring at David as he cowered in the sand. Victor approached, hands in his pockets.

"Hey, David." David looked up at him. "You don't know what my life has been like, after I left you. As it turns out, it's infinitely better. What do you think about that?"

"I'm so sorry," David said. "I never meant to— I was scared. I was a fool."

"Yeah, maybe." Victor rocked back on his heels. "And maybe I should hate you for it. But I wouldn't have found Sava if you hadn't sent me here." He gestured toward Sava, and David flinched. "I wouldn't have started painting again. I wouldn't have learned more about Lukos or learned what it's like to love someone more than any of your philosophers could have guessed. Still, I'm not going to thank you for it." He turned to Aurelia. "I hope you dumped him."

"Oh, yes."

"Good. You deserve better." To David, Victor said, "You should get back on your boat. We're done here, you and I."

"But Victor, I …" David glanced from Victor to Sava. "I still love you. You know I do."

"I don't think you know what love is," Victor said. "And I won't be the one to teach you."

"You heard him," Aurelia said. David knelt there a moment longer, looking lost, until Sava took a step forward. David scrabbled back on his hands and knees, then turned to run back to the boat.

"*That* was your old mate?" Elena laughed. "You aimed too low, Owl-Eyed."

"She says I should have had higher standards," Victor translated for Aurelia, who smiled at Elena.

"She's right. You won't come back with us, Victor?" Aurelia gestured to David, who was already scrambling into the boat. "He won't be with us long. I'm dropping him off in Staria, and he can find his own way home."

Victor shook his head. "I'm home already."

Sava, who understood enough of the language now to get Victor's meaning, wrapped an arm around him, and Aurelia's eyes twinkled.

"I see that," she said. "Look at you, Victor, making me come all this way for nothing."

"Not for nothing. The look on David's face just now was worth a lot." Aurelia beamed, and Victor dug in his bag while she whistled to her crew. "I do have something for you. I was hoping whoever came here could take it back with them, and I trust you far more than I do David."

He handed his journal to Aurelia, who opened it and raised her brows. "What is this?"

"The first real book on Lukos," Victor said. "Maybe it'll be useful, teaching other people the truth of this amazing, wonderful home of mine."

Aurelia scanned the pages, eyes widening. "You know, you could be a professor with a book like this. A proper scholar, with the silver laurel."

"It would clash with my coat."

Aurelia looked him over and leaned in to hug him. "I'll come back," she said. "Write more books, and I'll take them to Gerakia. Then I can visit with praise for your talents, instead of terrible exes."

"Much preferable. Thank you." Victor paused, looking out over the sea. "How long are you here?"

"Not long. The sea is dangerous, this time of year."

Victor smiled. "Next time, you should come during the summer. Stay for a while. It's beautiful here."

Aurelia looked around the gray, dreary beach and up to the hills of yellow grass and rivers of mud. "Really? Well, you did say you were an artist. I suppose you can find the beauty in everything."

"Maybe so."

"Speaking of beauty," she said, glancing at Elena, "why don't you introduce me?"

Aurelia left that evening, carrying Victor's book under her arm, while the gathered Lukoi lit fires on the beach to watch the ship unfurl its sails. Victor watched, too, leaning into Sava's side. He felt no twinge of homesickness as Aurelia's rowboat left the shore, no ache for the warm summers of Gerakia as the ship raised anchor.

"I might paint this," he said, as Elena waved to Aurelia. "The ship, and the fires."

"We'll look for more paints for you tomorrow," Sava said, as they turned toward the low hills. "And maybe a new quill, for your second book."

"Who says I'm writing another?"

Sava kissed him, and Speedy went scrambling over the grass, a muddy, meowing bundle of fur. "I know you, my mate," Sava said. "You have more to learn, and more to tell. And plenty of time to tell it."

"You're right." Victor took Sava's hand, and as they left the shore of Lukos behind, the wind pushed at his back as though guiding him home. "I think I do."

A new season approaches in the Spring of the Wolf, the next adventure in the Seasons of the Lukoi series!

SPRING OF THE WOLF (Seasons of the Lukoi Book 2) available soon!

# ABOUT THE AUTHOR

Iris Foxglove is a shared pen name between two longtime fantasy readers, Avon Gale and Fae Loxley, who are committed to writing fun, escapist dark fantasy featuring decadent, kinky stories, intricate worldbuilding and unforgettable characters.

Loved the book and want to help indie authors produce more unique content to enjoy? Leave a review on Amazon, Goodreads or wherever you like to review books. Don't forget to tell a friend!

Connect with Iris:

Twitter: @irisfoxglove
    Email: irisfoxgloveauthor@gmail.com

If you're interested in receiving information on new releases, as well as exclusive excerpts from upcoming books and bonus content, sign up for Iris' newsletter!

Iris also has a Facebook group if you'd like to check it out: Iris Foxglove's Poisoned Garden

If you're interested in monthly bonus content, exclusive excerpts and other perks, consider becoming a Patreon! Monthly content is available at just $1 a month!

# THANK YOU TO OUR PATRONS!

***House of Onyx***
Jae Dixon
Brittany
Kari Shanahan
Unpopular Onion
Gail Morse
Justy

***House of Gold***
Amy Schaffer
Andrea Canada
Anna
Anonymous
Brooklynapple
Catherine Dair
Elle Porter
Eva Wild
JaneBuzz Jane
Kendall
Nix Rodriguez
Rosie Hallen